The Golden Age of Red

DOUG VILLHARD

MABEL
MABEL PUBLISHING

Copyright © 2024 by Doug Villhard
Book cover art copyright © 2024 by Danielle Villhard
All rights reserved.
No part of this book may be used, transmitted, or reproduced in any manner whatsoever without the written permission of the publisher. For information regarding permission, visit mabelpub.com.
ISBN 979-8-9865378-4-9

Cover design by Danielle Villhard

The Golden Age of Red is a work of fiction. The roles played by Red Grange and his family in this narrative are fictional; however, the imagined characters in this novel do abide by the generally known facts of Grange's real life. Specific incidents and dialogue, and all characters with the exception of some well-known historical public figures, are products of the author's imagination and are not to be construed as real, including the chronological order of events. Where real-life historical public figures appear, the situations, incidents, and dialogues concerning those persons are entirely fictional and are not intended to depict actual events or to change the entirely fictional nature of the work. In all other respects, any resemblance to actual persons, living or dead, events, or locales is entirely coincidental.

*This book is dedicated to my sons,
D.J. and Drew,
whose love for sports
has renewed my own.*

THE FIRST QUARTER
∽ Seeing Red ∾

CHAPTER 1

"Showtime," C.C. Pyle says, standing just off stage and signaling Clem, his trusted house manager, to dim the lights.

The sold-out 1,500-person audience, sitting a few blocks from the University of Illinois campus at the start of the 1924 school year, steals one last admiring glance at the Virginia Theater's ornate trim, hand-painted murals, and marble statues. Pyle never calls the Virginia a "theater." He prefers "palace." His silent partner and bankers, however, call it a money pit.

Every time Pyle steps out to find his mark on the darkened stage, memories from earlier in his career still sting. Actors he worked with in his 20s have enjoyed successful movie careers. But now, at 42, Pyle has been forced to give up his struggling acting career and his desperate attempts to produce movies and manage starlets. Instead, he finds himself stuck in the Midwest night after night, faking the role of theater owner extraordinaire.

On cue, Clem flips on the spotlight. Basking in the polite applause, Pyle, now fully illuminated, admires his own attire. His double-breasted suit coat, matching vest, pinstriped pants, and Italian leather shoes—all convincing knock-offs of the latest New York City designs—look fantastic.

Although fit and trim, Pyle wouldn't be complete without his signature cane, a symbol of the wealth he portrays. Adjusting his monocle to look down at the cane's handle, he's nearly blinded by the fake rubies, diamonds, and pearls that adorn the ornate grip.

He tilts his fedora slightly, giving the audience a hint of his thick sandy gray locks, which perfectly complement his trim mustache, just as the feather in his hat always matches the color of his pocket handkerchief and tie. On Fridays, he wears green—the color of a sold-out audience, the color of money, a color that remains just out of reach for him.

"Tonight's film is a masterpiece of cinema," Pyle declares to the eager audience. "You're sure to love *A Woman in Paris*, directed by film legend, Charlie Chaplin."

The audience, mostly college couples on dates, erupts into thunderous applause. Most wear suits and the daring new rage of shorter, flapper-style dresses.

"For the past few years, Charlie hasn't starred in a movie, and I remind you, he's not on camera in this one either. Instead, he is the film's director, giving us a rare glimpse into the mind and soul of the most genius entertainer and storyteller of our time. The only way this evening could be any better is if my good friend, Mr. Chaplin, whom I used to perform with back in the day, were here himself to preview the movie."

Murmurs ripple through the audience as they wonder if their local theater host really used to know Chaplin.

"He will be in nearby Chicago tomorrow, and, as advertised in the papers, I had *hoped* he might drop by tonight, but sadly, it didn't fit his schedule."

Disappointment washes over the faces in the audience. Pyle knows the only reason these college kids would give up a Friday night to see an art movie was the opportunity to see Chaplin in person.

"But I trust you will understand that a man of Mr. Chaplin's unrivaled fame and talent has a demanding schedule."

Pyle continues consoling the audience, oblivious to their shift from disappointment to sudden euphoria as the 35-year-old Charlie Chaplin, in a fancy blue suit with his graying hair slicked back and a clean-shaven face, steps out on stage and pretends to sneak up on Pyle.

"Chaplin sends his deepest regrets," Pyle says, ignoring the growing excitement from the crowd until Chaplin taps him on the shoulder. Pyle feigns surprise and hugs Chaplin to the delight of the audience. The crowd is on its feet now, cheering wildly. After what feels like an eternity, the college kids finally settle back down into their seats.

"Of course, you wouldn't let us down," Pyle says to the world's most famous entertainer.

"I always have time for a friend," Chaplin replies in his distinctive English accent, signaling to the organist to begin playing the popular tune of the same name.

Chaplin and Pyle launch into a duet and are soon joined on stage by two tall showgirls, a brunette and a blonde, in sparkly short dresses. Their long, professional dancer legs add to the spectacle. The four of them step along to a flawlessly choreographed dance number.

Pyle keeps up with the initial dance sequences but soon steps aside, giving the audience what they want: Chaplin and the showgirls alone on stage, commanding both the song and the dance with their synchronized movements, a routine they have honed night after night while promoting this film across the country.

As the dance number reaches its crescendo, Pyle interjects himself for the final few moves, hits the song's last notes, strikes a pose, and basks in the applause. Chaplin and the showgirls bow, wave, and exit the stage as Pyle attempts to resume his introduction to the movie.

However, the audience has no interest in hearing from Pyle. They don't even want Chaplin to return. Nor do they want the showgirls. They want someone else.

"The Tramp!" a fraternity member in the audience shouts. "We want The Tramp!"

Pyle attempts to calm the college audience as they chant, "Tramp!" While Pyle tries to regain control, he turns to find none other than Charlie Chaplin strolling back onto the stage, now adorned in the costume of the most iconic character in film history, complete with a derby hat, black suit coat, baggy gray pants, checkered vest, oversized shoes, ribbon tie, curved bamboo cane, and a fake black mustache. The audience is on the brink of hysteria.

The Tramp initially pantomimes shyness before shuffling into some of his most famous movie routines, including reenacting scenes with the showgirls now dressed as Keystone Cops, who repeatedly attempt to capture him while maintaining perfect rhythm with the organist's melody.

Having grown up watching Charlie Chaplin films, the college audience is at the ideal age to fully appreciate his antics. They erupt in laughter as they witness The Tramp evading the showgirl cops by walking a fake tightrope, boxing, window washing, and balancing what appear to be buckets of water. The Tramp culminates this comedic spectacle with a new routine that involves distracting the cops by making two potatoes perform a tap dance.

The showgirls eventually manage to handcuff The Tramp's wrists in what seems like the end of the line for him until he miraculously finds a way to slip out, leaving the audience in disbelief as they realize the showgirls are now handcuffed to each other while The Tramp bows and makes a clean escape.

The audience is clamoring for more as Chaplin and the still handcuffed showgirls take a final bow, posing with Pyle amid a flurry of flashes from newspaper photographers. Pyle signals to Clem, who lowers the screen to play a few newsreels before the movie starts.

Backstage, Pyle takes a moment to catch his breath, his mind drifting back to the recent Great War and the influenza pandemic, when audiences flocked to theaters just to watch newsreels. Today, only a few years later, and with the economy roaring, the reels are much lighter, featuring movie stars, new automobiles, and sports heroes like Babe Ruth.

Pyle lingers to ensure everything is in order before heading upstairs to the theater offices, located near the projection room at the back of the building.

As he opens his office door, Pyle is not surprised to find Chaplin rummaging through his desk while the showgirls raid his secret liquor cabinet.

Realizing Pyle has entered, Chaplin doesn't hide his nosiness, continuing to rifle through Pyle's private papers as he gestures to the women.

"Be dolls and make C.C. and me a drink," Chaplin demands.

"Make your own drinks," the brunette snaps back. "We're off the clock."

The women instead take turns trying on The Tramp's hat and fake mustache between sips of booze, while giggling and unabashedly exchanging kisses on each other's necks.

Pyle walks over and knocks a few legal notices and past-due bills out of Chaplin's hands. Chaplin gets the hint, slips past the amorous women, and pours himself and Pyle each a double.

Quality liquor isn't easy to come by these days. Chaplin doesn't seem surprised that despite Prohibition or any legal or financial situation Pyle might find himself in, he will always have a fully stocked liquor cabinet.

"Do you remember the first rule of show business?" Chaplin asks, holding out a drink for Pyle.

"If it's not in the newspapers, it didn't happen?" Pyle replies, attempting to put his papers back in order.

"The other one," Chaplin clarifies.

"Always leave them wanting more?"

"Come on," Chaplin chuckles, shaking his head. "You know the first rule of show business."

"Ah, yes," Pyle recalls, abandoning the worries on his desk, crossing the room, and taking the drink from Chaplin. "Always give the audience what they want."

Chaplin nods in agreement as they clink glasses.

"Even if it destroys your bank account?" Chaplin asks.

"Even if it destroys your soul," Pyle replies.

Pyle downs his drink and wipes his upper lip with the back of his hand, wondering if he even has a soul any longer. Meanwhile, the showgirls have discovered Pyle's other hidden cabinet, which contains a small movie player ready to project onto the office wall. They flip the switch before Pyle can stop them, and a screen test of a stunning eighteen-year-old girl appears. The black-haired starlet makes all sorts of faces while posing in different directions, flaunting her beauty and voluptuous figure.

"You're still obsessing over her?" Chaplin asks.

"Margarita Fischer?" the brunette asks. "Is that her from back in the day?"

Pyle, embarrassed, wants to turn off the projector, but he's paralyzed whenever Margarita flickers on screen. She still takes his breath away, just like she did all those years ago when he shot the test footage.

"I saw her at a party recently in Los Angeles," Chaplin says. "I mentioned I was going to drop by Champaign, Illinois, to see the great C.C. Pyle."

Pyle is filled with questions: How did Margarita react? How did she look? What was she wearing? Is she still letting that idiot Harry manage her career? Worse, is she still living with him? A thousand more questions swirl in his mind as he crosses the room and turns off the projector. Even though he is ashamed the showgirls discovered his hidden film stash, it pains him to flip off the switch. He could watch Margarita all day, and he often does.

"Okay, let's get this party started," Chaplin says. "On the train ride out here, I promised these ladies I could talk you into showing off your infamous belt buckle."

"He won't shut up about it," the brunette says.

"But we do sort of want to see it," the blonde adds.

All eyes are now on Pyle as he simply shakes his head, reminded of loves and opportunities lost, bad memories piled up like the papers on this desk.

"Nobody wants to see that."

"No, we want to see it," the brunette insists.

The women plop down on the couch, dragging Chaplin with them, sitting attentive and ready. Pyle hesitates, but his inability to resist a captive audience is one of his many weaknesses.

He begrudgingly grabs his jeweled walking cane, straightens his suit, and stands before Chaplin and the women. It's been years, but he slowly begins to unbutton his double-breasted suit coat. The women's and Chaplin's anticipation increases with each unfastened button.

As he loosens the last one, Pyle playfully reveals the final piece of his millionaire costume. He throws open his suit coat, and the little light in the room radiates off his oversized belt buckle, jeweled to match his walking cane. He gets the reaction he desires as the women come to realize the diamonds, rubies, and pearls on the buckle strategically spell out his initials—C.C.

The sparkling belt buckle is as sensational as Chaplin advertised. The showgirls are beside themselves. Even the periods in the initials appear to be made of genuine diamonds. It's all the women can do not to reach out and touch it, wondering if it's real.

"Now, tell them what C.C. stands for?" Chaplin prompts.

The stage manager, Clem, suddenly bursts into the office, saving Pyle from having to reveal his nickname.

"We have a big problem," Clem says, sweat dripping down his black cheeks and soaking the chest of his denim shirt.

With the office door standing open, Pyle can hear a chant emanating from the theater audience. He'd been warned by other theater operators this might happen. Audiences don't want to see an art movie about a woman in Paris. Chaplin himself broke the number one rule in show business. He isn't giving them what they want. They want The Tramp.

Pyle follows a cheetah-like Clem down the stairs to the back of the theater. Clem, a decade younger, often refers to Pyle as the only white man to ever show him kindness and respect. He's remained loyal, running everything behind the scenes since Pyle took him in all those years ago.

Clem takes the stairs two and three at a time. When Pyle finally catches up on the main level behind the last row of seats, he finds that the audience isn't saying "Tramp." They are chanting "Red. We want Red!" Pyle is confused.

"Red Grange," Clem clarifies.

"The football player?" Pyle asks.

"They want to see the newsreel again."

Now Pyle understands.

"Well, Clem, give the audience what they want."

Clem darts off, and the chanting relentlessly continues until the movie abruptly shuts off, causing the audience to cheer. The projectionist scrambles and quickly gets the newsreel playing again.

Chaplin and the showgirls catch up to Pyle in the back row of the theater just as a title screen on the newsreel reads, "Meet Red Grange. University of Illinois. All-American."

The newsreel then cuts to grainy and jerky black-and-white footage of a football player standing on a field preparing to catch a kickoff with a jam-packed college stadium surrounding him. Except, there is something special about this football player. Pyle can see it immediately when number 77 for Illinois catches the ball and takes his first step forward.

Red moves differently than the rest of the pack. Rather than running, he appears to be gliding or floating just above the grass, effortlessly changing direction, impossible to catch.

He pumps his legs and swivels his hips in a way that makes him look nothing short of superhuman as he flashes by would-be tacklers, expertly using his blockers and stiff-arming the final defender until there is nothing left but to gallop out in the open field to the adulation of the crazed college stadium, which holds substantially more people than the Virginia Theater ever will.

The only other time Pyle has ever seen this much grace and agility is the countless hours he's watched Margarita Fischer on the test reel up in his office. But standing here in the back of the theater, he finds watching Red Grange and the massive crowd he commands to be even more intoxicating. Pyle can't help but notice that with each swivel of Red's hips, the young women in the audience cry out even more passionately than they do for a Rudolph Valentino movie.

Suddenly, the newsreel cuts to a close-up of Red on the sidelines. The college girls in the audience nearly faint as he removes his leather helmet and runs his fingers through his thick hair.

Despite his young age, Red has the mature good looks of a seasoned movie star with the muscular body of an Adonis. But the brooding shyness about him makes the girls tremble. He never quite looks into the camera or fully smiles, as though he's teasing the world, leaving everyone breathless.

Pyle has certainly noticed Red in the papers, given his breakout performance as a first-year All-American for the Illini last season, but Pyle has been so busy getting the theater up and running that he didn't realize what a huge following Red has amassed.

"I have to cast him in my next film," Chaplin says, finding himself starstruck.

"I'd like to cast him in our bedroom," the brunette showgirl replies with full agreement from the blonde.

"He must live around here," Chaplin realizes. "Let's invite him up to the party."

At that moment, Pyle begins to form a different plan in his mind, one with the potential to finally change his fortunes. He doesn't want to cast Red or party with Red.

"I want to *own* him," Pyle says under his breath.

"You all serious about meeting Red?" Clem interrupts, having dashed back down again from the projection room.

Clem points to the theater's back row, where a lone chair is now empty. The seat is still wobbling as their eyes move from the chair to the closing exit door.

Even in real life, Red dashes so fast that none of them had laid eyes on him. He moves like a phantom, Pyle thinks to himself, or a ghost.

"Red and I have an arrangement where I save him a seat in the back each night, and he arrives just as the movie starts," Clem explains. "He insists on paying and everything. He just wants to time it right to sit alone in the dark and enjoy a movie. No football. No fans. No fuss."

As the newsreel ends and *A Woman in Paris* resumes, the crowd again begs to see Red. Chaplin and the showgirls join in and lead a new chant by shouting, "One more time!"

Pyle wants to see Red again, too, many more times. His mind races at the possibilities as he instinctively adjusts his green tie.

CHAPTER 2

The following Monday morning, Pyle and Clem make their way across campus to the Zeta Psi fraternity house.

Pyle always starts off the week wearing a blue tie with a matching handkerchief and feather. Blue, the color of the sky, symbolizes endless possibilities. However, as they near Red's fraternity house, Pyle realizes he has competition as he and Clem are forced to navigate past newsreel-men and newspaper photographers assembled on the street.

Already waiting in the foyer are owners of several local auto dealerships, haberdasheries, insurance agencies, out-of-town newspapermen on assignment, media representatives from the Big Ten Conference, and even an aspiring all-girl trio singing act known as "The Baker Sisters," accompanied by their pushy stage mother, who is wielding a large camera.

It takes Pyle a moment to realize that everyone is lined up in a first-come, first-served fashion, which becomes apparent when a young boy, who should be in school but was there first, aggressively repositions himself in front of Pyle, holding a football to be signed.

Fraternity men are constantly moving between the upstairs and side rooms. One of them, a handsome ox of a young man nearly bigger than Clem and Pyle put together, recognizes Clem and immediately shakes his hand.

"This is Earl Britton," Clem says to Pyle. "He's why Red always breaks loose on those long runs. Earl blocks for Red."

"Red hardly needs me to break loose," Earl replies, shaking Pyle's hand and suddenly recognizing him. "Hey, you're the Millionaire Movie Guy."

Before Pyle can acknowledge his local fame, Earl's eyes move on to what Pyle holds in his other hand.

"Freebies go in the baskets," Earl instructs.

Pyle now sees baskets lined against the wall filled with samples, flyers, coupons, and vouchers from all the business owners in town who hope to entice Red to frequent their establishments.

Earl takes the free movie passes from Pyle's hand and dumps them into one of the baskets, but not before keeping a handful for himself. As other fraternity men pass through the lobby, they grab the rest of the movie passes and other items from the baskets for themselves, too.

Then, six freshmen sorority pledges, each holding a pair of scissors, barge into the lobby, disregarding the line's order. In their orange sweaters and long skirts, the college girls march up to Earl; the bravest of them demands his attention.

"Tell Red the Delta pledges are here," she instructs. "We're not allowed to attend class until we get what we came for."

Having handled this request before, Earl shouts out, "Deltas," in all directions until twenty or so fraternity men assemble in the already overcrowded foyer. Everyone steps back to make room as the sorority girls form a line.

"Let's see it, girls," Earl shouts, igniting the enthusiasm of the assembled fraternity brothers.

"Three, two, one," the bravest girl shouts as her fellow pledges launch into a choreographed cheer. "Illini are Orange, Roses are Red. We've come for a lock of our hero's head."

Pyle can't help but turn to Clem and smile at the ridiculousness of it all as the girls finish their routine.

"Harold Grange is a mighty man; we're here to say we're his biggest fans."

The six girls summon the courage to lift their skirts in unison, revealing the tiniest sliver of skin just above their knees, evoking whistles and cheers from the fraternity men. Earl beckons a young fraternity pledge forward. The young man awkwardly approaches the line of girls. The pledge hands each girl a lock of red hair, eliciting shrieks of excitement as they rush out the front door, clutching their hard-earned trophies. Pyle's grin widens as he notices the young pledge's convenient hair color. As the pledge turns around, the back of the kid's red hair is haphazardly shorn and dotted with bald spots.

Abruptly, Earl checks his watch and shouts, "Time for class!" As if conjured from thin air, around fifty more fraternity men materialize, forming a line from the stairs to the front door. Earl snatches the football from the young boy who's been waiting patiently and tosses the ball up the stairs. Along the way, various fraternity members propel the ball upwards until it momentarily disappears from view. Soon, the ball makes its way back down.

The young boy's face erupts in sheer joy as he discovers a fresh "Red Grange" autograph scribbled right under the laces. The boy tucks the football under his arm and bolts out the front door, emulating his hero from the newsreels.

As the fraternity members form a path down the stairs, a figure emerges from the upstairs platform, revealing the man they've all been eagerly awaiting. He steps out on the landing and descends the stairs.

All eyes in the room are drawn to his fiery red hair, even before they can make out his famous face. Anticipation builds, sending goosebumps across everyone's skin, including Pyle's.

Clad in an orange letterman's jacket, the man descending the stairs resembles the figure from the newsreel, but Pyle, having watched the film a thousand times since Friday night, notices subtle discrepancies.

This Red Grange appears slightly younger and smaller than his newsreel counterpart, even if his facial features are almost identical. The others in the lobby remain oblivious to these differences, but Pyle's suspicions are further aroused by the notoriously camera-shy star's apparent eagerness to bask in the attention. He glances at Clem, who confirms his doubts.

"That's Red's younger brother, Garland," Clem whispers.

The trio singing act, their mother, and the other businessmen in the lobby eagerly chase after the imposter as he bolts out the front door. Earl leads the way, surrounded by a fraternity security force and a throng of photographers and newsreel-men capturing the crowd's march toward campus.

Pyle and Clem are still watching the scene unfold when a sudden gust of wind sweeps through the lobby, strong enough to dislodge the blue feather from Pyle's hat and send it soaring into the air.

Pyle turns back to the foyer, realizing that someone or something must have just flown down the stairs while they were distracted. Pyle's gaze shifts to the side door, which is already closing shut.

Twice, he's missed Red.

The blue feather now catches Pyle's eye as it dances in the air, but his attempts to grab it only push it further from his grasp. Clem intervenes, motioning for Pyle to extend his palm and remain still. Patience is not Pyle's forte, but, eventually, the blue feather gently lands in his outstretched hand.

Pyle gets the hint. He'll need to employ a different approach if he's ever to secure a meeting with the elusive Red Grange.

CHAPTER 3

Red, having bolted out the side door of the fraternity house, continues at a brisk pace for several blocks, only slowing down once he ensures he's in the clear. Always looking to avoid unwanted attention, he's grown accustomed to skirting the campus perimeter by discreetly entering through the back doors of classroom buildings and slipping into the last row of already-started lectures.

After a few blocks, he bounds effortlessly up the stairs to his classroom building. With his hand resting on the door handle, Red notices a particular car parked on the street. It's his all-time favorite, the Wills Sainte Claire Roadster. He's never seen one in person before, but he recently bought an entire magazine dedicated to the vehicle, memorizing every photo and word within the publication's pages.

Drawn toward the mesmerizing machine, he steps away from the building to get a closer look. Nearly the shape and size of a casket, the car is essentially just an engine with a compact two-seat cockpit precariously perched behind it. Its bodywork is a harmonious blend of curves and angles. This one is painted in a rich, deep burgundy and is complemented by signature dual exhaust pipes, oversized fenders, and whitewall tires. As Red's auto magazines proclaim, it's more than just a sports car; it embodies the freedom and optimism that has roared across the nation since the end of the Great War.

The prospect of seeing the automobile up close is thrilling, but the sudden sight of a beautiful woman, apparently its owner, lifting the hood further excites Red. She messes with a few wires, leaves the hood open, climbs back into the cockpit, and attempts to start the engine, only to be met with frustration.

As he draws closer, Red's fascination with the car has now shifted to the woman. She's a few years older than him, in her mid-20s, with reddish-brown hair that mirrors his own. Her trim yet voluptuous figure is accentuated by the new trend of a shorter skirt. Frustrated by the uncooperative car, she angrily removes her jacket coat, revealing a sleeveless blouse that grants her more freedom to work on the engine.

She leans in again for further inspection, and Red can't help but notice more exposed thigh than he's ever seen outside of clandestine magazines his fraternity brothers have shared with him. Her focus remains on the engine, oblivious to her appearance as she fiddles with wires and tubes before making another futile attempt to start the car.

Red's proximity to the open hood allows him to admire the car's intricate engine, a sight that rekindles his fascination with the machine. He notices the overhead valves designed to facilitate more efficient combustion at higher speeds. The recent innovation of the crossflow cylinder head ensures an efficient flow of air into and out of the engine.

Right away, he spots why the car is failing to start. Instinctively, he reaches out to fix it, only to have his hand slapped away.

"The last thing I need today is a college boy making things worse," the woman says, using her body now to block his access as she continues her troubleshooting, ultimately failing yet again to start the engine.

Her frustration is palpable as she raises her hands to her head in exasperation, her once fiery curls now a disheveled mess. Her lips are pressed into a thin line, further emphasizing her growing impatience. Yet, despite her frustration, Red notices the determination that burns brightly in her endless brown eyes. She's not ready to give up the fight as she jumps back out of the driver's seat to once again experiment with adjusting combinations of wires and valves.

Red again offers his assistance, but she cuts him off.

"Back off, rich boy," she snaps. "If I have what it takes to buy a car like this on my own dime, then I sure as hell have what it takes to get the damn thing to start."

Red takes the hint and starts to walk away as she resumes tinkering with the engine, except he can't resist clarifying one thing.

"I'm far from a rich boy," he asserts. "I'm just a working-class kid who happens to love cars, and this car in particular. I have a poster of this engine—not even the car, but this engine—on my wall. I go over it every night, taking it apart in my mind and putting it back together. And I know, for a fact, you are messing with the wrong valve."

She outright ignores his remarks. Thus, he turns to leave, betting she'll still be struggling with the car when his class ends. Maybe she'll come to her senses by then. He's about to cross the street when she finally calls out to him.

"Fine!" she yells. "Fine. What is it? I've adjusted every tube, wire, valve, and combination of each."

Red now has his opening to glide back over. With his left arm, he reaches in next to her, barely brushing up against her bare skin as he adjusts a tiny valve, and with his right hand, he leans into the cockpit and turns the ignition. The engine roars to life without him even giving it any gas.

Without saying a word, she watches as he quickly puts back some of the other tubes and wires she had messed with and gives the engine one last admiring look before closing the hood tightly, using his toned hips to provide extra force for good measure.

In a flash, he's now holding out her coat to help her back into it. Instead, she rips the jacket from his hand, hops into the convertible cockpit, and slams her door shut.

23

"I would have eventually figured it out myself," she says, her voice laced with determination.

"Regardless," Red replies, "I'd like to thank you."

"Thank me?" she says, putting the car into gear. "You want to thank me?"

"Never in my wildest dreams did I think I'd ever get to see something so beautiful up close," he says.

She stares him down before shifting the vehicle into first gear. She starts to pull away, but not before one last parting thought.

"You're welcome."

He watches the car of his dreams—and maybe the woman of his dreams—zoom into the distance. The best part of the entire exchange was she had no idea who he is. That's his real dream in life—to be mistaken for just another college kid.

He watches the Wills Sainte Claire Roadster and the fiery auburn hair of its owner until she completely disappears from view. As he turns to head to class, he's stunned by another sight: a scrawny freshman girl barreling toward him, her eyes locked on him with a determined gleam, a pair of pointed scissors clutched in her hand.

Red's God-given gifts extend beyond his ability to run fast and elude tacklers. He also possesses an innate ability to analyze the entire field laid out before him and predict the movements of all the players. From this skinny girl's gait, he can tell she's about to leap into the air and make a wild attempt at snipping off a lock of his famous hair.

Red effortlessly swivels safely out of the way, just as he's done thousands of times on the football field. Except, he also notices that she's overextended herself, and, as a result, after flying past him, she's going to end up face down on the pavement, most likely with the scissors lodged into her ribcage.

Though this all plays out in less than two seconds, part of Red's gift is that the world around him magically slows down in these situations, allowing him to weigh his options. In this case, he sighs as he determines that the right thing to do is disarm the girl with one hand while gently easing her to the ground with the other, ensuring she doesn't hit her head on the pavement.

In a split second, he accomplishes both tasks, and the girl suddenly finds herself in the arms of the famous Red Grange.

Red offers to help the girl back up, but she unexpectedly bursts into tears, remaining sprawled on the ground. Now he's in an even worse predicament. Her sobs grow louder, prompting him to sit down next to her on the pavement, still holding her scissors and protecting her should a car come down the road.

If she doesn't snap out of it, he will miss class. Red doesn't place much value on his schoolwork, but the NCAA keeps track of his attendance. He eventually offers her his handkerchief, which she accepts, blowing into it with a messy display of disgusting noises. She attempts to return the soggy handkerchief to him, but he gestures for her to keep it forever. It's the last thing he wants back now.

Sitting alongside her, watching for cars, he takes another look at the skinny girl with her pimply face and loose Delta sorority sweater. He wonders if the woman he just met in the Roadster ever went through an awkward phase like this girl.

"Who put you up to this?" Red finally asks the sobbing girl. "It was Peggy McCaffrey, your pledge master, wasn't it?"

The girl nods, still on the ground crying uncontrollably.

"You tell Peggy I want to talk to her."

Between sobs, the girl blurts, "Peggy says I'm to be voted out if I don't get a real lock of your hair. Peggy says, 'no second chances.' I'm to turn in my sweater immediately if I don't get a real lock today."

"Why would anyone want to join a stupid sorority that makes you do this? I'll never understand."

"Because my grandma was a Delta. My mom was a Delta. My sister was a Delta. And Peggy says she doesn't care. She had to take me on Selection Day, but says she doesn't have to initiate me unless I can prove myself."

Her tears intensify, but Red has witnessed this scenario many times before. He'll help anyone who genuinely needs help, even if they don't fully appreciate it, like the woman with the car. But helping a girl get into a sorority will never be high on his list. If he gave a lock of his hair to everyone who asked, he'd be completely bald.

"Listen," he says to the girl, "my personal opinion is you should forget the Deltas, focus on your studies, and trust me that none of this will matter one day. If it were me, I'd take off that sweater and throw it in Peggy's face."

However, he can tell by her expression that she could never do that.

"But I am going to do something for you," he says, causing her eyes to light up slightly. "Look closer at that handkerchief I handed you."

She opens it a bit, revealing her disgusting snot, and spots in the lower corner the embroidered initials "H.G."

"My real name is Harold Grange."

The girl's spirits lift now that she possesses a treasure no other Delta pledge can match. She immediately sits up, clutching her newfound trophy.

"Did your mom sew this for you?" she asks.

"Coach Zuppke's wife sewed that for me," Red says. "It's just me, my dad, and my little brother."

"The famous Coach Zuppke? And you gave it to me?" she says, regaining even more color in her face, though snot is still trickling down her nose.

Red takes her hand that holds the handkerchief and raises it to wipe off the rest of her face. Once finished, he notices that her confidence has returned, and she's now sporting a new winning smile.

He helps her up and hands back her scissors. She boldly gives him a big hug, pressing her bony body against his as tight as she can squeeze. It appears she has no intention of letting go, as he merely pats her on the back, still looking out for cars.

Then, suddenly, he hears the distinctive sound of a snip. The girl dashes away. Red feels the back of his head and confirms that a large chunk of hair is missing. She's got spunk, he has to admit. He's lucky she's not also running off with his ear.

As he watches her run away with her prize, he realizes there may not be a single person on campus who won't do whatever it takes to get a piece of him.

CHAPTER 4

Later that afternoon, the Illinois football team, clad in practice jerseys, lines up on the goal line for wind sprints.

Warren Brown, a young sports reporter for the *Chicago American*, watches from the empty stands of the new Memorial Stadium, a cigar in one hand and a notebook full of nickname brainstorms in the other.

Baseball great Babe Ruth is The Sultan of Swat. Golf great Bobby Jones is The Georgia Peach. Boxing great Jack Dempsey is Kid Blackie. Even thoroughbred Man o' War is The Galloping Comet. Babe Ruth even has a second one: The Great Bambino.

So far, none of the nicknames Warren has attempted for Red have been picked up nationally. He's tried The Red Flash, The Iceman, The Phantom, and his favorite, The Red Tornado.

Warren is confident he can get something to stick. He has to. Coining a nickname will surely be his ticket out of Chicago to a nationally syndicated column.

Down on the field, an assistant coach blows a whistle, and a hundred young men take off sprinting. By the fifty-yard line, three players emerge far ahead of the pack—Red Grange; his brother, Garland; and Red's lead blocker and friend, Earl Britton. Warren watches in awe as they finish at least twenty yards ahead of the others when his thoughts are interrupted by a loud voice he knows all too well.

"Garland is almost as fast as his brother in the straightaway," Head Coach Robert Zuppke points out, his thick German accent nearly filling the empty stadium as he sits beside Warren in the stands. "But it is the ability to break loose that sets Red apart."

Zuppke's petite stature is noticeable even when sitting. He's clearly too small to have ever seriously played the sport himself, but everyone knows Zuppke compensates for his physical limitations with unwavering tenacity and a brilliant strategic mind.

Warren has reported that the older generation of great coaches like Fielding Yost of Michigan despises the younger Zuppke's unorthodox methods. Left to their own devices, Yost and other old-schoolers would be happy to simply field the biggest players and run the ball straight up the middle for eternity.

But the growing legion of casual sports fans love Zuppke. After all, he is responsible for nearly every major innovation in football over the past few years. Zuppke has masterminded the huddle, the screen pass, the spiral snap, the linebacker position, and the flea flicker. Zuppke also perfected the "I" formation, the quick kick, the onside kick, and even the fake punt. Yost and his ilk often derisively label Zuppke, even publicly in the press, as "Mr. Razzle Dazzle."

It famously burns Zuppke that Notre Dame's Knute Rockne gets credit for inventing the passing game when it was Zuppke who had perfected it earlier as a coach at the high school level where there was no national press in the stands. Not only does Warren have the greatest player on his beat, but, in his opinion, he also has the greatest coach.

"It's a shame the NCAA doesn't allow freshmen to play," Warren says. "Think Garland could be as good as his brother Red when he's eligible next year?"

"Are you kidding? Und you cover sports for a living?" Zuppke replies in his quick German banter that barely keeps up with the intense pace at which words form in his mind.

29

"There will never be another Red in the history of the game. Never. I have seen the greatest und it is Red Granche."

Warren suppresses a giggle over Zuppke's mispronunciation of Grange's name as he quickly jots down the coach's perfect quote. From watching national reporters, he learned that an out-of-the-blue direct question is the best chance to elicit a gem.

Both men watch in silence as the players catch their breath. Soon, the whistle blows, and the players sprint back the length of the field.

Instead of finishing twenty yards ahead of his teammates, this time, Red, unmistakable in his number 77 jersey, finishes thirty yards ahead of them, with Garland right behind him. Earl has fallen behind and is now indistinguishable from the pack. As Red crosses the end line, Zuppke clicks the stopwatch he's always holding and jots some numbers down in his notebook.

"This week's game could be the biggest in sports history," Warren says. "You. Michigan. Co-national champions last year. Your nemesis, old-school Yost, across the field from you. And here in this beautiful new stadium."

"If it's the biggest game, then why am I talking to a Chicago reporter?" Zuppke says, motioning to the empty stadium. "Where's the national press?"

"In New York City. You know they can't miss the annual Army-Notre Dame game," Warren replies.

"I know they don't respect Western football," Zuppke says. "To them, football is all about the East, where it originated. But they don't have giant stadiums in the East like we're building out here. Und, they don't have teams like Michigan und Illinois who draw boys from the cornfields instead of rich prep schools. Und no one besides Illinois has Red Granche."

Zuppke motions to the field while getting his stopwatch ready again. Warren watches the players line up for their third one-hundred-yard dash in a row. The whistle blows, and this time number 77 beats his teammates by over forty yards, with

Garland at a distant second and Earl still nowhere to be found. Zuppke clicks his stopwatch as Red crosses the end line, again writing in his notebook.

"Imagine if Red goes pro," Warren says.

The words have barely come out of Warren's mouth when Zuppke's face turns bright red in anger.

"Never say that," Zuppke shouts. "Und never say that to him. We can't risk poisoning his mind. He can never be allowed to lend credibility to the abomination of a game that is pro football."

Bingo, Warren congratulates himself, rapidly recording Zuppke's German rat-a-tat ramblings in his notebook.

"Pro football is a bastard version of a great amateur game," a fiery Zuppke continues. "They draw a thousand fans at best per game. We draw sixty-seven thousand. Their fans come to see blood, und they get it. We play for the pride of one's school. One's state! The sooner that joke of a league goes bankrupt—und for good this time—the better. How dare you even put Granche und the pro game in the same sentence?"

"But just imagine what he could do for the NFL."

"I'll imagine nothing of the kind," Zuppke growls. "How could you say that? The NFL has zero integrity. They prey on poor college students, offering them one-game under-the-table contracts and sneaking them off on Sundays to play under assumed names. Rich Eastern Ivy League kids turn the cash down, but my state school kids are ripe targets. That cheating league couldn't care less about risking kids' reputations und eligibility. They are just looking for a one-game ringer, an edge. I'd never allow Red to legitimize a league that aims to ruin college football."

Zuppke abruptly stands to leave, but not before pointing out to the field.

"You want your story?" Zuppke shouts. "Here's your story. Look at him. Look at Granche."

The team is now running their fourth one-hundred-yard dash in a row. Most of the players can barely move, except for

Red. He beats the entire team this time by over fifty yards. Zuppke shows Warren the time on the stopwatch.

"It's faster," Zuppke shouts. "Each time Granche runs, he's faster."

Warren stares at the stopwatch in disbelief. He wouldn't believe it if he hadn't seen it for himself. No mortal man can do that.

"Granche is going to graduate after next season, und he's going to become an ambassador for the amateur college game," Zuppke declares. "I have it all planned out for him. He's going to take over for Valter Camp."

"*Walter* Camp? The *inventor* of football?" Warren says, making sure he heard Zuppke correctly.

"Yes. Valter Camp, the *organizer* of football, und is about to retire. Granche is going to take over for Camp und chair the Rules Committee. Granche is going to take over selecting the All-Americans from Camp. Granche might even become the commissioner for the entire NCAA. He's going to make sure football stays amateur und that boys play for their home colleges. No recruiting. No athletic scholarships. No booster money. No cheating. He'll make sure players play for pride. Unlike the pros for $50 a game, selling their souls for blood money."

"You sure you're not still just sore over Taylorville?"

Zuppke's eyes shoot daggers at Warren, causing Warren to wonder if he's gone too far by bringing up a scandal he broke a few years ago. Illinois and Notre Dame players got caught playing a game the Sunday after Thanksgiving for money—most likely organized by the Chicago mob—and Zuppke and Knute Rockne, despite having no part in it, were almost forced to resign.

Warren thought that story would propel him to the national level, but it didn't. Zuppke swiftly expelled all the players involved, forcing Rockne and Notre Dame to do the same. In doing so, Zuppke maintained his image of running the cleanest program in all of college football despite the irony of having a group of his players wrapped up in the sport's biggest scandal.

Red has since dominated all the headlines coming out of Illinois, and Zuppke became the champion for amateurism. Meanwhile, Warren is still stuck covering the same old beat.

"But why shouldn't Red be allowed to cash in on his fame?" Warren asks. "Babe Ruth does it. Movie stars do it. Even big-time college coaches do it. Rockne and you both have endorsement deals with Rawlings."

"College football players are *amateurs*," Zuppke replies, his face turning red.

"Look around at your new gargantuan stadium," Warren says, motioning to the sixty-seven thousand seats surrounding them. "Does this feel amateur? College football hosts the largest crowds in all of sports. Illinois and Michigan together are poised to gross a million dollars in ticket sales over the season."

"Those funds go back to the athletic program to create even more amateur opportunities: track, wrestling, gymnastics…why am I talking to you? You know this. I'm tired of you attempting to bait me with your *amateur* debates."

Zuppke begins to walk away again until he calms himself down enough to return with one final thought:

"My wife Fannie und I love Harold Granche as if he were our own son. He's everything that's good about college sports: being a good teammate und becoming a better man. He embodies the amateur athlete. His humility represents the best of mankind. Pro football is the opposite. Want a quote? Granche will never degrade himself by playing in that blood circus."

With that, Zuppke storms off for good, leaving Warren scrambling to jot down as much of Zuppke's tirade as he can remember. He could write faster were he not struggling to balance his lit cigar.

The national columnists, like his favorite, Grantland Rice, more poet than reporter, can blow smoke rings while composing masterpieces. It's all Warren can do to keep his cigar from setting fire to his notebook.

As excited as Warren is to have an exclusive Zuppke quote or two, what he really needs, if he has any hope of escaping the amateur stage, is to get back to coming up with a nickname that sticks.

His obsession with finding the perfect one for Red not only keeps him awake at night, it haunts him.

CHAPTER 5

Coach Zuppke's tiny apartment is only big enough to have two football players over at a time for dinner, and Red has realized that's exactly how Zuppke likes it.

Zuppke has a tradition of inviting his captains over before each game, and this season Red and Earl have earned the honor. Even though Red learns more from Zuppke at those dinners than he does at practices, he's mostly fixated on Mrs. Zuppke. He watches her wait on them with an affection bordering on hero worship. Growing up, he played a similar role in his father's tiny apartment.

The table in the kitchen is barely big enough for three, so she doesn't even bother to set a place for herself. Red assumes she'll eat later, similar to how he'd often first feed his dad and brother and then scrounge for himself.

Red observes it's all Mrs. Zuppke can do but keep the food coming because Earl and Red—and all boys their age—can eat all night. The quicker she plops mashed potatoes and pork chops onto their plates, the quicker they devour it.

Once Red's younger brother, Garland, arrived on campus earlier this year, Mrs. Zuppke caught Red sneaking food into his pockets to take back to the fraternity house for his brother. Athletic scholarships are forbidden by the NCAA. Red's father works extra shifts to make tuition payments. There's often no money left over for food. Red asks himself daily why he plays football, making millions for the university, rather than getting a part-time job.

Since the day she caught him stashing food, they have developed a system where she has a basket made up on his way out that he can take with him. As such, he's finally starting to learn to settle in and enjoy himself at these meals instead of feeling guilty that Garland is missing out.

Familiar with her husband's routine, Mrs. Zuppke, after a few rounds of food, wheels in a little chalkboard so Coach can make a few final strategy adjustments before sending the boys home to rest up for the big game.

The Zuppke's keep the chalkboard in what should be the dining room but is instead the art studio. On top of being a famous football coach, Zuppke is also an accomplished painter. The room is filled with expansive watercolor landscapes, which document the Zuppkes' exotic off-season travels.

One time, Mrs. Zuppke confided in Red that every year that went by without her getting pregnant led instead to another summer trip. And every trip conceived dozens more paintings for which she had to find a home. Her husband has almost as many paintings as he has football players.

Zuppke was a teacher before he was a coach, so getting a piece of chalk in his hand is his real comfort zone. A coach who can teach is essential given that football, which evolved from rugby and soccer, is a game where coaching from the sidelines is prohibited. The first page of *Walter Camp's Rules of Football* reads: "Football is a game played to be played by the players using their own muscles and their own brains." Coaches and reserve players must sit on the bench the entire game. They are not even allowed to stand. Coaches can discuss plays in practice and at halftime but not during the game.

Football is also a game of endurance. If a player comes out of the game, he can't return until the next half. If he comes out in the second half, he can't return to the game. Players must know how to play both sides of the ball—offense and defense.

Zuppke isn't just teaching his captains. They are his coaching staff. He's training them to think like him when they are on the field, as it becomes their job, not his, to call the individual plays during the game.

"With Red's speed, we've been able to run the same offense ever since you two have been on varsity," Zuppke reminds Red and Earl in his thick German accent while drawing Xs and Os on the chalkboard. "We stack our blockers either here to the right or the left, and Red runs around them, und Earl throws the final block that springs him free straight down the sideline."

The boys are very aware. That has indeed been their modified "I" offense the entire time they've been at Illinois. Because freshmen aren't allowed to play on varsity, Red and Earl scrimmaged against the varsity nearly every day in practice their freshman year utilizing this offense. Except they achieved something that had never happened before at Illinois under Zuppke. Red and Earl's freshman team would routinely beat the varsity. That same "I" offense has been beating Big Ten opponents ever since.

"Us running variations of this play over und over again is what Coach Yost and Michigan are watching on the game film preparing for tomorrow," Zuppke says. "It's all they have to work with because it's all we ever do."

Now, Zuppke puts down the chalk momentarily and leans in as if to whisper the deepest and darkest secret to them.

"But I'm going to finally let you in on something. I've made you run only this offense on purpose this whole time. For years, I've been preparing for tomorrow's game against Michigan. We're going to surprise them with something different. I've been setting them up the entire time."

Both boys look at each other in disbelief.

"It's all I've had to listen to," Mrs. Zuppke confirms while making sure their glasses and plates remain full at all times. "He had to tell somebody, so I've had to keep this a state secret for years. Thank God it is about over."

"Fannie, you love talking football strategy even more than me. Admit it," Zuppke implores her, but she shakes her head.

It never dawned on Red before now that a husband might talk privately about his work with his wife. He has no idea how a traditional household works.

"You boys ready for it?" Zuppke says. "You ready for the big reveal of the plan?"

Earl nods excitedly between bites, and Red is ready too, but he suspects, or rather hopes, he knows the plan. Zuppke erases the chalkboard with his sleeve, preparing to unveil his masterpiece for the first time.

"Red is going to start off following the blockers just like always," Zuppke explains as he draws a diagram looking similar to the standard play until he takes the chalk and suddenly sketches a violent S-shaped line in the opposite direction. "But then Red is going to cut back. He's never cut back before in his entire football career, even in high school. But tomorrow's the day. He's going to cut back."

Earl appears thrilled with the plan but has a burning question.

"Where am I?" Earl inquires.

"This X. Earl, you are going to pull first und cut back even before Red."

Coach redraws it again; this time, the X that represents Earl cuts back before Red's X follows.

"Und they'll never see you two coming. I'm counting on it working the entire first half before they figure it out."

Earl is ecstatic, as is Coach. Mrs. Zuppke, shaking her head, chimes in.

"But I keep telling him all Michigan would have to do is watch Earl, and they would see it coming," Mrs. Zuppke points out.

"But they won't," Coach says adamantly. "They will only be watching Red. I've made sure of it for years. All eyes must be on Red until it is too late."

Earl is enamored with the plan. He absolutely loves it, as Coach knew he would. Earl is a selfless soldier, born and raised to do whatever his coach or commander tells him.

Now, all eyes are finally on Red, but Coach and Earl are so excited about the plan that only Mrs. Zuppke notices the concern on Red's face.

"What is it, son?" she asks.

"It's just not what I was expecting," Red replies.

"Exactly," Zuppke interjects. "No one will see it coming."

"No, I mean, I was assuming you were going to say it's about time I became the decoy. Or I do the blocking and we spring Earl for a change. That's what I assumed this dinner was about. I've been thinking about it all summer, and I'm confident mixing it up will work even better."

The whole room falls silent. Zuppke simply exhales and looks down at the floor, trying to gather his thoughts and prevent an outburst of emotion he might regret. Earl is too afraid to say anything.

"It's just that all this fuss about me is ridiculous," Red says. "I get my name in the papers simply for being the last guy to touch the ball and cross the goal line. But it takes an entire team to make that happen. Not to mention coaches. Not to mention strategy. Not to mention Mrs. Zuppke feeding us so well the night before."

She dismisses Red's compliment, gesturing as if it's nothing.

"I'm just the last guy after everyone else does their jobs, and I have to take all the fame for it. I'll never understand it. Let's spread it around a bit; then they'll really never know what's coming. Sometimes, it's me. Sometimes, it's Earl. Sometimes, it's Chuck. Let's spread the offense out. Why's it always me?"

Earl is too afraid to say anything in front of Coach, so much so that he refrains from eating or making any noise. Mrs. Zuppke knows her husband has never coached a talent like Red Grange before. No coach has ever coached a Red Grange before. She's been around football long enough to know that this is an extremely rare conversation taking place with a once-in-a-century talent.

"Why's it always me?" Red repeats.

"Why's it always you?" Zuppke finally shouts. "Because it's your God-given gift. He gave us all one. Earl's is to block. Mine's to coach. Fannie's is to put up with all of us leatherheads und let me draw Xs und Os on her back in the middle of the night. Und yours is to find an opening und run through it. This game is designed to allow us all to use our God-given talents for the good of the team. The team!"

Zuppke lets that sink in a bit before continuing.

"Why's it always you, Granche? I'll tell you why. Because in big games, teams have to lean on big players. Earl is the best blocker on the team. The best I've ever coached. He sacrifices himself every single game so we can win. Don't you, Earl?"

Earl nods.

"Und your sacrifice, Granche," Zuppke says, pointing his finger in Red's face. "Your sacrifice is greater. I'll admit it. Your sacrifice is greater than all of ours combined. Yours is immortality. We all pay a price. I'm afraid that's just the price you must pay for this team und this university to achieve greatness. You'll be immortal. That's your sacrifice. Is that so bad? To be the star?"

The last thing Red wants in the world is to be immortal. "Sacrifice" is an interesting way to label it. He's always viewed being the star as a burden. And if Zuppke's cutback strategy works, that burden is about to multiply exponentially.

CHAPTER 6

The night before big games, or any night for that matter, Red longs to disappear into any story that isn't his own. He's about to knock on the side door of the movie theater to have Clem let him in when he notices a Ford Model T dealership has moved into the commercial space in the front of the building, right next to the ticket booth.

Red stops in his tracks to admire the latest version of the mass-produced car through the large store-front window. While straining to see into the dark showroom, a familiar voice interrupts him.

"That car could sell itself," Pyle says, now standing next to Red, dressed as dapper as ever. "But the owner of the dealership is too cheap to pay to keep the lights on at night. I told him, when promoting a new opportunity, don't agonize about the cost. Focus on the reward."

Red has never met C.C. Pyle, but every college kid knows him as the Millionaire Movie Guy. Red would be fortunate to have one of Pyle's suits or even one pair of his Italian shoes. He can't help but notice that today's feather, tie, and handkerchief are all the color orange. Everything in town is orange tonight, reminding Red that he'll never be able to fully escape the pressure of tomorrow's big game.

"Want to see the tin can up close?" Pyle asks, pulling a ring of keys out of his pocket.

"No, I don't want to bother anyone. I was just going to pay to see what's left of the movie."

"It's no bother," Pyle says, opening the door. "You're not going to believe what's under the hood."

Before Red can refuse, Pyle lets them in, flips on the lights, and props open the hood. The moment Red catches a glimpse of the engine, he can't help but move closer.

"I couldn't believe it myself," Pyle says, "the cylinder head is...."

"Detachable."

Red has studied how this innovation allows for maintenance, repairs, and modifications without having to disassemble the entire engine block. However, getting an opportunity to disassemble an entire engine block would be Red's dream.

"Do you know what it's made out of?" Pyle asks.

"Aluminum. To facilitate heat transfer away from the combustion chambers."

"Impressive," Pyle says, patting Red on the back.

"Oh, there are plenty of guys at the fraternity who know more than me about cars," Red says. "I'm still learning. But there is one thing for sure I don't know."

"What's that?"

"How they got it in here. Was the window removed?" Red asks. "Wait, don't tell me they took it apart?"

"I offered to remove the window for a modest fee, of course," Pyle says. "But instead, they spent the entire day taking it apart and putting it back together in here."

Red disappears into that thought. He would have skipped class to help. If he could get away with it, he'd even skip the game tomorrow against Michigan to watch them do it again.

"When I was in California working in the film industry, I had the pleasure to witness every car on the market and models not yet on the market," Pyle says. "Movie stars drive them for free. Have you ever been to California?"

"California? Are you kidding me?" Red laughs. "I've never been anywhere."

"Other than making motion pictures, I spent most of my time out there helping movie stars make decisions. What car to drive? What role to take? Helping them decide whom they can trust. Especially helping them realize who they couldn't trust. I got paid to negotiate deals. But my real job was just being someone they could talk to."

Red's eyes shift from the car to Pyle.

"Fame is a fascinating creature," Pyle continues. "It's not actually tangible, but yet it is all-consuming. It can swallow you. It can own you. Or, you can learn to control it. You can tame it. Own it. Make it work for you. I helped movie stars not just to embrace fame but to turn it into gold."

Red watches as Pyle adjusts his orange tie.

"That being said, you wouldn't believe the pressures a famous person endures," Pyle adds. "I wouldn't wish it on anyone. But once it happens, I am the guy to help."

Pyle moves to the front of the car and closes the hood.

"But now I own movie theaters and real estate, and California is a world and a lifetime ago," he says, walking back to hold the door open for Red. "They still come to see me, you know? Charlie Chaplin did just the other night. Still seeking my advice. Can you believe that? The most famous entertainer in the world comes all the way to Champaign to hit me up after all these years."

Now that is amazing, Red thinks, stepping back outside.

"You know how I help them?" Pyle asks. "Do you know what the simple trick to it all is? When the whole world wants something from you, and you don't know what to make of it all? Know how I help?"

Red would love to know the answer to that question.

"The trick is very simple," Pyle says, motioning for Red to step fully outside so he can lock the door. "You gotta talk it out, is all. Find someone you can trust and talk it out. In the end, it's not that hard. It's just that no one can do it alone. Everyone needs someone to talk to. Even Charlie Chaplin."

With that, Pyle locks the door and heads toward the theater.

"You going to turn off the lights?" Red asks, admiring the now illuminated car in the window.

"The owner is inside watching the movie," Pyle says with a wink. "When he comes out and the crowd gathers around his new dealership, he'll thank me."

Indeed, Red imagines, he will.

"Come on in," Pyle says. "Clem has a seat saved for you. You can still see what's left of the picture."

Red doesn't answer. He's content to stare at the new car through the illuminated window.

"Suit yourself," Pyle says, entering the theater. "If you change your mind, I'm never hard to find."

Red is lost in thought, continuing to admire the car for close to an hour, thinking about how he would have gone about taking it apart. However, if he doesn't move on, the movie will let out, and the theater crowd will soon swarm, not around the car, but around him.

As he cuts through an alley on his way home to the fraternity house, he imagines the world would love to stick him in that lighted showroom window and charge the public to gawk. Pay double to touch him. Ten times to own a piece of him.

Red snaps out of his thoughts when he spies the Wills Sainte Claire Roadster from the other day parked against a curb in the alleyway. All cars are worth his attention, but especially this one. He only has a moment to reacquaint himself with its lines and curves compared to the Model T when an alley door bursts open, and the unforgettable woman he last saw driving away barges out dressed to the nines, auburn hair flowing, a large man in pursuit of her.

As the alley door closes, Red hears a jazz band playing inside and catches a glimpse of people drinking. Everyone in town—even the cops—knows where the speakeasies are located, but as long as they stay tucked away, the whole nation seems content to look the other way.

The large man catches up to the woman and shoves her against the car. Red's instinct, of course, is to step in. But from the spunk he saw in her earlier today, he suspects he won't need to. He's correct as she immediately fights back and subdues the large man with a well-placed knee to his groin.

Red can't help but admire her tenacity. Except the man is considerably larger and, out of nowhere, smacks his hand across her chest, sending her bouncing off the Roadster and onto the pavement.

In a flash, before the man can advance on her, Red slams into him, sending him sliding across the pavement and crashing into the curb.

Red attempts to help the woman to her feet, but she won't let him even touch her. When she finally stands, she takes a good look at Red and shakes her head.

"Again, the college boy," she says to herself as she dusts off her dress and reaches for the car door. Red steps back to give her room, but out of the corner of his eye, he senses movement from where he left the man on the pavement. The woman has a better vantage point, and Red can tell from her eyes that the large man is doing more than just advancing on them.

Red turns and has a split second to decide what to do, given that the man is not only filled with rage but is also now lunging at him with a knife. Red can easily avoid the man and the blade, except that doing so would result in the man flying past him and into the woman.

Red analyzes multiple scenarios in his mind before finally settling on the one that will hurt everyone the least. But it's still going to hurt.

CHAPTER 7

Red matches the steps of the auburn-haired woman as they ascend the stairs to her apartment.

His summer job of lugging one-hundred-pound ice blocks up flights of stairs behind housewives is a breeze compared to the task at hand: balancing an unconscious 200-pound man over his shoulder.

The woman unlocks her apartment door and gestures toward the living room.

"Drop my idiot brother on the floor or wherever you like," she instructs, ducking into the bathroom to retrieve something. "He gets drunk like that and thinks he can drive my car."

Red, who wouldn't even consider leaving his worst enemy on the floor, looks the living room over and decides to ease the idiot brother onto the couch, even propping his groggy head with a pillow.

Red's eyes take in the apartment's surprising starkness. Despite driving a flashy car, the woman's living space is remarkably standard—small, sparsely furnished, with bare walls and tables.

Clutching a first-aid kit, she strides out of the bathroom and brushes past him into the kitchen. She begins setting up a station on the kitchen table while heating water on the stove. Her interactions remain matter-of-fact, devoid of eye contact, and focused purely on the task at hand.

Her averted gaze gives Red a chance to study her again. The women in his life have either been shrieking coeds or the older wives of his coaches. This woman is a refreshing middle ground: a few years older than him with an effortless confidence that he's only observed in movie stars.

She slides out a chair from under the table and gestures for him to sit.

"I have to go," Red declares, stepping toward the door. "They'll start a search party for me if I don't get back."

"Who, your college buddies?"

"Maybe the whole state," Red mumbles to himself.

"You can't leave with your shoulder bleeding like that."

He reaches back to touch his shoulder, his fingers coming away sticky with blood. His shoulder had stung during the altercation in the alley, but the pain had subsided. He had no idea he was bleeding so badly.

She moves toward him and gestures for him to raise his arms. He reluctantly complies, and she carefully unbuttons and lifts his shirt over his head, ensuring it doesn't further aggravate his injury. Standing on her toes, she fully removes his shirt, ignoring the reveal of his muscular chest. She again motions for him to sit at the kitchen table, which he does.

She hands him his bloodstained shirt to hold, revealing a slash marring the back of the fabric. Red wonders if he'll be able to get the blood stain out and salvage the shirt. It's one of only three shirts he owns. Without warning, she applies antiseptic from her first aid kit to the wound.

The shock to his body causes the muscles of his torso to tense. Most of the guys on his team have some form of muscular definition from the routine of practices and calisthenics. But Red has the body of a Greek god from working an ice truck all through high school and his college offseasons.

"Carbolic acid," the woman says, wiping the excess with a towel. "If I'd warned you I was about to apply it, it would have hurt even more."

"Acid?"

"I spent half the war in Europe treating wounds," she replies, messing with her supplies, including, Red notices, a suturing needle and thread, which she begins to prepare. "Tincture of iodine also works well, but it stains the skin. Sodium hypochlorite—basic bleach—is more available and less irritating but doesn't do the job as well. Boric acid works the best, but you'd need to be unconscious to handle that pain."

Red watches as she nonchalantly prepares the needle and thread.

"So you were a medic?"

"I was trained for a lot more than that," she says, dipping the needle into the boiling water.

Red braces for the hot needle to puncture his skin while trying to remain as brave as possible to impress this woman.

"What else were you trained for?"

Instead of feeling a needle stick into his shoulder, she flicks his ear with her finger, which smarts even worse than the carbolic acid. Instinctively, he grabs his ear to stifle the pain, and when it finally does stop stinging, he realizes she's finished stitching him up and has even taped a bandage over his wound. He didn't feel a thing.

"I'm trained in many forms of deception, but the specifics are classified," she says, putting away her supplies and using some of the boiling water to prepare two cups of instant Red E Coffee. She scoops in a few spoonfuls of powder, stirs it up, and places two mugs on the table.

While the coffee is cooling, she takes the bloody shirt from him, and he watches her expertly remove the stain using cold tap water from the sink. He would have used the hot water, and he can tell she's a pro by the way she never rubs the actual stain, instead working from the outside edges toward the center. For the most stubborn parts, she abrasively applies salt.

Once she's satisfied, she sits down next to him, and using what is left of the thread on her needle, she sews the gash in his shirt just as quickly as she mended his shoulder. She lays the shirt out on her lap to dry, pushes one cup of coffee toward him, and starts in on the other. It all happened so quickly that Red still sits shirtless across from her in awe.

"What, you don't like coffee?" she says, lighting up two cigarettes and handing him one. But he doesn't take it either.

"No caffeine or nicotine? Jeez, no drugs. Let me guess, no alcohol either?"

"It's illegal."

She scoffs, alternating between her coffee and cigarette.

"I'm sorry about your brother," Red eventually says to make conversation.

"He slices your shoulder, and you feel bad for him?" she asks, shaking her head, appearing to finally take a better look at Red and, for the first time, his sculpted physique.

"Well, he's your brother," Red says.

"He's a pain in the ass. But he's family."

"Family is important."

She takes another drag of her cigarette and looks Red over again.

"I know who you are," she finally says.

Red knew remaining anonymous was too good to be true.

"You're some kind of superhero, aren't you? Car expert by day? Saving damsels in distress by night? Masquerading as a college student?"

Her words elicit a smile from Red, her eyes scanning him like Sherlock Holmes piecing together a puzzle.

"I pegged you for a typical rich college kid," she declares. "But with that physique, you're clearly a laborer of some sort. You work construction or something to pay the tuition? What's your name anyway?"

Without thinking, Red starts to say his name, "Re...," but then corrects himself. "Harold."

"Well, nice to meet you, Re...Harold," she replies with a sly grin. "Not that you asked, but I'm Polly."

She gulps down her coffee and immediately starts on the second cup. She seems content to sit silently, her gaze fixed on him.

49

"Are you married?" he asks.

"Now I know you are a college kid. No common sense," she retorts, holding up her empty ring finger. "What's next? Are you going to ask me if I have kids? Or did you assume I'm maybe a war widow or something? At my age, I'd surely have been married, right?"

Red had indeed considered all those possibilities.

"No kids," she declares matter-of-factly. "If I were a man, maybe I'd have had a dozen kids by now. How fun. But as a woman, no thank you."

Red can't hide his bewilderment, a reaction Polly fully expected. It's not her first time launching into a dissertation on this subject.

"I'd love to teach a class about how the world really works," she says to him. "Let me guess, you grew up watching your mom cooking and cleaning your whole life, and how could all women not be like her, right?"

Red could easily correct her assessment of his upbringing, but he doesn't. He's tired of being misjudged, just like she's clearly tired of assumptions being made about her.

"And your big plans after college are to put your degree to work and get a job, right?"

He nods in agreement. That's everyone's goal after college.

"And then have an amazing career in something...I don't know, insurance, maybe?"

He nods again. He'd be proud to have a job like that.

"And then work your way up the ladder, buy a house, go on business trips, play golf, something like that?"

"Something like that," he agrees.

"And what if you marry and have two or three kids along the way?" she asks, not waiting for an answer. "Who cares? Right? Great. Doesn't slow you down for a moment. You may even want to have a good time girl on the side if your wife gets boring. The world is your oyster, right?"

Red wouldn't put it exactly like that, but he can't deny that it is often how the world works.

"And what if I want to have all those things? A career, hobbies, freedom, a fling on the side. How does that work for me as a woman if I'm married with kids?"

Red has never thought that through before. In all the years of watching the wives of his coaches and the mothers of his friends, the question of what a woman wants outside the home has never crossed his mind.

While caring for his brother and his dad, he'd never even asked himself what he wanted. He never had time to think about himself. He was always serving others.

"Enough of my lecture. Let's get you back to patriarchal expectations before that search party really forms," she says, standing up and holding open his shirt for him to put his arms into. "I'm sure you've got better things to do than get a lesson in feminism from me."

But he isn't ready to go. Not even close. He could watch and listen to her forever.

"Hurry on now," she says. "I don't want you here when the knucklehead in the other room wakes up. I'm out of thread for both of you."

Red eventually obeys, leans forward, and puts one arm into the shirt, forgetting his wound and bandage, only to wince as some pain reminds him of it.

"You better take it easy tomorrow," Polly says, helping his other arm into the shirt before turning him around and kneeling in front of him to assist with the buttons. "It's a good excuse to lay around and do some homework or something. Everyone deserves a lazy Saturday."

Each button she fastens seems to bring her closer and closer to him. Eventually, she finishes, straightens his collar, leaps up, and opens the front door to show him out.

"Thank you," he says to her as he stands and steps out into the hallway.

"Again, you thank me?" she says, shaking her head. "For what?"

"For...," Red searches for the words. "For the adventure."

"Well, if you ever see me around town again, how about next time...you mind your own business and quit trying to save me?"

He's taken aback but gets the courage to look her in the eyes before she closes the door, expecting maybe the slightest smile to form on her face. But it doesn't.

Before the door shuts, she pauses with one final thought.

"Or, maybe next time, I'll save you."

CHAPTER 8

Michigan at Illinois
Saturday, October 18, 1924

Lined up in formation, awaiting the whistle, Red enjoys a moment of serenity before receiving the opening kickoff. Game day in Champaign is electric.

On this hot autumn day, the stadium is at full capacity with sixty-seven thousand in attendance, not counting another twenty thousand fans that the fire marshal wouldn't allow inside. Many of them are taking turns holding children on their shoulders or standing on trucks, peering over the north wall, desperately trying to get a peek at this historic matchup.

Late morning editions of the local newspapers printed that more cars are in Champaign today than in Europe. The Illinois State Police temporarily changed the highways from Chicago and Michigan, so all the lanes run south into Champaign.

Red's entire hometown of Wheaton—just west of Chicago—sits with Red's father, Lyle Grange, in a designated section in the front row near the goal line.

Lyle is an imposing figure who towers above the crowd. The muscular physique he earned laboring as a Pennsylvania lumberjack comes in handy working as Wheaton's city jailer. Garland is right beside his father in the stands, wishing he were old enough to be on the field, sharing the glory.

Red has endured pageantry all morning. After the flag raisings, field dedication speeches from politicians, military plane flyovers, national anthem, pep band performances, student section cheers, cheerleader routines, ROTC marches, pregame warmup routines, fireworks, a moment of silence for all alumni who died in the war, endless renditions of the Illini "Oskee-Wow-Wow" fight song, and eventual coin toss, the time has finally come to play the actual game.

Earl waits for the kickoff, lined up ten yards ahead of Red. He sneaks a look back, signaling he's ready for their secret play. Red reluctantly nods back at him, hoping Michigan scouts aren't already tipped off. He stretches his arms just a bit, loosening up his bandaged shoulder one last time before going to battle.

To say Red's teammates are fired up would be an understatement. On top of Coach Zuppke's brilliance in terms of strategy, he's also a master at preparing players mentally, which is especially needed given that the opposing Michigan team outweighs every Illinois player across every position.

Assembled in the locker room earlier, before they came out on the field, Zuppke barged in, mad as hell, holding a piece of paper.

"I found this letter under my office door just now," Zuppke said, so angered he could barely talk. "It's from Coach Yost. You can see the Michigan letterhead at the top, plain as day."

Zuppke, tiny compared to his players, held the letter high enough for everyone to get a glimpse of the yellow and blue Michigan colors before lowering it so he could read it out loud to his troops.

"The letter says, 'Coach Zuppke, I instructed the conductor of our train to keep the engine running,'" the little German coach shouted, painfully reading each word. "'Because we expect to have your Illini boys so whipped by halftime, they won't dare return from the locker room.'"

After the reading of the letter, the players were even more red in the face than their coach. They slammed their fists against lockers, kicked over chairs, and stomped their feet.

Coach allowed their rage to run rampant until finally raising his hand to demand their attention.

"It goes on to say a few more disparaging things, which I don't have the heart to read to you," Zuppke declared, utterly disgusted. "And it closes by saying the most un-Christian thing I've ever read. I can't...I...I could never say it."

The boys were even more livid at this point.

"What's it say, Coach?" Earl shouted. "What's it say?"

The boys quieted down. They wanted to hear it, but Zuppke kept shaking his head that he wouldn't dare. Finally, a voice yelled out from the back of the room.

"Coach, what's it say?" Red demanded with the authority only he could command, completely quieting the locker room. "Go on, Coach, we can take it. What's it say?"

The boys could tell by Zuppke's face he would never say it were it not that Red had asked him to do so. Zuppke took a deep breath before struggling to read it aloud.

"The letter simply ends with," he said, choking as he gathered the courage to finish. "It ends with, 'Zuppke, you and your Illinois boys are all a bunch of pussies.'"

At that moment, the noise in the locker room was reported to reach a level that the sixty-seven thousand fans out in the stadium wouldn't match the rest of the afternoon.

The entire Illinois team, now lined up in front of Red on the field awaiting the kickoff, will never forget, for the rest of their lives, their beloved coach having to read that despicable word. They stand ready to pound Michigan into the dirt when the whistle finally blows to start the game.

Michigan, having won the coin toss and electing to kick, not surprisingly, given Yost's old-school strategy that values field position over all else, sends the ball sailing into the air with eleven Michigan killers instructed to do one thing: knock Red Grange out of the game.

Red tracks the ball soaring against the blue autumn sky. He takes a few steps forward, gracefully receives the ball, and tucks it safely under his arm. Before even taking his first step,

55

he assesses the entire field of play, as his orange teammates match up perfectly against the yellow, paving the way for his standard run to the right and around the end.

Red follows his blockers and dashes to the right with all eleven Michigan yellows determined to annihilate him. All eyes in the stadium lock on Red, mesmerized not just by his speed and agility but by the gracefulness with which he appears to float effortlessly across the field in contrast to the huffs and puffs of the other players.

The crowd anticipates a hole developing for him on the right, but after a few more strides, Red does the unthinkable, defying all football logic of the day. Instead of shooting through the hole, he cuts back in the other direction.

As Michigan scrambles to adjust to this unexpected change of course, they are so off balance that Earl, out of nowhere, having cut undetected ahead of Red, forces two Michigan players to the ground with a simple stiff arm, taking out a third by sacrificing his body.

Coach Zuppke, on the sidelines, and Mrs. Zuppke, in the stands, were the only people in the entire stadium who saw Earl pull in the opposite direction before Red. The rest of the crowd sees that the only one left in Red's way is Michigan's quarterback—the most athletic player on their team—who plays back as the last line of defense.

Red thinks to himself, "If Earl can take out three guys, what kind of a teammate am I if I can't beat one?"

He races along the Michigan sideline, flashing past a team that hasn't lost a game in two years. They barely turn their heads in time to witness Red blast past the last defender, cross the goal line, and touch the ball to the ground.

The crowd goes wild, led by Lyle Grange's section, which has cheered on Red's touchdowns ever since his playing days in Wheaton. An uproar of sound from the stadium blows past the twenty thousand still in the parking lot and envelops the entire town of Champaign.

Red immediately turns, not to bask in any form of glory, but to thank as many of his teammates as possible for their outstanding blocking. Earl kicks the extra point, making it 7-0 less than a minute into the game.

Up in the press box...

Young sportswriter Warren Brown and the rest of the press corps are at a loss for words. Before Warren could even get his cigar to light, the unimaginable has just happened.

The only distinguishable voice in Warren's vicinity is that of WGN radio announcer Quin Ryan, who desperately attempts to describe the cutback, barking the description into a telephone receiver that will be wired back to the broadcast towers in Chicago and then disseminated to hundreds of thousands of Midwest listeners huddled around radios at saloons, high schools, VFW halls, and living rooms. All he can think to say is, "I'm not kidding, folks. I'm not kidding. Red Grange has just scored on the opening kickoff."

The announcer will have to say, "I'm not kidding," over and over and over again throughout the first quarter because each time Illinois scores, Michigan elects to kick off to Illinois, which adheres to the common strategy of valuing field position over ball possession. Red scores again. And again. And again. Warren listens as the radio announcer attempts to describe four Red Grange touchdowns in less than twelve minutes against an undefeated Michigan team that hadn't given up this many points the entire last season.

After the initial ninety-five-yard kickoff return that successfully used Zuppke's cutback, Red scored on running plays of sixty-seven yards, fifty-six yards, and forty-four yards to the complete and utter hysteria of the record-setting crowd.

Warren studies the field as Illinois huddles for a well-deserved water break after scoring four touchdowns by the twelve-minute mark of the first quarter. As the team lines up to go back onto the field, Warren notices Red holding his shoulder. Then he watches in awe as a substitute player comes in for Red. Red tries to wave him off, but Zuppke is adamant that Red is to come out of the game. Red has no choice but to tuck his head and jog off the field.

The crowd spontaneously erupts into a standing ovation for Red that delays the game for ten whole minutes until Zuppke gets permission from the referee to allow Red to stand from the bench and take a bow. When he reluctantly does so, the cheers erupt even louder.

Warren does his best to type away despite the hysteria that has swept across not only the stands but also the press box. But the Red Grange legend isn't over yet. He returns in the second half to score a fifth rushing touchdown, intercept two passes on defense, and throw a pass to one of his teammates for a sixth touchdown.

An exceptional college player might tally fifty total yards throughout an entire game. But by Warren's count, Red has finished this game with over four hundred yards, only having played in three quarters of the 39-14 blowout, cementing not just Illinois' status as the best team in college football but the single greatest individual athletic performance of all time.

Warren attempts to capture in words the way Red kept cutting back over and over throughout the game, creating a phenomenon where he would disappear within the scrum of players, like a surfer disappearing under a curling wave, only to eventually reappear out of thin air on the other side, unscathed, and off to the races. No mortal man could accomplish what he just witnessed.

Looking back over his notes, at one point, he even typed, "Red would have to be invisible to pull off those runs."

"Or supernatural," he says to himself, his eyes suddenly lighting up. "Or, a ghost!"

CHAPTER 9

After the game, fans mill about the stadium's grounds. There is too much congestion on the highways to consider driving to Chicago. Besides, everyone wants to see if they can get a piece of Red.

Champaign police officers escort Red from the stadium, lights and sirens flashing, driving at one mile an hour to avoid pedestrians crowding the car. The persistent crowd follows, flowing to his fraternity house, forming an eight-block radius of tens of thousands of fans.

As the police cars pull up in front of his fraternity house, Red is swarmed when he steps out. Everyone wants to touch him. His hair. His legs. His arms. His face. Anything they can reach.

His lumberjack of a father, Lyle, barrels through the throngs of screaming fans and lifts Red into the air in a violent bear hug before imploring Red to shake the hands of just about everyone from his hometown of Wheaton; they aren't going to leave until they get to acknowledge their hero.

Every face from Red's childhood crowds around him. Former teachers. Former coaches. Shopkeepers. High school classmates. The mayor. His grade school principal. Fathers shamelessly reintroduce their daughters to him. Everyone seems to expect him to remember them.

Red's expression to each one of them, externally, is nothing but gratitude and appreciation. Over and over, he thanks everyone for taking the time to drive down and watch

59

him play. Deep down, though, he's dying. Absolutely dying. Until today, fame has been a nightmare. After today, he fears it will be a living terror.

Lyle shepherds forward one person after another—for what seems like an eternity—to congratulate Red. Garland is more than happy to entertain everyone waiting in line. Maybe next year, Red thinks, when Garland is eligible for varsity, his brother will take some of the heat off him.

Red is interrupted by that thought when his father brings over two prominent businessmen whom Red doesn't recognize, both wearing pinstripe suits with matching orange ties.

"Meet the Kaan brothers," Lyle says in his boisterous voice. "Big Illini boosters. They own the largest insurance agency in Chicago. They offered to fly me home on their plane tonight so I don't miss my shift tomorrow. And, get this, they want to set you up with a summer job."

A desk job far away from all of this hysteria would be perfect. He doesn't know anything about insurance, but he'd love to learn. Red wonders whether doing a good job over the summer could earn him a full-time position. He even remembers some of his older fraternity brothers talking about their summer internships in big companies and being relegated to having to work in a basement. Even that sounds amazing to Red, especially the opportunity to blend in with the other college interns.

"Don't worry," one of the Kaan brothers says, interrupting Red's daydream. "You won't have to learn actual insurance or anything. Or even go into the office. We'll just take you around to meet customers. Entertain them on our boat on the lake. Play golf. We also have a place in Panama. You'll love it. You won't have to work a single day in the office all summer. We promise."

The Kaan brothers shake Red's hand as if it's a done deal, and then they go back to yacking it up with Lyle. Red doesn't even have a chance to dwell on his disappointment of it not being a traditional job before Peggy McCaffrey, arguably the prettiest girl in college, pushes her way right up to him along with an entourage of the other gorgeous girls from her sorority. In tow is the skinny sorority girl who had successfully cut a real lock of Red's hair.

"Agnes said you wanted to see me," Peggy says, eyelashes flapping in full-out flirt mode. "I assume it is about the big dance tonight."

Peggy hands him her dance card and a pencil in front of the entire crowd.

"I have one spot left," she says. "I saved the last dance for you, Red."

Garland, Earl, and all of Red's friends cheer in support. Even Lyle looks at Red as if to say, "Well done, son."

Red wants to tell Peggy straight to her face to knock it off and stop sending girls after him, but this isn't the time or place with mobs surrounding them.

The dance card has spots for the names of ten boys; sure enough, the last spot remains blank. He signs on the remaining line and closes the book. She clutches it to her chest and runs away, shrieking along with her entourage, having just secured the prize of prizes. Later, however, when she goes to show off his signature, she'll instead discover he wrote "B. Nice."

Flashbulbs start going off all around him. The media have caught up to him. Newspaper reporters lob questions in all directions. The scene is unruly and out of control with reporters shouting over each other until Earl steps in and shields Red from them.

"One at a time," Earl shouts, leveraging his imposing figure, making it clear that no one will get to speak to Red until they establish some order. "Just a couple of questions, and then I'm gonna get Red into the house."

The reporters compete for attention until one dominant voice rises from the rest.

"How'd you do it?" the loudest reporter yells over the others. "How'd you make all those runs against that Michigan team?"

Red takes a deep breath and answers the only way he knows how: honestly.

"With our coaching and our blocking today," Red says, "anyone could make those runs. Even my grandma in Pennsylvania could make 'em."

The entire crowd laughs, but Red didn't intend for that to be funny. He meant it. And she's in a wheelchair.

"Why'd you pick jersey number 77?" another reporter yells out. "Why 77?"

"My freshman year, we all stood in a line, and the guy before me got 76, and the guy after me got 78," Red says to the further laughter of the crowd. That's just what happened.

More questions pour in until Warren pushes up to the front, awkwardly balancing his pen, notepad, and a lit cigar. It's all he can do not to drop all three of them or light his notebook on fire when he yells his burning question over the top of the pack.

"Why'd you come out of the game?" Warren asks, quieting the crowd and the press corps, who had forgotten about that curious coaching decision. "In the first half? Why'd Zuppke take you out? You missed the whole second quarter."

Everyone is now waiting for Red's response. He's about to answer when someone far in the distance, nearly out of sight, catches his eye. He squints to confirm his suspicion. Auburn-haired Polly leans up against her Roadster, wearing a white dress and hat, illuminated by the setting sun against the sea of orange fans.

"Why'd you come out of the game?" Warren repeats, waiting with the rest of the crowd for a response.

Before Red can answer, Earl cuts in.

"He was dog tired," Earl says. "You'd be dog tired too if Michigan's eleven were trying to murder you."

Everyone agrees, and the reporters write that down, many attributing the quote to Red himself. Questions keep coming as Earl shepherds Red into the fraternity house.

As the reporters follow after them, yelling questions, Warren stands in place with an entirely dissatisfied expression. "Dog tired?" he jots down into his notebook, followed by twenty more question marks.

No sooner does Earl shepherd Red safely through the front door of the fraternity house than Red slips out the side door, glides undetected around the perimeter of the crowd, and hops into the passenger seat of Polly's getaway car.

CHAPTER 10

In the press box at the Polo Grounds Stadium in Upper Manhattan, the nation's most acclaimed national sportswriter, Grantland Rice, puts the final touches on his column chronicling the Army-Notre Dame game, which has just unfolded on the field below.

Known for his quiet eloquence and mighty prose, the slender, middle-aged bard not only effortlessly holds and smokes a cigar, but he can do so while typing. Like a basketball player dribbling with both hands between his legs, the cigar glides from one hand to the other, to his mouth, and back again in a way a local writer like Warren could only wish to emulate.

In between blowing perfect smoke circles, Rice has the distinct honor this afternoon to not only tell the story for his audience of how Notre Dame surgically dismantled Army's defense but to do so knowing that each word he types will be syndicated to millions of readers across the country who rely on him to paint a picture of the sports heroes and their travails, stories to which readers have grown addicted since the war ended.

The task at hand is to describe Notre Dame's acclaimed backfield, which consists of the best quarterback, the two best halfbacks, and the best fullback ever assembled on one team in college football history. Rice had recently overheard a Notre Dame press assistant talking about how this Notre Dame backfield reminded him of the title and characters of a

new Rudolph Valentino movie, which was all the inspiration a genius like Rice needed:
> Outlined against a blue-gray October sky the Four Horsemen rode again. In dramatic lore they are known as famine, pestilence, destruction, and death. These are only aliases. Their real names are All-Americans: Stuhldreher, Miller, Crowly, and Layden.

He pauses for a moment, happy with the Four Horsemen bit, the title of that Valentino movie, but wondering if it is too presumptuous for him to label each of the four as "All-Americans," especially since Walter Camp, who bestows the honor, has never before given that many accolades to a single team's backfield. Not to mention that Camp's list won't be released until the end of the season.

However, Rice is convinced if ever the time has come for a single team's backfield to be recognized for all four positions it will be this 1924 Notre Dame backfield, especially after today's dominating performance.

Rice hasn't fully decided whether to cut the phrase "All-Americans" or not when he hears a buzz coming from the other reporters in the press box. First, he hears someone saying, "Look at this off the wire." Another says, "That can't be true."

Rice is intently eavesdropping now as some reporters have started making phone calls to confirm what they just read. He hears them saying, with a telephone receiver in one hand and the speaker in the other, "The what?" "A ghost?" "Galloping who?" "Over four hundred yards?" "Six touchdowns?" One by one, after the calls conclude, he watches as his peers put fresh sheets of paper into their typewriters to file an additional story on top of the game they just witnessed. Some of them do not even bother to finish their original story on the Notre Dame game.

At this point, Rice feels he has no choice but to exercise his long legs, which came in handy back in the day when he played for Vanderbilt, and walks over to read the wires himself. He wasn't much of a football player, but he was good at reading the field, using his intelligence as a weapon and anticipating the play.

He barely makes it through the first few paragraphs of the wire when he rushes back to his typewriter and immediately scratches out "All-Americans" from the prose he had just typed. There is no way the entire Notre Dame backfield is going to get all four honors after the extraordinary feat that just took place in Champaign.

Rice spins his own fresh sheet of paper into his typewriter and pauses a moment for final inspiration to strike before composing a poem, which he often includes in his columns. He begins:

A streak of fire, a breath of flame,
Eluding all who reach and clutch;
A gray ghost thrown into the game,
That rival hands may never touch.

He has no idea at this time how his "gray ghost" stanza or his "Four Horsemen" metaphor will be remembered. He's published millions of words in his career and intends to publish tens of millions more. But, as he finishes his day's work, he knows one thing for certain: he's not going to miss another opportunity to witness first-hand for his readers the legend of Red Grange.

Illinois has an upcoming game at the University of Chicago against legendary coach Amos Alonzo Stagg, who is fielding a team of eleven men this year that is even bigger and stronger than Michigan's. National reporters rarely go further west than The University of Pennsylvania in Philadelphia to cover college football, but he'll be making the trip to Chicago.

Four Horsemen or not, Rice is now possessed by The Galloping Ghost.

CHAPTER 11

Taking a long drag of her cigarette, Polly is parked a few blocks from the Virginia Theater and sitting beside a young man who, as a result of tomorrow's papers, she's told, will surely be launched to the meteoric levels of Babe Ruth, Jack Dempsey, Bobby Jones, and Man O' War.

"Today was the first football game I've ever seen," she says between puffs. "It reminded me of the war. Violent, but yet there were rules and structure. The way you played, however, was something different. You were above it all. Floating. Untouchable."

She watches as he shrugs off her compliment. He's handsome, she'll give him that. She admires his strong jawline, high cheekbones, sparkly blue-gray eyes, and broad shoulders.

"I'll really be all over the papers now," Red says, looking out at revelers stumbling along the streets of Champaign. My dad has career ideas for me. So does my brother. So does Coach. So does Earl. I made the attention far worse out on the field today."

"What? You should be on top of the world. You do love football, right?"

"I do," he says. "It's the rest of it...."

"The rest of it can't be as complicated as the game itself. Before I watch another game, I need you to explain something to me."

"Anything," he says.

67

"Explain why Michigan kept kicking off to you."

"Um, well," Red fumbles a bit.

"It's just stupid. Why give you the ball? I'd never give it to you. And to do it over and over."

"I'm trying to think of the best way to explain it. I wish I had some chalk or something," he says. "Or, I could show you how I was taught. Except I'd need...well...I'd need your hand."

She immediately offers him hers. She senses from his trepidation and the way he awkwardly interlocks his fingers with hers that it might be his first time holding a woman's hand.

"Pretend I'm the offense and you are the defense," he says, pushing his hand gently against hers until she pushes back with enough resistance that they equalize. Then he pushes a bit harder until their entwined hands are closer to her than to him. "So I'm the offense and trying to score."

She catches on as he keeps their hands closer to her.

"At this point, I have momentum. I'm pretty close to scoring," he says. "I have what is called 'good field position,' giving me more options."

She nods.

"Now let's say you've got me pinned down on my end," he says, moving their hands much closer to him. "Even though I have the ball, look how close you'd be to scoring, especially if I screwed up. In this situation, we're taught to punt it away to be safe."

"I noticed sometimes you even punt on first downs."

"You have to keep your opponent on his toes."

"Then why don't you pass the ball more? You rarely do. Teams only hand off. It's too easy to predict a run play is coming when that's all you ever do."

"Have you ever held a regulation football?" he asks.

She shakes her head. He unlocks their hands so he can use both of his to show her the enormous size of the ball.

"The football evolved from a soccer ball to a big rugby ball. It's just too big to throw very far or accurately. It's too round and not pointy enough. It wobbles in the air."

"But you threw a touchdown pass at the end of the game," she says.

"Zuppke had me practice all summer. Garland and I threw the ball back and forth probably thousands of times. My dream is to complete a pass to my brother next year when he's eligible."

"Why can't freshman play?"

"Ask the NCAA that one. I don't know. They have lots of rules. It must be similar to the military. The top brass makes the rules, and the rest of us take orders."

"You got that right. Except, that's a dumb rule. Not to mention the litany of penalties that get called. And why can't you freely substitute players into the game like basketball? How come when a player comes out, he has to stay out?"

"Like soccer, the game is designed to test the endurance of the players, but I hear you on the penalties. Every year, Walter Camp adds more and more of them, making the rulebook even thicker."

"And all that business about your dad, brother, Earl, coach, and your future," she says. "Who's your mentor? Who is your coach off the field?"

"I don't have a coach for that," Red admits.

"Find one," she says. "You need to quit worrying and enjoy life more. You should be on top of the world. Find a good advisor. Someone who knows a thing or two."

"What about you?" he says. "You're smart. How about you advise me?"

"Easy. My advice would be to take the option that pays the most money."

"Well that settles it," he says jokingly. "Problem solved."

He smiles at that thought, yet she can tell he has something else to say. She loves how cute it is that he has to muster the courage to talk to her.

"How about you watch a movie with me?" he asks. "One's about to start. My buddy Clem will let us in the side door. I still pay, though."

"After the big game, that's what you want to do? A party is raging on at your fraternity house and you want to see a movie?"

"I don't just want to see a movie. I want to see it with you. I'm asking you on a proper date."

She's been expertly trained to never show any weakness, including expressing admiration or affection for others. As a result, she never smiles, even when she wants to as much as she does right now.

But what a cute kid, she thinks. *The world's first genuine superstar.*

CHAPTER 12

The day after Red's historic game, Tim Mara wonders what he's gotten himself into as he pays his $1.50 admission and enters Cubs Park to watch the Chicago Bears play.

Not even a week ago, against his better judgment, he agreed to shell out $500 for the exclusive rights to launch a new NFL team in New York City. Once Mara finalizes the lease agreement to play at the Polo Grounds, he intends to name his team after the baseball team that plays there—the Giants. The same would have happened in Chicago, except naming a football team after a baby bear just wasn't going to cut it for Bears owner George Halas.

The irony, though, is that the Cubs fill this stadium. The Bears, if you count the hundreds of free tickets handed out, are lucky to draw one thousand fans who could sit anywhere they want but prefer to stand along the actual sidelines, just off the field, jeering at the players, throwing beer, and vehemently booing the referees. Most of the fans haven't slept, given they stayed up watching boxing matches the night before, partied at speakeasies until dawn, and then slept outside the stadium until the gates opened.

Unlike a professional baseball game, Mara notices no kids or families in the stands. The fans are drunk, stupid, and obnoxious. The entire experience for them is about one thing: witnessing extreme violence. The more blood, the better.

Mara is learning that teams are lucky if they practice once a week. Many of the players are dock hands, laborers, construction workers, wrestlers, boxers, and vagabonds who play for one reason and one reason only: to get a chance to hit somebody.

Mara watches the violent scene play out on the field below him, realizing his three-piece suit is out of place in this crowd. As a tall and slender thirty-six-year-old businessman, he looks and dresses the part of extreme generational wealth, even though he wasn't born into it. He began his transformation into this lifestyle at age ten when he had to quit school to support his mother by running bets for bookies up and down Wall Street.

Today, he owns the largest bookmaking business in New York with the highest-volume betting windows at each of the five largest NYC racetracks, including Belmont Park. Like these Bears fans, his customers are anyone willing to make a bet. But his real customers are the wealthy elite who own the horses. Their bets are the real money. To win them over, he had to become one of them.

Mara searches high and low for a stadium worker. Cubs games sell food and drinks. Fans apparently bring their own food and drink to Bears games, so there are hardly any paid stadium workers on game day. Mara eventually finds someone who looks like they might work here.

"I'm looking for the Bears owner."

The worker points toward the field.

"I can see that everyone is down there," Mara explains. "But which one is George Halas?"

"That one," the worker says, pointing him out on the field. "He just made the tackle."

Mara's first glimpse of Bears' owner/player George Halas is of Halas standing up after making a violent play and spitting blood out of his mouth toward the sidelines. Halas smiles and wipes his face to the absolute joy of the fans. They love him. And they love getting spit on.

Mara can hardly believe his eyes.

"Is there someone else I can speak with in the Bears organization?" Mara pleads to the worker. "Someone in charge of ticket sales? Or advertising?"

"That's also him," the worker says, pointing to Halas again.

"What about the back office stuff? Leases? Player contracts? Media relations?"

The worker looks at Mara like he is crazy and again just points to Halas.

"Next, you are going to tell me he's the coach, as well?" Mara jokes.

The stadium worker doesn't have the patience to listen to any more dumb questions and walks away, leaving Mara to realize that even in a big market like Chicago, owner George Halas wears all the hats, including player and head coach.

Mara could have chosen any of the fourteen thousand empty seats, but he elects to slide into the seat closest to him to watch his first NFL game. Like most Americans, he didn't attend college and is still learning the sport. For the most part, Mara would even publicly admit that he has no idea what is going on on the field below him.

But he knows one thing: this same sport drew sixty-seven thousand fans just the day before at the University of Illinois and fifty-five thousand fans at the Polo Grounds to watch Army-Notre Dame. Every Saturday, college football games draw more fans than the Chicago Bears have today. Even tiny colleges draw more than the Bears. Even high schools.

Something, Mara is convinced, is amiss with pro football. The fan bases for college football teams draw alumni, parents, students, and, recently, after the war, entire states who have transferred their national pride in rooting for America to win the war to their favorite state colleges doing battle with teams one state over.

Mara knows Major League Baseball is organized in big cities like New York, Boston, Chicago, Philadelphia, Detroit, and St. Louis. He is sitting in Chicago, the NFL's largest city.

The other NFL cities are ones he's never heard of, places like Frankford, Racine, Rock Island, Hammond, Akron, and Kenosha. If there was ever an opportunity to invest in a sport, it is pro football.

Eventually, the game ends in a non-riveting score of 6-0 with only field goals and no touchdowns. Mara stands after the game to introduce himself to Halas, but then sits back down when he realizes all the work Halas still has to do after the game.

He watches as Halas sorts through the cash collected from the gate, gives half to the other team, and then pays his players fifty to a hundred dollars apiece for playing in today's game. Halas pays the guys who got hurt a little more. A couple of others appear to ask for help for one reason or another, and he pays them some extra as well. When the gate receipts have run out, with more people standing in line to be paid, Halas takes out his wallet to settle the remaining debts.

Once the money is settled, Mara watches as Halas cleans up the field to get it back in shape for another event happening in the stadium later that night. Almost two hours after the game, Mara is finally able to walk up to Halas and shake his hand.

"I'm Tim Mara," he says. "I'm the dummy buying the exclusive New York City rights."

Mara is nearly a head taller than the short, stocky twenty-nine-year-old Halas. As Mara shakes his hand, he can't help but notice the distinctive scar running down Halas' right cheek, adding a touch of intrigue to his already rugged post-game appearance.

"Ugh, New York," Halas replies.

"You're not excited to have another major city in the league?"

"I'm not excited to come up with the travel money to get my team that far."

That's the other problem with the NFL, Mara thinks to himself. The owners often don't have any personal money to invest. He's now realizing firsthand the challenges of keeping the fledgling league alive week to week.

"Look," Halas says, making his way toward the elevated train, "I have to go. I need to drop the score and stats from the game off at the newspapers. They won't even send reporters to the game. I haven't seen my wife and kids since early this morning. My daughter, Virginia, is going to forget what I look like. I need to shower and have dinner with them. Maybe sleep. And get ready for work tomorrow. My family already hates this crazy dream of mine to own a football team, and the later I get home, the longer they'll have to worry that I got seriously hurt or worse out there today."

That's a lot of information for Mara to unpack, but he has one burning question.

"What's your day job?"

"I'm a civil engineer."

That's another thing, Mara realizes: the players, coaches, and owners don't make anywhere near enough for football to be their full-time job, yet they risk their lives playing it.

"Listen," Mara says, "before you go. I have one idea for the league I'd like to run by you. Just one. And then I'll let you get home to your family."

"Fine, go on," an exhausted Halas replies.

"Red Grange," Mara says, smiling, expecting an enthusiastic reply.

Instead, Halas shakes his head and starts to walk away as Mara chases after him.

"What? The NFL needs a star. We need a Babe Ruth."

Halas keeps walking toward the train as Mara chases after him.

"You don't think Red Grange is the guy?"

Halas makes a fist at his side, attempting to isolate his anger, before finally turning back to Mara.

"Have you done any homework at all? Any research before you got into this?" Halas says, so severely agitated now that the last thing Mara would ever want is to be on a football field lined up against Halas' level of intensity.

"Do you know who Red Grange plays for?" Halas continues. "Do you know Bob Zuppke? He'll never allow Red to play in the pros. Ever. Zup wants to see the NFL go bankrupt for good. Zup loves only three things: God, his wife, and college football. In a close fourth place is Red Grange. Zup loves Grange like a son. And do you know where pro football falls on Zup's list of priorities?"

"I'm assuming the bottom?"

"Almost," Halas says, but his rage slowly turns into sadness. "I'm just beneath pro football on his shit list."

"Why you?" Mara can't help but ask.

"Because I used to be his Red," Halas admits. "He's not about to let the pro game corrupt Red like he believes it did me."

At this point, Halas has lost all of his energy for further conversation, turning to walk away.

"So you're not going to make a play for Red?" Mara shouts after him.

"No one can," Halas replies. "It's a fool's errand."

Mara watches Halas board the train and race home to his tiny apartment. After Halas is well out of sight, a sly smile forms across Mara's face.

He didn't get to be the largest bookmaker in New York without knowing the odds, and those can't be set without gathering inside information. His strategy is all coming together between what he's confirmed on this trip and the details he's currently gathering in Champaign.

CHAPTER 13

Clem barges into Pyle's office with an urgent look on his face only to discover Pyle now has two film projectors going, allowing him to simultaneously enjoy Margarita Fischer on one screen and Red Grange on another.

"Put all that away," Clem says frantically, stepping back outside. "They are coming. They're coming up."

Pyle flips off the projectors and tucks them away in the hidden cabinets just in time for Clem's formal knock at the door. After knocking a few more times, Clem slowly opens the door and peeks inside.

"There are some students here who want to see you," Clem says in a tone loud enough for the students to hear. "I already told them you were too busy, but they insisted."

Clem starts to shut the door when Pyle yells out to him.

"It's okay," he says, "if it is quick."

Clem turns into the hallway and says a few muffled words to whomever is out there before officially opening the door to Pyle's office.

Clem holds the door open as Red, Earl, and Garland respectfully enter the office to find Pyle poring over maps. Without looking up, he motions for them to sit on the couch, which they do. Clem shuts the door and takes a seat at a chair near Pyle's desk.

While they are waiting for Pyle to finish, the boys look around his office. Framed photos of every movie star the boys

77

have ever seen cover the walls. Posing next to these recognizable movie stars is a smiling Pyle.

A particular photo frame on Pyle's desk catches Red's attention. It's his all-time favorite actress, Marion Davies. Sure enough, she's standing there smiling with Pyle's arm around her waist.

"She's my favorite, too," Pyle says, coming around his desk, grabbing the frame, and handing it to Red. "That was taken almost a decade ago, the night I introduced her to William Randolph Hearst. Next thing you know, Hearst ships his wife off to the East Coast, builds the Hearst Castle, and guess who lives in that castle with him still today?"

"Marion Davies," Red answers. "Wow. You know her."

"I know them all," Pyle says. "I was just going over some plans to build more theaters, and I still have that thing I need to do for Charlie Chaplin. Remember, Clem?"

Clem is confused at first but then nods to confirm.

"But what can I do for you boys today?"

The three of them all look at each other to decide who is going to speak when finally Garland goes first.

"Mr. Pyle, I'm not sure if you follow college football?"

"After the amazing Michigan game, I watched you beat DePauw 45-0 and Iowa 36-0," Pyle says quickly. "You guys are on your way to back-to-back national championships."

"Well, as result of that, Red is all over the papers now," Garland continues. "All the papers. Everywhere. As a result, he has a ton of opportunities being thrown at him. Earl and I have been trying to help him sort it all out. But, well, we don't always see eye to eye."

Earl nods in agreement.

"That puts Red in a tough spot," Pyle says. "His best friend on one side, and his brother – his *family* – on the other."

"I feel like we could work it out ourselves," Garland says, "but Red suggested...well...he said, we should see what C.C. Pyle thinks about it all."

Pyle lets loose his winning smile. He's pleased as punch to have been considered.

"My goodness," Pyle says. "Clem, how many times have we helped people in similar situations?"

Clem's unsure how to answer.

"Too many to count," Pyle answers for him. "Red, so you want my advice?"

Red nods.

"It's a pretty simple process," Pyle explains. "First, we list all the opportunities, putting them all on the table, and then we list the pros and cons for each, and then, well, and then it always becomes clear what to do. How does that sound? Clem and I follow this process all the time for the movie stars that pass through here. What do you think the stars do up here in my office while the movie is playing?"

"Well, one of the opportunities doesn't have a con," Garland cuts in. "It's clear cut and dry."

"So is another one of them," Earl adds, staring Garland down while Red closes his eyes in frustration.

"Clem, I think I see the issue," Pyle says "Boys, you're not helping Red when you don't have an open mind to the good and bad of each opportunity. We'll find out shortly, but if I had to guess, I'd assume the option each of you likes is not the best option for Red, per se, but for you two personally."

They begin to protest until Red quiets them, imploring them to listen as Pyle continues.

"I think that is why Red asked for me. I don't have a horse in the race. Red, you are wise to seek my counsel. Very wise at your young age. I'm impressed."

Red nods as if to say, "Thank you," but Garland and Earl are still steaming mad at Pyle's accusation they are in it for themselves.

"Red, let's have you tell me the options in your words," Pyle says. "Clem is going to sit at my desk and write them down exactly as you say them."

This suggestion surprises Clem, but he complies, reluctantly moving to Pyle's desk in search of pen and paper.

"Go on now, Red, tell us what's going on?" Pyle implores him.

Red doesn't want to have to verbalize it all, but he closes his eyes and gets started.

"Coach Zup wants me to be the next Walter Camp. Start by being his assistant coach before eventually becoming the 'ambassador,' as he calls it, of the 'great amateur college game.'"

Red opens his eyes, ready for everyone to jump all over the idea, but Pyle holds his arms out for everyone to remain quiet.

"Red has the floor now," Pyle explains. "Red, lay it all out. We're just here to listen. Keep going."

"Garland and Dad want me to work for the Kaan brothers—the insurance boosters. They are offering perks to Garland and Dad, as well."

"That's why you like it," Earl says to Garland, unable to keep his mouth shut.

Garland is about to fight back when Red calms them.

"Earl knows there is no money in it, but he wants me to play pro football with him," Red says. "The NFL barely sells any tickets. The most a player can make is only a few thousand a year."

"Football is what you're best at in this world," Earl says. "I know you love it. God gave you a gift. You should use it for as long as you can."

"Dad says insurance is forever," Garland says. "And they have a place in Panama we can use any time. And they have their own private planes."

Earl and Garland almost start fighting until Pyle regains control of the meeting and settles them all down.

"What else?" Pyle asks Red.

"Those are all the things," Red says. "What do you think?"

"Ambassador of the college game, insurance, and pro football?" Pyle confirms. "That's it? Those three?"

"Doesn't that seem like plenty?" Red asks.

"Red, you are a comet, a blazing meteorite, the hottest commodity in the world. I thought you'd be bringing me endorsement offers. Book offers. Movie offers," Pyle explains. "Clem, imagine if I dialed up my movie executive friends about Red doing a screen test? They'd leap at it. I bet they wouldn't even bother with a test."

Clem does his best to nod.

"Red, I bet Marion Davies would jump at the chance to star in a film with you. Remember, the title cards do all the talking. You'd just have to occasionally smile and run around a little on camera. Flex a little. You're pretty good at running around, aren't you?"

Red's eyes widen at this possibility, which he'd never considered. He could never sing and dance or even talk on stage. But silent movies, well, he might just be pretty good at that.

"Imagine sitting in the back of one of my theaters and seeing yourself up there on the screen, not in a newsreel but in the actual story?"

Surprisingly, Garland and Earl both love the idea.

"He could be the next Rudy Valentino," Garland chimes in. "The Latin Lover."

"Or an action star like Douglas Fairbanks," Earl adds.

"Couldn't you see Red up there on screen, Clem?" Pyle asks without allowing him to answer. "He'd be Valentino and Fairbanks all rolled into one. An action star men love and a heartthrob for the ladies."

Earl and Garland start going back and forth with ideas of characters Red could play. "Football star." "International spy." "Race car driver." Pyles watches as Red lets out a smile or two at each possibility. It's the first time he's ever seen Red smile.

81

"And Earl," Pyle says to him, changing the entire tone of the meeting for a moment. "I'm sorry to say, but we have to rule out playing for an NFL team. Too much risk for too little reward."

A second ago, Earl was having so much fun, but now his temper is about to flare when Pyle suddenly lets loose his winning smile.

"I wouldn't advise playing for *an* NFL team. If I were Red, I'd form my own league. Play in big cities. Hire former college coaches to coach. Recruit college players who actually know the game and can block. Fill the stands with wholesome families. The NFL is a joke. But a *Red Grange League*? Now you'd really have something."

Earl, Garland, and even Red don't know how to react. They never thought of such a possibility.

"I thought you guys were sorting through real offers," Pyle says to them, shaking his head in confusion. "I read in the papers that the postal service is now delivering a truck full of mail a day to the fraternity house. What's in all those letters?"

Red's face flushes. Garland, however, grins ear to ear and is ready to answer, but Earl cuts him off.

"Some of the mail is little kids wanting stuff signed," Earl says. "Red stays up late at night, answering as many of them as he can. I try to help. I'm getting pretty good at faking his autograph."

"And the rest?" Pyle asks.

"We put it in the trash," Red interrupts, looking at his brother sternly.

"You say to put it in the trash," Garland says, turning and smiling at Pyle and Clem. "But the rest is girls. So many girls. You wouldn't believe the photos some of them send."

"Oh, I think we would," Pyle corrects him. "I think we would. This is not our first rodeo, boys. Clem, even Rudy Valentino would be jealous, I bet. He's getting a little up there in age, you know."

Clem nods in agreement.

"Red, you do have a lot to process," Pyle says, "but the volume of mail is only going to increase."

Red appears to shudder at the thought.

"I see the answer. I know what you should do. But I'm not sure if I should say it today," Pyle says. "See, I'm not your brother, best friend, coach, father, booster, or even a guy who makes movies any longer. I can't make decisions for you. However, a manager or an agent could take it all off your hands. You don't have to make any of these decisions yourself. I'm not sure if you realize that?"

"I hadn't," Red admits. "We've never discussed that or any of the big ideas you've brought up today."

"Here's what I suggest," Pyle says. "I suggest your brother and Earl promise to leave you alone about this for a while and let it all sink in, especially with the big University of Chicago game coming up. Can you two agree to give him space to think for a moment?"

It takes Garland and Earl a moment to agree, but, eventually, they nod.

"How's that sound to you, Red? You take some time on your road trip to Chicago to reflect and come see me when you're ready. Lay it all out. Pretend I'm your agent. I'll listen and give advice."

Pyle can tell by Red's face the weight of the world may be on him even more now.

"Let me take Clem's notes with me, at least," Red says, "so I don't forget all we talked about."

"Sure thing. Clem, pass those notes over."

Clem can't hide the sudden look of panic on his face. He reluctantly starts to hand the paper to Pyle when, at the last moment, Pyle waves him off.

"Red, let me type them up for you. I'll estimate how much money you can make with each, as well. You have enough on your mind without having to sort through Clem's chicken scratch."

Red nods and Clem can't hide his relief of not having to turn the notes over.

"Okay, now let's get you three boys out of here," Pyle says, waving his hand toward the door and standing up. "Go back to college. Enjoy yourselves. Play your big Chicago game. Trust me, now is the time of your lives because pretty soon, regardless of the path you choose, you'll one day be sitting at a desk like mine, poring over boring piles of paperwork, like me here today, deciding where to place my next thirty theaters."

"Wow. Thirty?" Garland says.

"The next thirty of three hundred," Pyle corrects him.

The three boys' eyes light up in amazement at the thought. They each shake Clem's and Pyle's hands and let themselves out of the office.

After a few moments, Clem finally breathes a sigh of relief.

"You know I can't write and read," Clem says, maybe too loudly.

Before Pyle can respond, Red has stepped back into the room without either of them realizing it.

"Here's the thing," Red says. "I just wanted to thank you. It's refreshing to have an advisor to talk to who's already successful and has nothing to gain from me."

"Oh, my boy," Pyle says, putting his hands over his heart. "My pleasure."

"You have no idea what it means to me to have someone like you," Red says, looking at the floor, struggling to make eye contact. "Someone who's seen all this before. Someone I can trust."

Red starts to leave, but not before asking, "Do you want your door open or shut?"

"My door?" Pyle replies, flashing that winning smile yet again. "You can always trust that my door will be open to you."

CHAPTER 14

Red takes Pyle's advice and walks the streets of Chicago alone on the eve of the big game.

For every banner hanging out of an apartment window reading "Stop Red," there are three times as many banners reading "Go Red." In the past, when Illini played the University of Chicago, the banners always read "Stop Orange" or "Go Orange." It's not lost on him that, for this matchup, the town is painted Red.

He pulls out a piece of paper Pyle typed for him laying out Red's financial options. Like most average Americans, Red's father, Lyle, makes around two thousand dollars a year. Pyle estimates the Kaan brothers would probably pay Red ten thousand dollars a year. He'd make far less working for colleges. He could make tens of thousands with a hit movie. But he could make a hundred thousand if he owned an entire successful pro football league.

The choices are overwhelming, not to mention the bonus option Pyle outlined of Red owning a football league, starring in movies, and endorsing products. Red can't even bring himself to fully commit that number to memory. It's more digits than his mind can comprehend.

What's really weighing on him is yet another option, one not on that piece of paper but that frequently runs through his mind. It's not an option as much as a fantasy. It's one where he changes his name, moves to Florida, gets a normal job, and talks Polly into running away with him.

He still has no idea what she does for a living. Something about "information gathering" for bigwigs. She won't talk to him about it. She won't smile. But she does listen. And she does offer advice.

As he nears the hotel and sees the massive orange crowd of fans forming in front of the hotel, that fantasy of running away sounds very appealing to him whether Polly comes along or not.

Before he can glide around to the back alley, a businessman steps out in front of him and extends his hand.

"Tim Mara," he says, shaking Red's hand before he can get away. "Let me cut right to it. How'd you like to star for the New York Giants?"

Red is confused.

"I'd like you to play for us."

"I'm not that good at baseball," Red says, walking away. "I already turned down the Braves."

"Sorry, the football Giants," Mara corrects him. "We're making a go at a new team. We're going about it the right way by signing actual All-Americans to serious contracts. But we need a star and I've got my sights set on you. How'd you like to be the Babe Ruth of pro football in a new and improved NFL?"

Red has never heard of Tim Mara, and he's read nothing about a new NFL team. Men like Mara approach him with opportunities ten times a day, but few are fortunate enough to corner him.

"I'm late for a team meeting," Red says, deciding which side street will help him lose this guy.

"Fifty thousand in cash up front," Mara says back to him. "For just three home games at the Polo Grounds."

Red pauses for just a moment to get a better look at this tall, slender man with a friendly, confident face in a fancy, custom-tailored suit, the likes of which Red has only seen on one other person: C.C. Pyle.

"For three home games," Mara says again. "After next year's college season. After your last game. When you won't owe anything more to Zuppke or Illinois. Fifty thousand, and with more to follow."

Red takes a longer look at the man's serious face before rushing off.

"Think about it," Mara says, calling after him. "Three games after your final college season is over."

Red glides down multiple alleys, trying to process the conversation. *Fifty thousand dollars for only three games. Could that be a real offer?* He zig-zags down a few side streets and cuts back to the alley behind the team hotel. He's deciding which of the seven back doors to attempt when one conveniently opens out toward him, but no one exits.

He quickly peeks around the door ready to talk his way in, only to have an entire bucket of dirty mop water thrown right into his face. It's such a direct hit that water even goes up his nose and into his eyes. He can feel the dirty water sliding down his body under his shirt and into his shoes.

When he regains his eyesight, he sees the most adorable young brunette. She's around his age and wearing a hotel uniform, propping the door open with one foot and turning back into the hotel to grab a second bucket of mop water to throw out.

As she goes to throw the second bucket out into the alley, she spies him and halts her motion, causing the dirty water to splash right up into her face and down her white uniform.

After getting the water and gunk out of her nose and eyes and realizing they are now both in the same situation, a beautiful smile easily forms on her face. It's infectious, and soon Red is smiling, as well. Then her smile turns into the cutest laugh, and he can't help but join her, unable to remember the last time he laughed this hard.

The more they laugh, the more she gets a better look at him, and her eyes light up.

"Well, Mr. Red Grange," she says, barely able to form her words through her laughter, "let me be the first to welcome you to our fine hotel."

CHAPTER 15

Red is hiding out in the hotel's oversized coat room, wearing just a towel, his muscles on full display. All his clothes hang from a makeshift clothesline. He still can't help but laugh at his predicament as the young woman comes in, wearing a fresh uniform, her hair still damp.

"Really," he says to her, looking at her empty hands. "You found nothing for me to wear?"

"I thought long and hard about it while I was changing," she said. "First of all, all we have in the women's locker room are dresses. We didn't have your size, though I imagine you might look better in a dress than me."

Her adorable smile has returned; he just can't get enough of it.

"Second of all, I thought to myself, Helen Morrissey, you have a half-naked famous young football player trapped in your coat room. What's the hurry?"

Now, he really can't help but smile.

"So I'm being held hostage?"

"Just until I get a ransom note written. My friends are bringing me a pen and paper. Until then, I don't know. Maybe we can get to know each other a little? You good at small talk?"

He looks at her as if to say, "Seriously?"

"I'm kidding. My friends are bringing you some clothes. Although, if I'm being honest, I might have told them to lollygag. But just a little."

89

"I get it now," Red says. "You're one of those vaudeville funny girls masquerading as a hotel housekeeper."

"I am a coat and hat check girl, mind you. Look at the square footage in this room. This is all mine. Which I prefer to mop myself, is all. Not to mention, I designed the cataloging system."

Red takes a better look around at the various types of coats and hats hanging neatly on racks and shelves. He sees everything from trench coats and fur coats to fedoras and flowery women's hats. Even luggage and bicycles are tagged and organized. In particular, a familiar hat with an orange feather catches his eye.

"Impressive," he says, his eyes lingering on the hat he knows well.

"Now, I don't know, maybe we should engage in some small talk? How about you ask me the craziest thing someone has ever checked," she says.

He plays along, "Okay, what is the craziest thing?"

"Well, I think that is pretty obvious," she replies. "It's you."

Before he can react, the door flies open, and into the room barges a gaggle of other young women who work in the hotel, all wearing different types of uniforms. The moment they see Red only wearing towel, they shriek. The women can barely contain themselves, moving closer, seeming like they might claw him to pieces.

With all her might, Helen forces her friends back out the door, but not before removing the clothes from their hands and tossing them to Red.

"Sorry about that," she says. "They were under strict orders not to come inside."

Red can hear the other women giggling outside the door, trying to force their way back in as Helen blocks them.

"You don't need any further assistance, Mr. Grange?"

He sizes the clothes up for a moment.

"I'm good."

"Wonderful, wonderful."

She exits and almost closes the door but then opens it again as the women whisper something to her.

"I'm reminded that I'm also required to say, 'my pleasure.'"

She leaves again, batting the women off, only to return one more time.

"Thanks for being a good sport."

"Honestly, it's been my pleasure," he says, causing her to blush.

He enjoys her adorable smile before she closes the door.

On the other side, Red hears Helen let out what he assumes was supposed to be a private shriek, causing him to burst out laughing.

As he dresses, no matter what he does, he can't get his new smile or thoughts of this refreshingly fun girl to go away.

CHAPTER 16

Halftime Score:
Illinois 14, University of Chicago 21
Saturday, November 8, 1924

Trainers work tirelessly to return a locker room full of bloody and bruised Illinois players to Stagg Field in Chicago.

Zuppke's staff are literal war veterans accustomed to patching up soldiers under fire. Repairing players under the wrath of a maniac German coach, however, is nearly as frightening.

With Zuppke yelling in their ears to do whatever it takes, the trainers stitch gashes, tape wounds, and pump the players with caffeine and cocaine injections. Any player taken out in the second half will be lost for the rest of the game. The trainers have fifteen minutes to do the impossible of bringing these boys back to life.

In anticipation of this game, Chicago's legendary coach, Amos Alonzo Stagg, has been recruiting the largest players he could find over the last three years. Stagg used his size advantage to harass Zuppke's smaller team relentlessly throughout the first half with a series of short running plays to wear down the clock, bang up the linemen, and keep the ball out of Red's hands.

Zuppke knows it would be 21-0 were it not for Red, who, through sheer will, scored twice. He played even better on defense, preventing Chicago from scoring more. But even Red Grange can't win this game by himself in the second half.

While the trainers work on the players' bodies, the little German coach focuses on their minds, starting with Earl.

"They're pushing you around like a baby," Zuppke shouts. "I didn't know you played the piano!"

Earl, confused, shakes his head, denying he does.

"You don't? Then why are you all fingers out there? Touching this guy, touching that guy. This isn't a game of fingers, Earl. Hit somebody! Do you hear me?"

Little Zuppke demonstrates this by forcefully slamming the massive Earl into the wall. Then he does it again. He's about to do it a third time when Earl finally stands his ground.

"That's it," Zuppke barks. "Like that. Nobody pushes you around. You got it?"

"Yes, coach!" Earl yells.

Zuppke then rummages through his coat pockets, frantically searching for something.

"I knew I should have burned this thing," he says to all the players in the locker room. "I just knew it."

He finally retrieves a piece of paper, its yellow and blue letterhead instantly recognizable to the team from the Michigan game.

"I kept Yost's letter because I intended to frame it in my office. But now, I fear it's cursed because Chicago is killing you," he proclaims, holding the letter up and inciting even more emotion than before.

"We're changing our defense," he barks. "We can't win if they keep scoring. Form a box behind the line. Granche, Earl, Chuck, you guys get up tight on the line. They're averaging five yards a carry. I want to see no more than two, so they can't get a first down und have to punt. We can't score if they control the ball."

He locks in on Red.

"They don't have the talent to do anything but pound the ball up the middle. You're going to have to be the one to step up to the line und stop them. Und if they do break through, you must hunt them down. You up on the line is the only way we're going to get the ball back."

"I have an idea, though, to score. A new play...."

"None of that nonsense. The greatest player has to make the greatest plays, or we lose. Do you follow me?"

Red nods that he does and refocuses.

"I'd follow you anywhere, Coach," Red replies.

God damn, Zuppke loves that kid.

He then turns his attention back to the entire team. Time to test if the caffeine and cocaine are kicking in.

"They do not score in the second half," he says resolutely. "They do not score."

The players are not reacting with enough enthusiasm to meet Zuppke's standard.

"Men, are you with me?" he barks. "THEY DO NOT SCORE!"

"THEY DO NOT SCORE!" his team roars in unison.

Zuppke hands the Michigan letter to Earl, who hesitantly accepts it.

"Dammit, Earl! What did I say about using your fingers?"

Realizing, like a fool, that he is indeed holding the paper with his fingers, Earl grabs it with both fists and tears it into a million pieces, each rip amplifying the team's emotions.

Minutes later, they take the field, practically breathing fire.

CHAPTER 17

The momentum in the second half changes dramatically. The first unlucky Chicago player to line up opposite Earl gets immediately knocked out of the game. Zuppke's defensive adjustment is a masterpiece. Chicago can't generate enough first downs to score, forcing them to punt repeatedly.

The forty-four thousand fans are on the edge of their seats every time Red gets the ball. Tickets sold out a few weeks ago, moments after Red's heroics at the Michigan game. Despite being a home game for Chicago, it doesn't feel like one.

At the top of the stadium, in the last seat in the last row of bleachers, an old man wants to say something, but he starts coughing so violently he can't get his thoughts out until Grantland Rice, sitting next to him, pats him on the back, trying to help him break his cough.

"Jeez, Walter," Rice says, "don't croak on me before you get to see whether Red can turn this game around."

Walter Camp, the Father of Football himself, steadies his broad shoulders and attempts to catch his breath. Camp was born during the Civil War, and he's been battling ever since.

When he first started playing football at Yale, the game was absolute chaos, with a hundred young college men on a field utilizing whatever primal method they possessed to get the ball from one goal line to the other—biting, scratching, kicking, clawing.

In Europe, college students played an elegant game of soccer. In the U.S., no one understood that game and found it boring, so they innovated by picking the ball up and fighting like savages, resulting in dozens of college player deaths per year.

In 1905, President Teddy Roosevelt intervened by threatening to ban the dangerous game of football. In response, Camp led the charge to organize the chaos. Each year, as his rulebook gets bigger and bigger, the game gains structure while staying true to its violence and brutality.

Camp established a line of scrimmage and limited the game to eleven men per team. He set up a system of four downs and established breaks between plays. He organized colleges into conferences, trained officials, planned schedules, and published an annual rule book that, among other things, set a uniform number of points for touchdowns, field goals, and extra points.

On this fine autumn day years later, Camp witnesses the crescendo of a life's work that has led to giant college stadiums and gargantuan athletic department revenues across the country. Violence is at the core of humanity. Camp found a way to organize and channel it. The NCAA found a way to monetize it.

The first half of this game was the best football Camp has ever seen. To see Red run, swivel, dodge, glide, shift, pivot, accelerate, drive, to see him compete at a level that will never be matched, brought tears to his eyes.

Camp spent his lifetime transforming the game of football from utter chaos into something that, at least today, has a sense of order to it. But Red has taken the game to another level. Camp's family and doctors urged him not to make the trip, but there was no way he'd miss the opportunity to see Red Grange in person. He even had to miss the annual Yale-Harvard game, a match-up neither he nor Rice have missed in their entire careers.

They both have reserved seats in the press box, but Camp prefers to sit out with the fans. Rice would sit anywhere to be next to his friend, who everyone fears doesn't have much time left.

While still trying to get his breath back, Camp observes the cost of Zuppke's "defensive box" strategy. Yes, Chicago struggles to score. But, with Red shifted up to the defensive line, they have free rein to hit him as hard as possible every play.

"Zuppke is going to get Red killed," Rice says grimly. "And he still has another game against Minnesota."

Walter finally spits some words out.

"He doesn't care about that game," Camp replies, coughing. "The Michigan game and this one are all he cares about this season. The rest don't matter to him."

"Remaining undefeated and winning another national championship doesn't matter to him?"

"Zuppke is looking out for all of college football by cementing Red's immortality," Camp explains. "He's grooming Grange to take over for me and preserve the sport."

Grooming him or sacrificing him? Rice wonders.

The game rages on with Chicago unable to score and Illinois still down by a touchdown deep into the fourth quarter. Illinois lines up on offense on their own twenty-yard line. They have to take a chance and make something happen. Camp observes Zuppke's facial expression on the bench when Red breaks from the huddle and lines up his team.

Rule Number One in Walter Camp's rulebook makes coaching college football difficult. It states that a coach cannot coach from the sideline. However, many coaches have found creative ways to cheat. They tape plays to the bottoms of water bottles to be read during timeouts or send signals through how they sit, take off their hats, turn their bodies, and even how and when they cover their faces. Coaches used to substitute a guy into the game just to send in a play, so Camp added rules against substitute players joining the huddle for two plays after they come into the game.

Camp can tell it's all Zuppke can do not to run out on the field himself and change the play as the ball is snapped back to Red, who appears poised to run the same cutback he used against Michigan. Chicago is ready for it and Red is about to get crushed.

Camp watches Red follow a few players to the right until Earl cuts left. The moment Earl pulls, Chicago's players trail him, creating a trap. Red follows causing Zuppke to throw his hat on the ground in disgust.

Suddenly, Red cuts back the original way, executing a double cut. Chicago was fixated on Earl and Red, oblivious to Chuck and the other players, who have already reversed their course ahead of Red. Camp can tell even Zuppke didn't see this coming. Red must have come up with the play on his own in the huddle.

A single tear rolls down Camp's cheek. Players modifying the strategy on the field is precisely what Camp has hoped for his entire career. He prayed a player like Red would come along, listening to and learning from a genius coach, but then taking it to another level by having the guts to improvise on the fly.

Camp watches Zuppke explode with energy, watching Red take off into the open field after the double cut. Zuppke scoots down the sideline bench, knocking his own players onto the ground. He's not allowed to stand, but the rulebook doesn't say he has to sit still.

Zuppke keeps scooting and cheering as Red breaks into an eighty-yard open-field sprint. Zuppke reaches the end of the bench, having knocked all his players off of it, adrenaline soaring through his veins, pumping his legs along with Red.

The Chicago crowd, momentarily forgetting its loyalties, rises to its feet, amazed to see The Galloping Ghost traverse the length of the field against a defense designed to prevent precisely that.

Red crosses the goal line, touches the ball to the ground, and immediately congratulates Earl for sacrificing himself to set up the run. Earl's kick then ties the game. With a few minutes left, the energy in the stadium is electric.

Chicago 21, Illinois 21.

Camp glances over at the press box. Reporters are typing furiously, their fingers flying across keys, documenting what may be the greatest comeback any of them have ever witnessed.

Illinois forces Chicago to punt again, but only after Red is slammed to the ground every single play. Chicago doesn't care about scoring. Taking Red out of the game continues to be their only strategy as they hit him over and over again with all they have.

Ordinarily, one would assume there wouldn't be enough time to score again, and Illinois would settle for a tie. But today, with Red on the field, nothing is ordinary.

Camp, along with forty-four thousand Chicago fans, dares to dream that Red has one more magical run left in him before the clock runs out.

Red receives the handoff and races off once more, stiff-arming several defenders. But one persistent tackler refuses to let go—South Chicago's Austin McCarty, who grew up playing on playgrounds littered with rocks. He's tougher than nails, even biting at Red's legs.

Camp watches as Red, unable to break free, carries McCarty with him down the sideline. This brief delay allows more tacklers to join the fray until Earl arrives, flying in to knock them all off Red.

The entire stadium erupts as a clear path to the goal line materializes. It's an absolute fairytale playing out in real life. Red is on his way to victory until a second wave of Chicago defenders crashes into him, slamming his head violently into the ground with just fifteen yards between him and the goal line.

He didn't score, but he's put his team within field goal range to win the game. Illinois starts to line up when, for the first time, Red is slow to rise. The final brutal hit to his head appears to have left him disoriented and unsure of his surroundings.

Earl lifts his dazed friend off the ground and attempts to steady him enough to take the snap and hold the football for Earl to kick.

"I'm already composing an epic poem in my head," Rice says to Camp. "All I need is a winning field goal to complete the last stanza."

Instead of sharing in the beauty of this moment, Camp's face is devoid of joy or expression.

"Penalty," he murmurs.

Just like that, the entire play is called back. Illinois committed a holding penalty before Red was even tackled.

Camp knows it's the one thing about the sport that can't be avoided if there is going to be any level of safety or order. Penalties are necessary. They are also the worst part of the game.

Zuppke explodes onto his feet in frustration despite the risk of an additional penalty for standing. He can yell and scream all he wants, but the referees' minds are made up. There are no appeals. What's called is called.

Due to the penalty, Illinois is pinned back almost to their own goal line. Red wobbles in a daze with no time left, and Illinois has no choice but to take a tie as the final siren wails.

Final score: Chicago 21, Illinois 21.

The home crowd erupts in a unanimous ovation. They are not cheering for the score, the game, their team, or even their players. This ovation is for the hero, number 77, carried off the field by his teammates and coach.

These fans witnessed the greatest player sacrifice everything. He suffered multiple blows to his head in the second half, never once leaving the game. He scored all the touchdowns for his team, amassing over three hundred yards. He made nearly all the tackles on defense, bringing Illinois back from the brink of destruction. He tied the game, giving his team an epic chance to win before eventually being carried off, unable to take another step. He had left it all on the field.

Rice pats his friend Walter Camp on the back. Camp accepts the pat, acknowledging that this is the closest he'll ever feel to heaven on earth. He has witnessed a testament to the beauty of the game he loves.

Today has been the pinnacle of his entire career. He can die satisfied knowing that, thanks to Bob Zuppke and Red Grange, his legacy will live on for eternity.

On the field...

Earl has to orient Red toward the locker room. He's never had to do that before, but then again, he's never seen Red, or any player for that matter, take as many brutal shots to the head.

He's not sure Red even knows what day it is as he helps his friend navigate through the fans who have rushed the field to touch him.

Earl repeatedly asks Red if he's alright, especially since Red keeps calling him Helen.

In the press box...

Warren momentarily forgets his professional role as a reporter. He stands and applauds in stark contrast to his peers, who furiously type their stories.

He'd hoped to have met Grantland Rice today. In his national columns, Rice exclusively refers to Red as The Galloping Ghost, forcing the rest of the sports world to do the same.

Warren planned to inform Rice that he himself first coined the nickname. But Warren forgets all his career ambitions, choosing instead to cheer for the greatest player to ever play.

In the stands...

Tim Mara joins in the applause, picturing a stadium twice this size next fall packed with fans eager to see Red Grange play for the New York Giants.

Also in the stands...

George Halas could never dream of his Bears drawing a crowd of this size. The only thing on his mind is finding a way to make peace with Zuppke.

In the corner of the endzone...

One man proudly displays an orange feather in his hat amidst a sea of Chicago maroon. Pyle endured the abuse of rival fans throughout the game, only to see them transformed into potential customers as Red's legend grew with every play.

Walking past him with Earl's help, Red is no longer just a son, a teammate, or a player. He belongs to the nation now. He's not simply a college athlete. He's America's hero.

With a draft of a golden contract tucked safely in his breast pocket, Pyle knows that, soon enough, Red Grange will also belong to someone else: C.C. Pyle, sports agent extraordinaire.

THE SECOND QUARTER
◯ Bottling Red ◯

CHAPTER 18

Ten years earlier...

Red and Garland walk home on a brisk fall afternoon, each with a pocket full of tip money from caddying at the Chicago Golf Club.

At twelve and ten years old, they can't take two steps without hip-checking each other off the side of the road or into the middle of the busy street. In the course of any five minutes, the two of them touch, shove, or worse dozens of times.

The Grange boys always cut through the Black part of town, and it is difficult not to notice the contrast between the homes that line the pristine golf course and the homes along this gravel road, which aren't much bigger than their tiny apartment.

As the brothers knock into each other, a tattered football bounces in front of them. Garland picks it up while Red turns to see where it came from. Dozens of Black kids their age are out playing in a sandlot, waving at Garland to throw the ball back. Instead of doing so, Red watches in awe as Garland tucks the ball under his arm and takes off, running down the gravel road.

Garland hasn't even run three steps with the stolen ball before the dozens of boys are after him. Looking back over his shoulder with a huge grin, Garland races the perimeter of the field, forming what Red begins to realize is a big circle connecting back to where Red is standing. Garland, who is

105

almost as fast as Red, gallops just out of reach of the gang of boys gaining on him.

Just as Garland is about to be smeared, he, with even more joy on his face, flips the ball to Red, and the mob of boys immediately shifts direction like a school of piranha.

Red doesn't have the luxury of surprise or a head start like Garland had. With his back to the busy road, cars whizzing by, he has only moments to decide his course of action.

He scans each of the boys' faces. Red knows them all. They've played together for years. None of them, including Red and Garland, know how football is supposed to be played. They play a different game where whoever has the ball tries not to get killed. That big smile on Garland's face is because he's set Red up for just that…to be smeared into oblivion.

Red gets a better grip on the old ball, which has been on its last leg for years. The simple act of tucking a football under his arm grants him superhuman powers. The field of play slows down for him in these moments, giving him time to calculate his first nine moves. However, the tenth is going to be the most fun.

A swivel of his hips to the left sends Martin right by him. A swivel to the right sends Ronnie flying in the other direction. Red knows those two are the biggest and fastest. For the rest, he puts his shoulder down, slams some, stiff arms others, fakes one way, jukes the other, dashes a few yards, retreats a few yards, and before the boys even realize what has happened, Red has made nine of his ten calculated moves to break loose. Except, Red knows by this point Martin and Ronnie have reversed course and are lunging at him from behind.

It's time for the tenth move. Red simply hands the ball back to an unsuspecting Garland just in time for his little brother to be pummeled. Along with Martin and Ronnie, the rest of the pack piles on Garland until the ball eventually pops loose. Ronnie picks it up, and now the pack is after him.

Garland peels himself off the ground with an even bigger smile on his face, launching into a chase after Ronnie. Red joins, too. They could play this game for hours. The boys fight to the death to get the ball. Then they fight to the death to keep it. The game ends when either they get called home for dinner or someone gets seriously hurt. But until then, they don't need officials, rules, structure, or adults to organize them. All they need is a little open space and a ball in any type of condition.

While the boys are playing, Luke Thompson stops his ice truck for a moment on the side of the road to watch. What initially catches his attention are two white kids in a sea of Black kids fighting and clawing with the best of them, killing themselves on the playground, having the time of their lives.

After a while, Luke, a muscular mass of a man, steps out of his ice truck and puts his fingers to his lips, making a loud whistle. It takes him a few whistles to get all the boys' attention before waving them over to his truck.

"I got a job for one of you," he says. "Just one. The strongest one."

He opens the back hatch of his truck, on which the logo "Thompson Ice" is etched. Refreshing cold air pours out as he lifts what appears to be the largest pair of wrought iron scissors the boys have ever seen.

The ice tongs have handles like scissors, but the pointy tips are curved to grip the giant block. The boys are amazed Luke can even lift the iron tongs, much less stab the ends deep into a solid block of ice, violently clamping it down before using his muscular legs to hoist the one-hundred-pound block of ice upon his shoulder.

He turns and slams the ice onto the ground in front of the boys with the iron tongs still attached and sticking straight up in the air.

"If any of you can lift the ice block," he says. "You got a job."

The top of the tongs comes up to the chest of the boys. Without hesitation, Martin and Ronnie are the first to try. Neither of them can get it to budge.

One by one, the other boys try. No luck, but in the process, they are having fun, cheering each other on, and laughing at each failed attempt. Luke is enjoying the show, as well. He even takes out a spike and knocks off a few ice slivers. It's no substitute for ice cream, but it's pretty close. They savor giant chunks between taking turns attempting to move the big block until it finally comes down to the Grange boys.

Garland steps up, and Luke immediately notices his athletic form and how Garland grips the tongs with his hands but uses his legs and shoulder to lift. Surprising everyone, including himself, Garland gets the ice to lift just barely off the ground. The other boys cheer for him, but Garland just doesn't have enough strength. He's spent and has to let go. The boys let out a collective sigh, patting him on the back, recognizing that he's come the closest so far.

Red is the only one left to try, but he's not interested, waving them off. He doesn't want the attention. Instead, he picks up the football to get back to playing, but the boys won't let him. They crowd around him, begging him to give it a go, chanting his name in encouragement. He remains uninterested until his little brother yells to Luke for all to hear.

"What's it pay?" Garland says. "More than caddying?"

"Ten times more," Luke replies.

Garland grabs his older brother by the shirt.

"You gotta try, Red. You gotta."

Red is still not interested. Luke wants him to. The crowd wants him to. Red just wants to keep playing their fun game.

"We need it. We need the money. Dad needs it," Garland begs.

Red gives in with a long sigh and hands his little brother the football. As he approaches the heavy wrought iron tongs sticking out of the ice, Red is reminded of the young King Arthur tale he learned in school.

In that legend, everyone in the world wants to be the one to pull the sword from the stone. Peasants try. Women try. Children try. Even priests and pastors try. The bravest of knights ride from all reaches of the land to try. No one can pull it out.

After the teacher read the story to them, Red remembers walking up to her privately and asking, "Why? Why does everyone want to be the king? The story never says why?"

The teacher looked at him as if he were crazy and declared, "Everyone wants to be the king."

Young Red puts his hands on the wrought iron tongs, steadies his legs, and prepares to lift the impossible burden onto his shoulders.

Ten years later...
Summer Break, 1925

Camera bulbs flash as Red effortlessly hoists a hundred-pound ice block onto one muscular shoulder and then another hundred-pound ice block onto his other, to the amazement of a crowd of adults and reporters.

Red is back home over the summer working his usual ice route in Wheaton, Illinois. Ten years after discovering Red's potential playing out in that field, a gray-haired Luke Thompson is loving the attention for his ice business. Red poses for publicity photos with throngs of beautiful women wearing beauty pageant sashes who also benefit from the attention.

Garland poses right along with his brother, with an ice block on each of his shoulders. The photographers mostly want photos of Red alone, but they take a few with Red and Garland together in anticipation of Garland joining his brother as a star for Red's upcoming senior season at Illinois. Reporters throw out questions between photos.

"How's it feel to have only three of the Four Horsemen named All-American? You beat out the fourth."

"I feel very fortunate that Walter Camp selected me before he passed away in March," Red says. "He leaves behind a remarkable legacy."

"Are you going to take over from him when you graduate?"

"My understanding is Grantland Rice is taking over for him for the time being," Red replies. "College football is in good hands."

"Think Rice will name you an All-American again your senior year? That would be every year you've played."

"I just do what Coach tells me to do," Red replies. "I don't chase accolades."

"Zuppke added a surprise game to the schedule this fall against undefeated Penn. Are you excited to head to Philadelphia and finally prove to the Eastern elites who's best?"

"Gosh, Penn's a great team," Red says. "I've never traveled anywhere near that far. I'm just hoping to get to see the Liberty Bell."

Red is always surprised when the crowd chuckles at his comments. He's serious. He does hope to sightsee in Philly. He's about to elaborate when Garland can't resist joining the attention.

"After we whip Penn, we're gonna ring that bell," Garland says, grinning wildly, hamming it up.

The reporters love a quote like that, scribbling like crazy in their notebooks, not noticing Red shooting his brother a look. Garland has a lot to learn. The last thing he should ever do in an interview is give the opposing team's coach a quote to rile up his team.

"Is it true you signed a deal with a Champaign movie theater owner to help you turn professional?"

Red takes a closer look out at the reporters. Sure enough, Warren is right in the middle of the pack, balancing a cigar in

The Golden Age of Red

the corner of his mouth, pencil at the ready, enjoying another one of his ambushes.

"Is it true?" Warren asks again. "Are you turning pro?"

The entire crowd quiets down, watching Red's face as he contemplates an answer. Before he can form a response, Garland cuts in again.

"He'll be back for his senior season," Garland says. "But all these wild rumors and such are not his biggest concern."

"What's his biggest concern?" Warren asks.

"Me. I finally get to play this year, and I intend to beat my brother out for All-American," Garland says, cracking up the throng of reporters, their pencils scribbling away.

Warren and Red stare at each other for a few moments, both of them knowing the question about Red turning professional wasn't answered. In the meantime, more photos are taken, easier questions are answered, and the scene winds down when Red and Garland continue on their route, earning well-needed money delivering blocks of ice all over town.

An ice route involves knocking on doors, making small talk with housewives, retrieving the ice from the truck, and lugging it into a home or climbing the stairs to an apartment. The hardest part, however, is squatting down and using every ounce of strength to maneuver the block into the ice box.

Now that Red is more famous than Babe Ruth, especially in Wheaton, the route is further complicated by his hometown wanting to see him up close. Young women push their mothers out of the way to be the ones to greet him at the door. Men ask Red about the upcoming season. Boys beg Red to stop and throw them a few passes.

Occasionally, Red and Garland get trapped in kitchens in the middle of the day with glammed-up housewives. The brothers are often asked to do other favors around the house: move and carry stuff, take cans down from high shelves, etc. More often than not, they are held captive until they manufacture an escape.

111

Lugging ice is the best exercise they could ever hope for in the off-season, and they make enough money to cover expenses for the entire school year. Unfortunately, the whole thing has become a daily circus that Garland loves and Red deplores.

Red knows Garland can't wait to take the field this fall, and Red has spent the summer bracing for an upcoming battle with Zuppke. He is plotting his arguments to be allowed to turn the spotlight over to Garland by handing him the ball as much as possible.

They finally get to a stretch of their route where Red can drive with just the two of them in the truck. It's Red's favorite part of the day. Or, it would be if his brother, over in the passenger seat, could shut his mouth.

"We could be in Panama right now," Garland says. "Beaches. Beer. Golf. Girls. Airplanes. A good job for Dad. But, no. You messed it up."

It's all Red can do to keep his eyes on the road, ignoring Garland running his mouth.

"Just tell me once and for all, did you sign that deal with C.C. Pyle to manage your affairs or not?" Garland asks. "Just tell me. You won't tell anyone. You must have. Didn't you? Where's Pyle taking you tomorrow? Why can't I go?"

Again, Red focuses on driving, trying to tune his brother out. They are coming up on the very field where Luke discovered them. Red loves seeing neighborhood kids still playing a form of Kill the Man with the Ball, a game forever stuck in time passed down from generation to generation.

"You know what you are?" Garland says. "Selfish. That's what you are. Selfish as shit."

Red slams his foot on the brakes sending Garland crashing into the dashboard. Thousands of pounds of ice blocks slam up against the back of the cab. Red struggles to maneuver the now-skidding truck to a halt on the side of the gravel road.

The kids playing on the field watch in awe as the door on Garland's side of the cab flies open, and the two brothers spill out, violently throwing punches at each other. All fistfights are brutal, but two brothers swinging at each other is major combat.

Garland and Red are down on the ground, clawing at each other's throats. Red wonders if today is the day he'll actually go through with it and choke his brother to death when he suddenly becomes aware that the kids have formed a circle around them.

Red believes he is far from being a perfect person or role model. However, he holds one thing pure in the world: doing right by kids. Though he'd prefer to choke his brother unconscious once and for all, he instead eases off. Looking around at these boys, he's embarrassed enough as it is. The moment he eases off, Garland throws a haymaker of a punch to the side of Red's head.

It has taken Red six months to recover from the multiple concussions sustained during the Chicago game. It's been months of headaches forming out of nowhere, avoiding bright lights, and having to steady himself while trying to walk to classes. Disorientation returns the moment his idiot brother lands a sucker punch.

Fortunately, Garland realizes what he's done and doesn't deliver additional blows, especially given that Red is now sitting on the empty lot dazed and confused.

"Is that Red? Red Grange?" one of the boys says.

"That's Red Grange!" another shouts.

Pretty soon the boys are all over Red for attention as Garland now has to switch from offense to defense to help his brother up to his feet and keep the kids at bay.

It takes Red a few moments, but eventually, he gets his wits about him. Just like in games, he'll always pop back up if he can just have a moment. Always. Under no circumstances is he to ever come out of the game. That's just how football is played. That's how it used to work when he played on this dirt field as a child.

Sensing his brother is starting to come back to reality, Garland forms a plan to give Red some space.

"You guys want to take us on?" he says to the boys. "Real football? Real rules? I'll take half of you. Maybe Red will take the other half. What do you say?"

"I'm on Red's team," they practically all yell until Garland promises Red will switch at some point and play for both squads.

While Red takes another moment to recover, Garland lines up the kids into two teams and goes over the basics: line of scrimmage, hiking the ball, blocking, running pass routes, and huddling up. He and Red will each be all-time quarterbacks and call the plays.

Garland has them all organized as he walks the ball back to his brother.

"Listen," Garland says, slyly forming the same smile he made years ago when he first picked up what might be the same ratty football on this very road. "Time to see which Grange boy is the real superstar."

Red would prefer to strangle his brother, but he can't help but form a smile of his own, looking at Garland holding out a football, inviting him to solve their differences in the American way.

114

CHAPTER 19

Pyle holds Red in suspense the entire drive. Red knows they are headed north of Detroit, but all the other details have been kept a surprise.

"You warned me there would be leaks," Red says. "I thought it might leak in the fall. Not this summer."

"Ignore it," Pyle answers matter-of-factly, brushing it off. "The whole rest of your life, there will be rumors, the price of fame. Remember the ridiculous story that ran last year of you playing a professional game in North Dakota? You had to prove your whereabouts for that day."

"I've never even set foot in that state," Red recalls. "I couldn't even find North Dakota on a map."

"Remember the story about how during games your eyes turn a shade of 'unhuman black,' granting you special 'x-ray peripheral vision,' allowing you to scan the entire field?"

"I had to look up 'peripheral vision' in a dictionary."

"You also had to allow a team of optometrists to examine you to prove you are indeed human."

Red shakes his head at that one.

"Deny. Deny. Deny," Pyle lectures. "Laugh it off. Deny again. It's as simple as that. Besides, soon I'll be handling the press for you. Remember when we met with my attorney friend who looked over all the NCAA rules and regulations? Remember what he said?"

"Stay clear from the NFL."

"That's right. All the NCAA rules have to do with not accepting payment to play professional football."

"Or signing contracts to play," Red clarifies.

"Which you haven't. But your name and identity are yours. No rules currently prevent you from making money doing anything other than being paid to play. You own your fame."

Pyle convinced Red to agree that he can feel out all forms of offers; however, despite Pyle's urging, Red refuses to sign or earn anything until his college season ends. Regardless of how loose the rules are, Red insists his only income will be from working the ice truck.

"Tomorrow, back in Chicago," Pyle says, "I have movie executives coming to the hotel. They are bringing Virginia Valli with them."

Red's eyes light up. Pyle knows Red has recently seen the dark-haired beauty starring in an Alfred Hitchcock silent film.

"It's just a screen test. You'll put on lipstick and run a little scene with Virginia in front of the cameras in the hotel ballroom. I have the scene—the script—in my briefcase somewhere. We'll go over it this afternoon on the way back. But it's all a formality. Don't worry a moment about it. What they really want is you under contract to film this summer, so they can release it the moment the last second ticks off the clock after you play your last game against Ohio State. The NCAA rules don't prevent that."

"I can't risk it. I can't do that to Coach Zuppke."

"I don't get it," Pyle says, shaking his head. "Zuppke profits off your fame. All college coaches do. What do you owe him?"

"The Taylorville scandal almost gave him a heart attack. I couldn't risk it. If something goes wrong, it'd kill him."

"It's just a film test. A little lipstick is all. You'll be fine. And they have directors and such to help you act out the scenes. You'll be great. You're a natural at everything you do. They are offering twenty-five thousand dollars for two weeks of filming. We can wait if you want and shoot it after the season, but I don't see the risk."

"I have to put on lipstick?" Red asks, looking genuinely worried.

Pyle doesn't answer given they've finally arrived at their destination. They pull up to a massive automobile factory near the St. Clair River just south of Lake Huron.

"No way!" Red says, looking at a row of display models showing off each car offered in the Saint Claire fleet.

Parked before them are a wide range of body styles: the five-passenger Gray Goose special touring car; the seven-passenger touring car; the four-door Brougham; the four-passenger coupe; the five-passenger sedan; the five-passenger Imperial sedan and town car; and, of course, the Wills Sainte Claire Roadster—Polly's car.

C.H. Wills, the factory's owner, is waiting for them out front with an outstretched hand.

Pyle knows Wills is Red's absolute hero. At 47, Wills displays the same serious demeanor as he does in the few photos of him Red has seen in magazines. He was once one of Henry Ford's highest-profile engineers. His fingerprints are all over the Model T, including its removable engine. Wills even designed the oval blue, cursive-lettered Ford logo.

Car magazines reported in great detail that after Wills and Ford amicably parted ways, Wills took his $1.5 million severance, sailed on his yacht for a while, and then invested in a state-of-the-art factory to build higher-end automobiles.

Wills' famously stern face remains so as he grasps Red's hand.

"America's hero right here at my plant," Wills says to Red. "The same young man who scored four touchdowns in just twelve minutes, destroying my beloved Michigan's entire season."

"Sorry about that," Red replies.

Wills leads Red through the factory, showing him off to all the plant managers. He signs autographs for hundreds of employees while witnessing firsthand how cars are made in volume.

Red has never seen such a magnitude of human labor working in concert to create beautiful machine after beautiful machine. The automobiles roll down the assembly line with sparks flying, hammers striking, and wrenches cranking. Red is so enthralled by the tour that Wills takes the opportunity to steer Pyle up to his office.

Once Wills and Pyle are alone, Pyle pulls a newspaper from his briefcase, lays it out on Wills' desk, and flips it open to a full-page Wills Sainte Claire advertisement. Pyle runs his finger along the copy.

"'Suddenly out of the inextricable tangle, with utter unconcern and the dash of Red Grange, there emerges one car,'" Pyle reads to Wills, emphasizing the ad's headline. "'The Red Grange of Traffic.'"

"What about it?" Wills says sternly.

"What about it?" Pyle replies. "All those years with Ford…did he have you just design his engines, or did he teach you anything about advertising? Anything about celebrity endorsements?"

Wills stares Pyle down for a moment. Pyle can tell he's sizing up his fancy suit, jeweled walking cane, and the rest of Pyle's impeccable apparel.

"Ford did teach me one thing," Wills says. "To spot a shake-down artist when I see one."

"Far from," Pyle replies. "That boy out there sacrifices himself on the field of battle for your enjoyment. For your entertainment. Also, for the love of his school, for the love of his coach, and the grandeur of amateurism."

Pyle, readying to unload his main point, stands taller.

"But his name and identity are his. His fame is his. Not the world's. And certainly not yours to profit from."

"And who are you?" Wills says. "Allow the boy to come up here and argue for himself. Otherwise, what's the point of that college degree he's earning?"

"Who am I?" Pyle says, reaching further into his briefcase, producing a signed agreement, and shoving it at Wills. "I am him. I'm his authorized power of attorney."

Wills flips through the agreement, realizing, with each sentence he deciphers, the magnitude of the document.

"Who am I?" Pyle says even more sternly. "I'm the one who defends Red Grange against serpents. Serpents lurking in the shadows. Serpents, like you, with the audacity to reveal themselves, daring publicly to extract profit by unlicensed association to his great name."

Pyle grabs the signed agreement back from Wills.

"Who am I? I'll tell you who I am," Pyle emphasizes. "I'm his friend. I'm his business partner. I'm his agent."

CHAPTER 20

Back in Chicago, Red sits in the hotel lobby looking over the script of the scene he's scheduled to perform the next day.

It calls for a shy college letterman to notice a pretty coed at a dance and gather the nerve to walk over and ask if she'd like to dance, only to be soundly rejected. As he embarrassingly walks away, she reveals she's only joking, and, to his surprise and delight, she drags him out on the dance floor, where two of them draw a crowd as they perform something called The Charleston.

Red takes a deep breath. The script requires a lot more than Pyle let on. Because silent films don't have dialogue, he'll have to convey the emotions of the entire scene through body language.

"You again," a woman's voice startles him. "You never call. You never write."

He looks up to see a familiar and adorable face.

"Helen. Helen Morrissey," she says. "Surely you remember me? We met in an alley. We got half-naked. Or, rather, you got half-naked. I rescued you. You were dripping wet. I, for one, memorized every moment of it. Ring a bell?"

"I remember," Red says, grinning. "You're impossible to forget."

"I read you got an awful knock in the head in that game. So I thought, you know, amnesia. That's why he didn't call. Or write. Or send me gifts. By the way, jewelry is my favorite. Aquamarine, to be exact. But amnesia can be the only explanation. That has to be it. I mean, look at me. What else could it be?"

"I was hoping you'd be here," Red says. "I was wondering if you might help me with something."

Sitting in the back of Helen's coat room, Red holds a mirror in one hand as he attempts to apply red lipstick. He runs the stick across his lips, swiping too far and leaving a smear on his cheek.

"And again, we start over," Helen says, wiping his face clean with a white cloth already riddled with many other failed attempts.

The bad news is he's terrible at this. The good news is he gets to feel her hand on his face.

"Okay, new idea, pucker up," she says. "Pucker those beauties up."

She puckers her lips to show him. He follows suit.

"Now dab it. Dab the stick to your lips. Over and over. Don't try to get it perfect, but keep the lipstick on your lips. Not your face. Pucker and dab. Go ahead."

His first dab is successful, but more pressure is needed to leave a mark. After a few more dabs, he's getting the hang of it, leaving blobs of red behind on his lips.

"Dab it harder," she says. "Keep it on your lips. Doesn't have to be perfect."

It is sloppy, but it's all on his lips.

"Now, use your fingers—not your pointer, your ring finger—to rub it in. Go ahead. Ring finger."

Using his fingers is much easier. He's able to smooth it across until he accidentally goes too far and gets some outside his lips.

"Now, use your pointer finger to clean that off."

He follows her directions. This technique works well for him.

"Excellent. Ring finger to smooth. Pointer to fix. Wipe your pointer on the rag from time to time. Good."

He's getting the hang of it.

"Someday, when you're a big girl, you'll be able to do it without your fingers."

That garners a grin.

"No smiling. Get it all uniform first."

Alternating between his ring and pointer fingers, his lips turn bright red and uniform.

"Who taught you?" Red asks between swipes of his fingers.

"My mother. She runs a boarding home south in Evergreen Park, outside the city. She works all the time, taking care of everyone. When I was a little girl, I begged her for about a year to teach me. She only had time to show me how I taught you, using fingers. Like most things, I figured the rest out the hard way, on my own."

She hands him the cloth.

"Now blot your lips against this cloth a few times. Lightly. Just to get the excess off."

He follows her directions perfectly. He's pleased with himself.

"Just one thing left to do now," she says.

"What's that? I think it looks good."

"All that's left now is to kiss me," she says, dead serious. "Gotta test it out."

She closes her eyes and puckers up, waiting on him. He thought she was kidding, but she appears not to be. He leans in to kiss her when her eyes pop open.

"Missed your chance."

He watches her put away the supplies, kicking himself for hesitating.

"Okay, now for the hard part," she says. "You really don't know The Charleston?"

"I've never even been to a night club. Besides, I don't drink."

"You don't have to drink to dance. Although, we are all better dancers when we do. But here we go. Stand up next to me. Face the same way as me and do what I do."

He lines up next to her, shoulder to shoulder.

"Ever squashed a bug with your shoe? You ever squish one? Like this."

She makes a squish motion with the ball of her right foot, and he immediately copies her.

"Very good. You're coachable. Now, start with your feet together. Right foot forward. Twist/squish. Bring it back. Left backward. Twist/squish. Bring it back."

He does it exactly like she does. When it comes to moving his legs, he's a natural. He's picking it up quickly.

"Repeat that over and over. Right then left. Good. Really squish it. Exaggerate the squish."

She shows him, and he perfectly copies her. He's got it.

"Now, swing your arms. Up when you squish. Back down as you reset. Like this."

Whatever she does, even if she only does it once, he mimics. She remembers it taking her what felt like forever to learn The Charleston, and he's already got it down pat after his first few attempts.

"Now you can have some fun. You can turn to one side. Spin around. Hold one hand out. Wave it. Good. Now quit copying me. Do your own thing. Improvise, like Jazz. Be creative. Vary it up."

In short order, the two of them are in perfect rhythm. He mimics some of her variations, cross steps, repeat steps, knees out, knees in, and masters all of it. She even takes his hands in hers to show him that the dance can work in conjunction with a partner. Playing off of another person, he comes to realize, is the real beauty of it.

He's loving every minute of dancing between the coat racks. She tries on some of the hats in the room. He follows suit. Coats, too. They are hamming it up, making each other laugh.

It takes Red a few more spins and gyrations before he realizes Helen isn't dancing any longer. He glances over to the counter, stopping dead in his tracks when he recognizes the customer she's helping.

With her jaw set, Polly, checking in a luxurious feathered hat and coat, patiently waits for Helen to fill out a ticket.

"I'm sorry to have made you wait," Helen says. "I was just just, um...."

"Wearing your customers' clothes," Polly says.

Helen quickly takes off the borrowed hat and jacket.

"I'd prefer mine stored, not worn," Polly says, taking her ticket and walking away, but not before slightly turning back toward Red. "Room 1245. Lose the lipstick."

With that, Polly strides toward the elevators, exuding confidence, radiating beauty, and turning the heads of every person she passes along the way.

"She's yours?" Helen asks Red, unable to hide her shock, watching Polly disappear into the elevators.

"She's not mine," Red says, returning his borrowed coat and hat to the rack and using the cloth to remove his lipstick. "She's not anyone's."

CHAPTER 21

Polly sits barefoot on her hotel bed. Her unbuttoned blouse hangs open as she leans forward to light a cigarette. There are no other chairs or couches in the room. Red isn't sure what is appropriate in this situation, so he elects to stand.

"What makes you think you can trust that coat check girl?" she asks.

"Helen?" Red clarifies. "What do you mean trust her? That's silly. Why would you ask that? Don't tell me you're jealous."

"Never."

"Never?" he asks, not loving her answer.

She shakes her head.

"Never? No jealousy whatsoever?"

She remains stoic.

"What are we to each other?" he wonders out loud.

She still doesn't answer, slowly drawing on her cigarette.

"Listen," Red says. "I caved and told my brother and my father I'd take them to Panama with those Kaan insurance brothers. Private plane. Beaches. They made room for Earl. I'm told the local women there love Americans. What about that? That make you jealous?"

She puffs out a smoke ring.

"Where were you?" he says. "Gone for over a month. Gone most of the summer. I tell you everything. You've told me nothing about yourself. Nothing."

"California," she finally answers.

"That's something. You were in California. Okay. That's a thought. Wow. Movie stars? I don't know. Were you hanging out with them? That's where my head goes."

"While I was out there, football came up sometimes. Lots of talk of a handsome University of Washington fullback."

"George Wilson."

"Yes, I'd bring up Red Grange, and West Coast sports fans would say, 'Red has nothing on George Wilson. Plus, he's a blond.'"

"Okay, that's working."

"What's working?"

"You're making me jealous," he says, pacing the room.

"He's got a pretty good nickname, you have to admit."

Red's aware.

"The Wildcat," she says. "Ernie Nevers at Stanford has an even better one...The Big Dog."

"Very cute," Red says. "You've been working your way through All-Americans. Are the Four Horsemen next?"

"Why are you pacing around like that? Sit next to me."

"Not unless you tell me one serious thing about yourself. Something truthful. Revealing. Your occupation. Something real. One thing."

"One thing?" she says.

"One thing. Your childhood. Your job. Your hometown. Your brother. A single hope. A single dream. When you were a little girl and didn't know any better, did you ever accidentally smile?"

She still doesn't. Even with that. Nothing. He's frustrated now and considers leaving.

"Ok, one thing," she says. "When you go to Panama, I want you to have a great time with your family and friends. Do whatever you want. And don't think one moment about me."

"That's your one thing? That's not a thing. Telling me to do whatever I want is not a thing."

"And when you get back, we'll pick right up where we left off," she says. "That's my one thing."

"That's not normal," he says. "That can't be normal. That can't be healthy. That can't be how relationships work."

"There's nothing normal about you, Red. You're famous. You're the envy of men, the desire of women. Hat check girls, to say the least. I'm perfect for you. One less thing to worry about. Never a need to tiptoe around me. That's my one thing."

Red stares her down. As far as he can tell, she's serious, puffing on her cigarette, confident in herself and the grip she has on him.

"I gotta go," he says, making his way to the door. "I'm sharing a suite with Pyle. We're going to go over the test scene for tomorrow. Virginia Valli, by the way. Maybe it's a kissing scene. What about that?"

"Do you ever talk to him about me?"

"Pyle? No. I don't talk to anyone about you. No one even knows you exist."

He starts to leave when he thinks of something.

"Why do you bring Pyle up? I'm seeing Virginia Valli tomorrow, and you bring up Pyle? Why?"

"I assumed you already mentioned me to him is all. With him being your partner. You signed, I assume?"

Red is livid. She asks him probing questions but won't answer his simple ones. But then something dawns on him.

They met when she conveniently had car trouble on his path to class. He's since told her everything. He's entrusted her with his innermost thoughts and strategies. He's outlined to her all his choices for after the season, even Pyle's idea of forming thier own professional football league.

She asked if he could trust Helen. The better question is can he trust *her*?

CHAPTER 22

For a guy who's never been far from Chicago, stepping off the plane in Panama in the heart of summer isn't just hot. It's scorching. The heat hits Red right in the face with the force of a linebacker. The same holds true for Garland, Earl, and his father, Lyle. In no time, their cotton clothes are soaked through with sweat.

Fortunately, it's an all-expenses paid trip. The Kaan brothers encourage them to charge anything to their rooms, even a whole new wardrobe. Once they are all outfitted in linen and shorts, it feels bearable.

Most of their days consist of fishing in the mornings and evenings, rounded out with beach time. They all have their try at golf, which Red loves but considers to be a hundred times harder than running with a football. It would be heaven were it not for the Kaan brothers and their top customers drilling him with questions all day long, forcing him to re-live his college games play-by-play.

"What were you thinking when you got out in the open on the first kickoff return against Michigan?" someone asks.

"I thought if Earl can take out three guys, who am I not to beat the last one."

Everyone laughs.

"What's Zuppke like?" someone else asks.

"Imagine being under fire from a German machine gun."

Some of the guys on the trip fought in the war. Sadly, they have first-hand knowledge.

"How'd it feel to have the penalty called to end the Chicago game?" someone else asks.

"I have no memory of the fourth quarter. I had to read about it in the papers."

Guys then chime in with their high school football injury stories and how they were proud to be coached to get right back up after an injury, rub dirt on it, and get back into the game, no matter how much your head is ringing.

"What about all the girls? Come on, what's that like? They must be all over you," someone else asks.

"I've never had any money to take 'em out on a date. I couldn't even afford to buy them a soda."

Someone remarks that, with his fame, Red can probably skip the meal altogether. Everyone laughs.

"All your best linemen graduated. Does Illinois stand a chance this year?" someone asks.

"Garland will make up for a bunch of them. Earl and Chuck already make up for the rest. With those three on the team, how could we lose?"

Guys correct him, saying that with Red Grange on the team, how could they lose?

"I saw a sign recently that read 'Penn Rules the East.' Does a Western team really stand a chance against Eastern football?" someone else asks.

"If Garland, Earl, and I melt in this heat, we'll never know."

Again, the uncontrollable laughter. Each day, someone eventually musters the courage to ask the toughest question.

"And, what will you do after your last game against Ohio State? Any thoughts of going pro?"

His father steps in to say, "Why risk his neck going pro when he could take more trips like this one? The Kaan brothers are talking about Cuba after Red's last game."

The customers are so excited about another trip they forget Red never revealed his plans. Also, by that time in the evening, everyone besides Red is generally so drunk they wouldn't even remember his answer. It's also the time each evening when their dinner is interrupted by the hotel manager, who, to the cheers of the men, leads a line of local women in a circle around the table.

When a girl meets one of their expectations, a man grabs her wrist to signal that she sit on his lap. Each time a match is made, everyone cheers. By the time they realize Red hasn't made a selection, he's vanished, and the wobble in his chair has long settled.

Despite having to disappear each evening, Red loves being on vacation with his dad, his brother, and his best friend, Earl, especially on the fishing outings. He loves seeing them patting each other on the back, working together to reel in large, exotic fish. All day long, he enjoys watching his family and friends laugh together.

The entire time Red is answering those same questions over and over again, he keeps telling himself that when his master plan eventually materializes with Pyle, his family and friends will be able to fish and travel as much as they want. Instead of being beholden to the Kaan brothers and their customers, they will soon answer only to themselves. Instead of telling the same old stories about old games, they'll create new stories and go on new adventures. He doesn't need to be anyone's puppet, nor will he ever allow himself to be one again.

Polly was right about one thing. He didn't once think about her on this trip, other than surmising who she's working for. Walking alone on the beach each night, he is thinking of someone else he'd rather visit when he returns—an adorable coat check girl.

CHAPTER 23

Weather during football season notoriously transforms from one extreme to the other. By the end of the season, teams are playing through snow and ice. But at the beginning of the season, in late August, especially during the early practices, it is hot as hell.

Zuppke's idea of practice, besides being four hours long in the brutal heat with few water breaks, is to simulate gameplay with the varsity playing an actual, sixty-minute full-out tackle game each day against the freshmen.

"You. You!" Zuppke yells to a brand-new freshman player, practically blowing a whistle through the kid's ear. "Why are you pulling at your sweater? What's in there? Ants?"

"It itches, Coach," the freshman says.

"It itches?" Zuppke says, perplexed. "Granche, get over here. Granche!"

Red jogs over.

"Granche, what are our uniforms made out of?"

"The finest of wool, Coach," Red says.

"Did you ever complain when you were a freshman?"

Red thinks about his answer for a moment before admitting, "I did."

The freshman's eyes are wide open now. It wasn't the answer he was expecting from the great Red Grange. The other freshmen perk up, as well. With the success of Illinois in recent years, there are double the number of guys trying out for the team. Fifty or so of the one hundred are considered to be the best players out of high schools across Illinois, passing up the University of Chicago and Northwestern. Unlike other schools, Zuppke doesn't believe in recruiting, especially out of state.

"Und what did I say when you told me your wool sweater itched?" Zuppke barks at Red.

"You said if I want to play football for the great state of Illinois…if I want to be part of something special…if I want to see even a minute of playing time…that I should…," Red stops, unable to finish.

"That you should what?" Zuppke says.

"That I should run five laps around the field, and if it still itches, I should run five more," Red says.

"Und, what did you do, Granche?"

Red looks out at all the freshmen. He remembers being one of them, dying in the heat while dying to be a part of Zuppke's team.

"Und, what did you do, Granche?" Zuppke repeats.

Red can't bring himself to answer.

"He ran five laps full out," Earl cuts in, getting in the boy's face. "Then he ran five more. Then he kept running until the itch was the last thing on his mind. Let's go! Ten laps! Go! Ten laps!"

Earl keeps shouting at the kid until he gets the hint and takes off to run his punishment for complaining. Watching the freshman sprint around the field, Red remembers an upperclassman yelling in his face, just like Earl is doing now. He also remembers not a single player ever complaining again all season about anything.

"Line back up!" Zuppke shouts, blowing his whistle.

The freshman coaches organize their squad while Zuppke gets right in the huddle with the varsity. Walter Camp's rules force him to sit on the bench during games, but the hell if he will do so during practice.

"We've been mixing up the freshmen to see who can play," Zuppke barks to the varsity. "We got the top eleven picked out now. Look at them over there. That's the makings of another national championship team in a few years. Look at them. Und they know it."

Red glances over at the hungry freshmen, remembering the historic day three years ago when Earl, Chuck, and he did the unthinkable and beat the varsity.

The current varsity is now locked in on Zuppke, awaiting orders. Except, that is, for one person in the huddle.

"The freshmen look like a bunch of pansies to me," Garland says. "Softies. All of them."

His reaction is so unexpected that the other varsity guys can't help but chuckle, forgetting for the tiniest moment that Zuppke is still in the huddle.

"Is that right, Garland?" Zuppke says.

"Just give me the ball, Coach," Garland replies.

They do just that. The ball is handed off to Garland. Earl and Chuck block. Garland barely takes two steps before he is absolutely pummeled by an amped-up freshman squad who's waited for an opportunity all preseason to shut Garland's mouth.

It takes a moment, but a dizzy Garland eventually rejoins the huddle.

"As I was saying," Zuppke continues, "we have some work to do."

Zuppke adjusts the offense after each play, moving varsity players around and trying new tactics. If he could be in the huddle, even if Illinois were playing eleven Horsemen, there is no way they could ever lose.

It takes almost the entire practice game for Zuppke to settle on having Earl join the linemen to beef up the sophomore line. He moves Garland to running back, the position Red has always played. Then he moves Red from running back to quarterback, giving him more flexibility to run, pass, and adjust the play at the line of scrimmage.

Warren, watching in the bleachers, loses control of his cigar. Unable to catch it, it burns the crotch of his pants. By moving Red to quarterback, Zuppke has transformed him into a triple threat. Red can keep the ball, hand it off to Garland, or throw it to Chuck. The highly recruited freshmen and their coaches find themselves at a loss for how to stop Zuppke's new "option offense." As such, it doesn't take long for Garland's mouth to start running again.

"Nice try, freshman… That's all you got?... Who taught you to tackle?... Itch my jock…." He's relentless. The more adjustments Zuppke makes, the more verbal jabs Garland lands between successful plays.

Just to have a little fun and catch the freshmen coaches off guard, Zuppke calls for a flea-flicker to end the practice.

The ball is hiked to Red. He tosses it underhand back to Garland. Garland runs to his right, drawing the attention of the entire freshman squad. Just as they are about to crush him, Garland sails a perfect pass to his brother, who has a wide-open fifty-yard path for a touchdown. The whole time Red is running, he's thinking to himself what a fun season this will be now that he finally gets to play alongside his brother.

As Red jogs back to congratulate the varsity, he notices both teams and the coaches have formed a circle around an injured player.

Red sprints back the fifty yards even faster, only to break through the circle to confirm his worst nightmare.

CHAPTER 24

Kids in wheelchairs line the hallway of a Chicago hospital. They sport a mix of casts, slings, and bandages. Some have grown so frail they are nearly unrecognizable to their families. However, all of their eyes light up as their hero takes the time to stop and talk to every one of them.

Red signs casts, footballs, bandages, and anything that might bring the slightest smile to their faces. After spending ample time with the children, he drops by a handful of adult rooms. While he despises talking football on paid trips and fundraising events, he'll do whatever he can to raise the spirits of hospital patients.

After he's met with all the patients, he allows the nurses to flirt with him, agreeing to take the phone numbers from the younger, single ones. Occasionally, a few married ones slip their numbers in, as well.

Once those visits are finished, he's able to make his way to his real destination down at the end of the hall. Red takes a deep breath knowing that entering this room will be harder on him than any patient he's met today.

In that last room, Garland looks helpless, lethargic from pain medication, and lying in his hospital bed with his right arm propped up to stabilize his shattered shoulder. Red's father, Lyle, acknowledges Red with a nod and asks all the nurses to clear out so he can be alone with his sons.

Red desperately wants to hug or touch his brother in some way, but eventually settles on holding Garland's left hand, the body part farthest away from the injured shoulder.

Squeezing Garland's hand and not receiving a squeeze back causes Red to tear up. His whole life, he's been to Garland a brother, a friend, and even a mother all rolled into one. Nothing is worse than helplessly watching a loved one lying in pain.

"It's gotta be surgery," Lyle says. "They can't get it back proper."

Surgery is the last thing any football player wants to hear. Lyle explains what the doctor told him. They are going to have to cut Garland open from his neck across his shoulder so that they have ample room to see what they are doing. Assuming the surgery is successful, Garland is expected to be in the hospital for up to two months. Incisions that big are always at risk for serious infection.

"He's already loopy," Lyle says. "Two months of morphine, and he'll have to wean off that on top of everything else. You've seen the degenerates around town, showing up in the jail, still hooked on that junk from the war."

Upon closer inspection, Red observes that Garland is ghost-like from the medication. Lost in a trance. Red is coming to terms with the fact that not only will he have to play his senior season without his brother, but the prospect of his brother ever playing again seems improbable.

At least it's not his knee, Red thinks to himself. Knee surgeries mean not only the end of a career but also a lifetime of chronic pain.

Red would do anything to reverse that last play in practice. He should have been the one to bait the defense. He'd do anything to change the past, anything to take the pain away from his brother.

"It's gonna cost mountains," Lyle says. "I'm going to have to pull Garland from school and use the tuition money for his surgery."

That burns Red, especially since he knows universities are prohibited from helping pay for players' medical treatment due to the concerns of affecting their amateur status. Families must pay tuition to play and must pay for medical care to avoid any hint of professionalism.

Red can draw tens of thousands of paying fans into the stands, generating astronomical revenues for athletic departments, but his own brother has to drop out of school to pay for surgery.

"I'm going to find a way to pay for it," Red says.

"Don't," Lyle says. "You're not his father. Or his mother. Those are my jobs. Yours is to finish up college and get a job. A good one, like the Kaan brothers are offering. Learn the insurance business."

"I'd love to do that, but you know that's not what they are offering. Do you really want to see them parade me around again? I felt like an animal in a zoo. People poking me in the cage while you and Garland lived it up in Panama."

Lyle's massive hands grip the metal railing of Garland's bed with such force it begins to bend. He's bigger than Red and Garland put together. When he gets mad, it's terrifying. At the jail where he works, they don't even bother locking the cell doors when he's on shift. What inmate would ever try anything with him standing guard?

"I didn't mean it like that, Dad," Red pleads. "I'm sorry. I didn't mean it, but you have to trust me to make my own decisions. I just can't do the Kaan insurance thing. I can't do it, Dad."

The metal railing is bending now. Red is certain his father will snap it in half if he continues squeezing. The only other time in his life he saw his father resort to extreme violence was when his mother died and Lyle nearly beat the entire hospital staff to death.

Thankfully, Lyle is older now. Red is eventually able to stare him down. At that moment, Lyle does something Red

137

didn't think he could ever do. Lyle starts to cry. Then shake. Then bawl like a 300-pound out-of-control baby.

"All Garland ever wanted was to be like you," Lyle spits out between sobs. "Now he's hurt. And you, well, I don't know what you're doing. No one knows what you are doing. I've failed you both."

His loud wailing causes the nurses to rush in, but they quickly realize they have no idea how to calm this beast of a man. Red takes another look at his inconsolable father and his comatose brother, questioning not if he's making the right decision but why he ever let Garland talk him into lifting that block of ice off the ground all those years ago.

CHAPTER 25

That evening, Red and Pyle wait in line at a flower shop behind a little old lady. Red looks out the window, past the daisies and tulips neatly arranged in buckets, across the street to a movie theater.

He'd love to see a movie, but not the one showing. The lighted marquee advertises *The Freshman*, released just in time for football season, a film about a college player named Harold.

"At least they had the good sense not to name him Red," Pyle says, taking a moment to smell some roses in the store.

The little old lady in front of them finally finishes her purchase, leaving Pyle and Red as the only remaining customers.

"Do you have any moonflowers?" Pyle asks the shopkeeper.

"What an odd request," the shopkeeper shoots back. "Why do you ask?"

"Because I'm told peonies bloom this time of night."

The shopkeeper suspiciously looks over Pyle and Red. After a while, he turns around to a wall of flowers, reaches his hand deep into them, and pulls up on a hidden lever, revealing a secret door through which Pyle and Red quickly disappear. The shopkeeper closes the door behind them.

Red follows Pyle down a winding, dimly lit corridor. Long shadows on the walls create an air of mystery as Red passes through multiple sets of velvet curtains that muffle the sounds of what lies ahead.

Jazz music fills Red's ears as they pass through the last set of curtains. A maître d' steps out and takes their hats.

"Mr. Pyle, welcome back," he says. "Mr. Grange, go Illinois! Oskee-Wow-Wow, young man."

With a wink, the maître d' leads them past dim oil lamps. Red, barely able to see, keeps his head down, focusing on the floor, hoping to avoid tripping. The maître d' drops them off at a reserved booth, where Red slides in after Pyle.

"Mr. Pyle, your usual is, of course, already on order," the maître d' says. "Have a wonderful evening."

Red finally dares to look out at the nightclub. Their table is at the heart of the action. He peers out over plush armchairs and polished mahogany tables into the expansive room. Chandeliers sparkle, casting a warm glow across the crowded dance floor and illuminating the jazz band on stage. Forbidden energy fills the dark space.

"Notice anything?" Pyle says to Red.

Red spies flappers in short skirts and bobbed hair, twirling on the dance floor. Men in pinstripe suits tap their feet and sway to the music. Nothing out of the ordinary. Except, come to think of it, all the men are exceptionally large. It's like a room full of Earls.

Red's first thoughts go to Al Capone, and he prays he's not here. Red discovers the significance of the large men only when George Halas, owner of the Chicago Bears, slides into their booth, sandwiching himself between Red and Pyle.

"Just a little team bonding," Halas says with a wink, his hand outstretched toward Red.

Red shakes his hand. He knows Halas. Over the years, they've met at Illinois banquets and such, but only when Zuppke wasn't present. Now that Red takes a better look, he also knows many of the Bears players in the room. Most played for Zuppke at some point. Some are the guys who were kicked out of college over the Taylorville scandal.

"I'll be right back," Pyle says, sliding out of the booth and leaving Halas and Red alone as the drinks arrive.

Red politely declines any form of alcohol. Halas gladly gulps down a few cocktails.

"You know what I love about this place?" Halas says.

Red shakes his head.

"No cameras, no reporters," Halas says, smiling. "And no Zuppke."

The mention of Zuppke sends shivers down Red's spine, even though he agrees. Down in this dungeon, they are safe to have a discussion.

"Look, this C.C. Pyle fellow claims he speaks for you. Before I deal with him, I insisted on some proof that he is who he says he is."

"Who does he say he is?"

"Your agent."

"I play football. And maybe act in films, as crazy as that sounds. But, yes, he handles the rest. He handles all my business affairs. So, I guess he is my agent."

"Fascinating. If this agent concept catches on, wow, that would really be something," Halas says, pouring another drink. "I don't know what I can offer a superstar. I guess your *agent* will tell me shortly. Competing with Mara and his New York City money won't be easy, but since I got you here, I wanted to remind you of one thing."

"What's that?"

"The pro game isn't college."

"I know. I snuck in and saw you play last year."

"That's funny because I snuck in and watched you play the Chicago game. I never saw anything like it in my life."

"Thank you, but the Bears game I saw, wow. Every pro player is huge and fast. Earl's who you really want. The "T" offense you've perfected is perfect for him. I just hope to find a way to contribute."

"You'll contribute," Halas says. "For one, you'll put butts in seats. But no one ever talks about your defense. If they kept

141

defensive stats, you'd easily have the record for the most tackles and interceptions. Those flashy touchdowns of yours get all the press, but you might be better on defense than offense."

"Nah, I'm sure there are better defenders," Red says.

"And the modesty," Halas continues. "Regardless, my guys are going to love you for something else. Here's the real value you'll bring to the team...."

Halas stands to make room for Pyle and five young women, who scramble over each other to get the chance to sit next to Red in the booth.

"I have to get home to my family," Halas says, fighting for Red's attention over the girls. "I'd love to see you keep wearing orange and blue."

Then Halas turns his attention to Pyle.

"I'll do what I can to make a good offer. But, regardless, I count myself lucky."

"Why's that?" Pyle says, with girls still jockeying for position next to Red.

"I get to tell my grandkids someday that I saw the great Red Grange play for Zuppke and Illinois," Halas says. "Nothing will ever compare."

The girls start lobbing questions at Red, offering to pour him a drink or lend him a cigarette. He fends them off the best he can, watching Halas move on, shaking hands, and hugging all his players before heading home.

Finally, Red looks closely around the table, realizing he recognizes the faces of all the girls who work various jobs at the hotel. Some of them even delivered clothes to him the day he found himself half-naked in the coat room. They all know Pyle, given he now lives out of the hotel suite, having left Clem back in Champaign to tend to the theater.

It dawns on Red that another person from the hotel may be in the club, as well.

Out on the dance floor...

Helen is lost in the music. All evening she's been telling large, older football players and some of Capone's mafia to take a hike. She's finally got a night off, and football players and thugs are the last thing on her mind. That is until one of them dares to grab both her hands and step in unison with her Charleston rhythm.

She's about to kick him in the nuts when she catches a glimpse of the famous smile and auburn hair. Red was a good dancer in the coat room, but, out on the dancefloor, he's even better. Stealing moves from Helen and the others near them allows him to improve with each song. Her smile quickly matches his. Together, they own the floor.

In the shadows...

Warren watches, piecing a story together that is shaping up to be bigger than any he'll ever break in his career. Grantland Rice's exposé about the Black Sox World Series cheating scandal launched him to national fame. And Warren's about to join Rice in the national press box. He can already taste the cigar smoke.

Back at the table...

Pyle is happy to hold court with the young women, offering stock market tips and promising to show them ticker charts and graphs he's tracking back up in his suite. He looks out at Red dancing, enjoying himself for a change. Pyle can't wait for the college season to finish. The big Penn and Ohio State games can't come soon enough.

The world is about to be Red's oyster, and C.C. Pyle is holding the fork.

CHAPTER 26

Illinois at Penn
Saturday, October 31, 1925

Two months later, on Halloween, Warren expects to be relegated to the bleachers upon his arrival at Franklin Field. Every national and East Coast reporter from Boston to D.C. is in Philadelphia today. He's shocked to discover that not only does he have a seat in the press box but it's right next to a spot reserved for his idol, Grantland Rice.

He looks out into the stadium. "Penn Rules the East" banners fly everywhere, and they should. The Quakers didn't lose a regular season game last year, and they are 5-0 to start this season. The sixty-three thousand Philadelphia fans in attendance love their University of Pennsylvania Quakers almost as much as they love the Liberty Bell.

Warren sets up his station just how he likes it with a typewriter, cigars, matches, notebook, pencils, binoculars, and stat sheets from Illinois' dismal start leading into this game. Three losses to Nebraska, Iowa, and, embarrassingly, Michigan, against whom Red scored four touchdowns in twelve minutes just a year ago. Their only win so far is against lowly Butler, whom they barely beat.

Per Warren's tally, Red has averaged an impressive 140 yards a game thus far, but the young sophomore line and the injury to Garland have proven too much for even Red to overcome.

Warren has reported that the only real offensive play Illinois has had success with all season is stacking blockers to the right and relying on Red, despite being a marked man, to smash through eleven guys almost on his own. As Warren has observed in his game reports, when a team can only run one play, it's pretty hard to win... even with Red.

The reporters in the press box highly favor the Quakers to win today, especially since the field is a muddy, soggy mess. Zuppke has complained publicly that Penn purposely didn't maintain the field's surface to slow Red down. Penn's groundskeeper gave a great quote to Grantland Rice, saying, "If you didn't know, it rains in the East. What's the matter, Western football? Is the Ghost spooked?"

Just before the opening kickoff, Warren is about to light his cigar when the great Grantland Rice sits down next to him. Nerves overcome Warren, and it takes him three tries with three different matches to light the thing. By now, he assumed Rice would have set up his station, but he hasn't.

Mustering all his courage, with a lit cigar finally sticking out of his mouth, Warren slowly turns to his right. Sure enough, Grantland Rice is sitting with no typewriter, no notebook, no pencils, no binoculars, and no cigar. Instead, Rice pinches the perfect amount of tobacco, taps lightly, leaves just enough room at the top, and, with a flick of a single match against his fingernail, lights a beautiful pipe.

Warren is starstruck. He doesn't snap out of it until Rice reaches over and grabs an ashtray just in time to catch falling ash from Warren's cigar, saving him from another burn to the crotch.

"Warren, what's your brand of sports journalism?" Rice says.

"My brand.... What?" Warren says, confused.

"I peg you for a traditionalist. First Amendment, free press, a watchdog for the public, holding those in power accountable, facts over narrative, illuminating stories that matter, voice for the voiceless?"

"Um, yes," Warren replies. "That's what we all are—journalists. That's the classic definition."

Rice nods, puffing gently on his pipe, producing a spectacular aroma.

The teams take the field. Illinois is set to receive. In line with the expectations of those in the press box, Penn kicks it far away from Red. Earl catches the ball and slogs forward in the mud, each step precarious, shifting more sideways than forward. All the players are in the same boat, practically running in slow motion.

Earl is eventually brought down by a gang of Penn players, who slam him into a pond-sized puddle in the middle of the field. Each player does his best to get the grime and slop off their hands and face. After a moment, they realize there is no point.

With decent field position, Illinois lines up as they have all season in the center of the hash marks and strong to the right. Red hands the ball to Earl, who runs to the right until the bigger Penn line drives him face-first into the muck, dunking him entirely under the water. Illinois runs this same play a few more times, getting nowhere before punting.

Warren records each play along with the yardage while noticing that Rice is recording nothing. His energy is spent on keeping the flame going on his pipe, which emits a blend of cherry and vanilla in contrast to the peppery smoke billowing from the cigars of Warren and the rest.

Penn punts it back to Illinois, who is stopped on their forty-five-yard line.

"Watch this next play," Rice says. "Look at Penn's defense. With Illinois always lined up to run Earl to the right, look how Penn overshifts in the same direction, anticipating. Do you see it?"

Warren nods. He does. He's never seen Penn play before, so he appreciates the inside scoop. However, if he didn't know which direction Illinois was headed, he couldn't tell which team was which. With their sweaters waterlogged, it's nearly impossible to tell who is who even at this early stage of the game.

"Now look what happens when Red is finally lined up to take the handoff from Earl," Rice says.

Warren watches both Penn and Illinois shift even more to the right. With Red set to get the ball, both teams overcompensate. Red is the only player on the field whose uniform is pristine, given he's yet to have any yardage or make any tackles.

"Now get your pencil ready," Rice says as the ball is snapped to Earl and handed to Red.

Red's head goes to the right as Illinois has run all season, taking the Penn defense with him. Except, Red doesn't run to the right.

Like a streak of lightning, he bolts left to the weak side, sprinting with his knees as high as possible, touching the ground only with the balls of his feet. This gives him perfect traction. Everyone else is slipping around, but he's clocked nearly as fast by Zuppke as if the field were dry. His pristine orange sweater stays untouched for fifty-five yards to the endzone.

He touches the ball down for a score and waits forever for both teams to slog their way down to set up for the extra point. Red kneels to hold, but Earl's footing is so slippery the ball goes nowhere.

Illinois 6. Penn 0.

Red has one muddy blotch on his uniform where he knelt to hold the ball for Earl. That's it. The "Penn Rules the East" record crowd goes silent.

Warren spins his head around to look more closely at Rice, still doing nothing but enjoying his pipe.

"And your brand of sports journalism?" Warren says. "You're from the future, I take it? You're a time traveler?"

"I do have a crystal ball," Rice says. "It's called befriending the greats: Babe Ruth, Bobby Jones, Jack

Dempsey, Bill Tilden, Bob Zuppke. I vacation with all of them. I consider them all dear friends."

Warren's eyes are wide open now.

"As a result of our friendship, they entrust me with their strategies. I was out here with Red and Zuppke late last night, watching Zuppke teach Red how to lift his knees to run in this muck."

"But you wrote the story about Zuppke's complaint with the field conditions," Warren says, realizing as he's saying it out loud that the report prompted Penn to make the field even muddier.

"Your brand of sports journalism is traditional," Rice replies. "What would you call mine?"

Warren is at a loss for words.

"Mine's entertainment," Rice says. "Ten years ago, what percentage of an average daily newspaper was dedicated to sports, would you say?"

"Less than one percent, maybe," Warren replies.

"Right, and it's twenty percent today," Rice says. "Sixty-three thousand people are here in this stadium, and it's not for the 'Freedom of the Press.' Not for 'facts.' Not for 'those in authority to be held accountable.' They are here to escape their ordinary lives. They are here to witness heroics. They are here to be entertained."

Penn elects to kick off rather than receive. Due to the wind, they can't kick it far enough away from Red. He picks it up and high steps, running it back sixty yards to the twenty-yard line, where he is tackled for the first time. He stands up with mud on the right side of his body, but a glorious orange streak still shows on his left. It's the only hint of color on any player on the field.

Illinois lines up heavy to the right. Penn is still determining whether they should line up heavily to match. Penn is lost in confusion and doubt as Red hands the ball to Earl, who runs to the strong side and gains five yards. The same confusion happens over and over again until Earl gets the ball to the two-yard line.

This time, Red is set to get the ball. Like always, he's the man to score. Red moves his head to the left, taking the defense with him. They are not dumb enough to fall for that again, tackling Red to the ground.

Except, Earl faked the handoff and crossed the goal line carrying the ball to the right. Penn is dumbfounded. Red is elated, hugging his friend. Again, Earl's footing is too slippery to get the extra point off properly.

Illinois 12. Penn 0.

The Penn crowd is silent. Dead silent.

Warren now understands why Zuppke allows him to attend practices. Writing about how Illinois only runs plays heavy to the right set up the first two touchdowns of this game. Zuppke baited a trap, and Penn is falling for it.

Now that they are down two touchdowns, Penn elects to take the ball. Given the slop, they can't get anywhere and are forced to punt, which is followed by an Illinois punt. The punts go back and forth into the second quarter until Illinois trips up and gets pinned down on their own one-yard line.

Earl is set to punt but slips, fumbling the ball in his own endzone. In this situation, Walter Camp considered it safer to just dive on the ball, which Earl does, taking a safety and giving up two points.

Illinois 12. Penn 2.

Red now looks like the other twenty-one players on the field. Soggy, muddy, indistinguishable.

Snow and sleet start to fall. The players were hard to see before, but now they are just apparitions in the mist. Except, that is, for one guy on Illinois who now gets the ball every play. He may be covered in the same mud, but something is different about him.

Red high steps, zigs, zags, and stiff-arms all who dare get near him, including a star Penn player whom he knocks unconscious and out of the game. The Penn replacement, sporting a fresh crimson top with yellow letters, is the only clean, recognizable uniform on the field...until one play later when a Red Grange stiff arm drives his entire body through the mud.

Play stops while the officials and his team attempt to dig him out and revive him. Both lines reset. Red scores another touchdown. Earl slips and misses another kick.

Illinois 18. Penn "Rules the East" 2.

The crowd has gone from cheers to silence to shock as the muddy players slog off the field at halftime. The Philly faithful can't distinguish their team's uniforms from Illinois'.

Rice taps his pipe, expertly keeping it lit.

"I gather you have an investigative story set to publish," Rice says to Warren, "of the traditional, hard-hitting journalism variety."

Warren is catching on to why he's sitting in the front row.

"Believe it or not, I debated the Black Sox situation before I set it to print," Rice continues. "I thought long and hard about whether I'd be tarnishing sports forever. I asked myself what the effect would be on the entertainment value if we uncovered that our heroes are actually human, revealing they succumb to greed and the other seven deadly sins just like the rest of us mortals. Where is the fun if everyone is always wondering if the game is fixed? I'm still not convinced I did the right thing."

"But you published," Warren says.

"I did because cheating is wrong. But what's Red done wrong?" Rice asks. "The Black Sox were downright cheating. They changed the outcome of the game for money. What's Red done?"

"A two-bit promotor flashing an agreement with Red's signature is running around the country lining up commercial opportunities for an amateur collegiate athlete," Warren responds. "The best amateur in the world. That's what."

"Lining up commercial opportunities for *after* Red's last game as an amateur. *After* the Ohio State game."

The Golden Age of Red

"Who can know for sure?"

"In all your years covering Red, have you any proof he's ever told a single lie?"

"Others have answered questions for him, but no," Warren admits. "I don't believe he himself has ever lied. I don't think he's capable of it."

"No matter what brand of sports journalism you subscribe to, traditional or entertainment," Rice says, "you owe it to the readers to corner him and demand a straight answer before you publish. Ask him straight up. Allow our hero to set the record straight. If nothing else, his fans deserve it."

Warren ponders Rice's advice as the teams jog back out after halftime, their hands and faces cleaner, but not the rest of them.

It's hard to make out the action through the fog, sleet, and snow, but deep in the third quarter, Illinois appears to be in field goal range, setting up for a kick with Red holding and Earl at the ready.

"Don't you find it odd," Rice says, "that Illinois would attempt a field goal when they can't even find the footing to make an extra point?"

Before Warren can answer, the Illinois center snaps it over Red's head straight to Earl, who tosses it to Chuck, who draws Penn's full attention before passing it to a wide-open Red for a Razzle Dazzle Bob Zuppke touchdown, reminding the East, one last time, that it is Western football that actually rules the sport.

Again, Earl misses the extra point.

Illinois 24. Penn 2.

The crowd snaps out of its shock. Sixty-seven thousand people on Halloween shift allegiance. They are on their feet, cheering for Illinois, cheering for Western football.

A few plays later, Zuppke pulls Red out of the game. He's amassed 363 total yards by Warren's count in ankle deep mud. Red grabs a blanket and tries to throw it over his shoulder, but he's too muddy, and it keeps sliding off his back. The entire

151

Illinois coaching staff wants to be of service. They all jump up, at risk of penalty, to fit the blanket around his shoulders. They just want to help in some way. To be a part of it. To be near greatness.

More and more of those on the sidelines come over to help. An army of people attempts to position Red's blanket just so. In the meantime, no one is watching the field.

Either team could have scored. A cannon could have been fired. The Germans could have invaded. A Headless Horseman could have ridden through the fog. A raven could have spoken. Anything could have happened on the field, and the crowd of sixty-seven thousand would have missed it. Same with the press box. Every single eye in the stadium is locked on making sure America's hero gets safely tucked under that blanket.

When the game ends with the final score of Illinois 24, Penn 2, the hypnotized crowd stands and cheers wildly for Red, the other team's star, successfully wrapped, walking off the field, desperate to escape the attention.

Red Grange has nothing left to prove to the East. Nothing left to prove to anyone.

Except Warren.

CHAPTER 27

Cross-country train porters, like anyone, have both easy and hard days at work. When their passengers are hyped-up college football players, media, fans, cheerleaders, and the entire Illinois marching band, porters have a singular regret: that they didn't call in sick.

Orange fills every train car today. The band tosses aside sheet music in favor of Jazz improvisation. Coed Conga lines wind between the aisles. Under a cloud of cigar smoke, alumni chant fight songs. There's no point in even cleaning the shoe polish off the windows. More will appear moments later, reading "Oskee-Wow-Wow," "Illini Rule the World," "Roaring Red," or "Zuppke is god."

Red can't hide on a train. Everyone wants to slap him on the shoulder. Every time they do, all he thinks about is Garland. The first thing he's planning to do when the train gets back to Champaign is to call his brother in the hospital. The surgery went well. The infection is under control. Weaning Garland off morphine, he's told, is the final step. Regardless, Red can't wait to get an update.

With the biggest grin on his face, Earl bursts into the rollicking train car, handing out a variety of newspapers he grabbed from the newsstand before they departed.

"Listen to this one," someone yells out, reading. "'As the game wore on and Grange electrified and thrilled those thousands, even the stricken and sore hearts of the Penn

153

faithful found room to acclaim Red Grange, the greatest of all football players.'"

Everyone cheers.

"And this one: 'When histories are written on the feats of redheaded warriors, Grange must be given his place with those old heroes, Richard the Lionhearted, Frederick Barbarossa, and Eric the Red.'"

More cheers.

"Another: 'This man, Red Grange, is three or four men and a horse all rolled into one. He is Jack Dempsey, Babe Ruth, Al Jolson, Paavo Nurmi, and Man o' War. Put them all together. They spell Grange.'"

The college kids rock the train, causing the porters, who fear a derailment, to brace themselves. Once the revelry calms down, Chuck shares a serious quote.

"Now, this is deep," Chuck says. "Settle down, listen up to this one."

After pausing for dramatic effect, Chuck reads, "'All that awaits Red Grange is immortality.'"

Everyone lets that sink in until, uncharacteristically for Red, he stands in his seat, holding a newspaper himself.

"I have one I'd like to read," Red says, hushing the crowd to where they could hear a pin drop, giving the porters their only moment of peace the entire trip. "It says, 'Earl Britton would open the way for the flaming helmet behind him, time and again punching holes in the Pennsylvania defense, which let Grange pour through.'"

Guys start patting Earl on the back, and he doesn't know how to react, given the spotlight has never been on him.

"'Perhaps it is only fair to say,'" Red continues reading, "'that without Britton, Grange would not have been anything spectacular.'"

"No, no," Earl says, trying to shake it off.

"Three cheers for Earl!" someone yells.

"Hooray! Hooray! Hooray!"

Earl stands and quiets everyone.

"Here's *my* favorite," Earl says, holding something out of view. "Red made the cover."

He proudly reveals the cover of *Time Magazine,* and sure enough, Red's face is on display for eternity. Recent issues have featured John D. Rockefeller, Thomas Edison, Charlie Chaplin, Henry Ford, and even the Pope. Red is the first football player to ever appear on the cover.

"You know who's never been on the cover?" Earl asks the crowded train car.

"Penn?" someone jokes.

"Penn never will. Eastern football is dead," Earl replies. Cheers ring out.

"No, guess who's never been on the cover?"

Earl makes everyone wait before revealing the answer.

"Babe Ruth. He's never been on the cover," Earl says. "What do you think about that, Red? You're officially bigger than The Babe."

Everyone is silent, waiting to hear what Red has to say.

"I know what would earn him the cover," Red says. "If Babe were on this team with you guys. With Zuppke coaching him, he'd be on the cover every week."

The loudest of cheers ring out. The band starts playing again. The porters appear to be considering jumping off the train and starting a new career.

It takes steaming through multiple states for the revelry to finally die down later that evening.

Red wants to doze off, but he can tell they are nearing Champaign by the number of "Go Red" banners hanging along the tracks, the number of banners and barns painted orange increasing minute by minute.

Warren plops down uninvited in the seat next to Red.

"I have something for you," he says, dropping a manilla folder on Red's lap.

Red wipes his eyes, focuses, and flips through the folder's contents for less than ten seconds before closing it and handing it back.

155

"It's all in there," Warren says. "The Bears. The Giants. Virginia Valli screen test. Movie offers. The Wills Sainte Claire shakedown. C.C. Pyle. Sworn statements of dozens of people up and down the East Coast, Florida, and California detailing Pyle rubbing a signed contract in their faces. It goes to print tomorrow. I have it all."

Red goes back to looking out the window. "Red the Hero," "Red the Man," "Red for President," and "Boy Scouts for Red," all flashing by.

"Unless you tell me it's not true," Warren says. "Tell me on the record I'm wrong, and I'll bury it. I'll rip the whole thing up. I'll burn it even."

Red continues to stare out the window. "America's Hero." "The Galloping Ghost." "In Red We Trust."

"I'm going to ask just once," Warren says. "Have you signed a contract to play professional football? If you did, that makes you a professional, even if you haven't been paid anything yet. Are you or are you not a professional?"

Red turns and looks Warren straight in the face.

"I've signed nothing with any pro team. I play for Zuppke," Red says. "Until the last seconds tick off the clock at the Ohio State game, I proudly play amateur football for my home state."

"And after that game?"

Red goes back to looking out the window.

"That's your final comment?" Warren asks.

The train slows as it approaches the Champaign station. Out the windows, the banners are replaced by something else. It's such an amazing sight that all the players crowd the windows. The energy level is building to a point in the train car that it quickly becomes the loudest it has been during the entire trip.

Red looks out the window to discover no less than twenty thousand people, waiting hours in the cold, organized in an energized mob around the train station. It takes a moment to make out what the crowd is chanting, but soon the chant is all that can be heard, even inside the train car.

"We want Red! We want Red! We want Red!"

The chant is deafening. Thousands of times louder than the chant in the movie theater when Charlie Chaplin visited. It's pandemonium outside. Suddenly, Zuppke bursts into the train car, demanding Earl and some of the other linemen help him, practically lifting Red out of the seat by himself.

"We have to protect Granche," Zuppke screams. "They'll tear him to pieces."

Zuppke grabs Red by his collar and drags him across Warren. The linemen, led by Earl, exit the train first, pushing the crowd far enough back that Red can at least step out on the platform. The moment the crowd sees his auburn hair, all hell breaks loose. Holding off the Penn, Michigan, and Chicago lines is one thing. This crowd is the fiercest opponent the Illinois line will ever face.

Red is well-protected by a wall of his friends and his coach, but a few hands still break through, poking at his face, eyes, and hair.

Red scans the scene, calculating his moves like he used to as a kid when Martin and Ronnie were bearing down on him during games of Kill the Man with the Ball. He sees his escape off the train platform to the right, behind the crowd. Earl has already found it, holding open the side door for him.

In a flash, Red fakes left before dashing right, putting his shoulder down, stiff-arming a few men, swiveling past children, and vanishing through the side exit before Zuppke even realizes Red had made the first move.

The moment Red gets through the side door, Earl slams it shut behind him, taking the brunt of the crowd upon himself.

Red's already calculated how he'll skirt the perimeter of town and hole up in Pyle's theater office. Just as he's through the side door, a look of terror shoots across his face. The crowd has outsmarted him. He tries to retreat back through the door, but Earl is blocking it on the other side.

Twenty thousand people march from the train station to the Zeta Psi fraternity house with their prize hoisted on their shoulders. Red is carried the entire way, touched on every body part imaginable, tossed around, and paraded down Main Street, where every single window of every single store proudly displays the same Chamber of Commerce poster of Red Grange scoring his fourth touchdown against Michigan.

In the blur, he notices the movie theater and sees that his one-time safe haven wouldn't have saved him. "Red Grange All Day Long," the Virginia Theater marquee advertises, promising game films and newsreels over and over throughout the day. Red gets a glimpse of Clem's concerned face as he's dragged past.

After a few miles of being carried, he's so confused that he doesn't even realize the crowd has finally taken pity on him by dumping him onto the porch of his fraternity house. Friends drag him through the door onto the floor of the foyer.

Even inside, he's not safe as the crowd forms a perimeter even larger than after the Michigan game, relentlessly chanting "We want Red!"

Eventually, the chief of police and fire chief fight their way into the house to convince Red that for the safety of all involved, he's going to have to open an upstairs window and say something to get the crowd to disperse.

Moments later, Red reluctantly appears in the open upstairs window. It takes forever for the crowd to quiet enough for him to say something. Before he starts speaking, he spots a familiar face in the distance.

Auburn-haired Polly is leaning up against her Roadster, wearing that same white dress and hat, illuminated once again by the sea of orange. There is no way to get to her this time. But a surprising feeling comes over him as he realizes he doesn't want to.

"I appreciate you, I thank you," Red says to the crowd. "But the victory goes to my teammates and Coach. They are the heroes. They've always been the real heroes."

The crowd cheers.

"Now, let's all get off to bed now. Believe it or not, we players have to go to class in the morning. Then we have the Ohio State game to prepare for."

The crowd goes nuts at the mention of Ohio State, but they respectfully quiet down again as Red holds out both hands.

"Always know, no matter what is said about me, I'm proud to play for the great state of Illinois. I may be Red, but I bleed orange."

He waves a few more times as the police and fire department begin dispersing the euphoric crowd. Red takes a brief moment to glance out at Polly and makes solid eye contact before shutting the window for good.

CHAPTER 28

Red sits on a plush sofa across from a fancy office door. The window in the expansive waiting room has a magnificent view of the University of Illinois campus, with students, faculty, and staff hustling about their day on a brisk mid-November Monday afternoon.

Standing outside in the hallway are uniformed police officers. Red has had no choice but to accept their escort services ever since Warren's story went public. Accusations that Red may have signed a pro contract are all that is being written about him now, sparking debates across the country about whether he should be allowed to play in the Ohio State game and putting Zuppke right back in the middle of a controversy a thousand times bigger than the Taylorville scandal.

Red can already see throngs of fans and media pooling outside the building. They followed him here and will remain a constant presence wherever he goes the rest of the day. They've figured out his class and practice schedule. Even he can't elude them any longer.

The door to the grand office finally opens, and a secretary motions that they are ready to see him. Red straightens his tie, attempts to push the wrinkles out of his cheap suit, and walks through the door labeled Office of the University President.

Powerful men more than twice his age are sitting on couches in a circle around a coffee table, smoking and sampling a rare scotch. All but one of the men stand and warmly shake his hand and introduce themselves.

In the room are President of the University of Illinois, David Kinley; Illinois Athletic Director, George Huff; Big Ten Conference Commissioner, John Griffith, who is also the Chair of the Executive Committee of the NCAA; Ohio State's Athletic Director, Lynn St. John; and lawyers representing The University of Illinois, the Big Ten Conference, Ohio State, and the NCAA.

As the men shake Red's hand, they congratulate him on home wins over Chicago and Wabash the last two weeks, which took Illinois' record from 1-3 before the Penn game to a now respectable 4-3 with just the Ohio State game left five days from now in Columbus.

It's daunting for Red to meet the entire Western college football establishment, but he's most intimidated by the person across the room who didn't rise to shake his hand. Jaw tightly set, face red with anger, hands clenched, Zuppke is a keg of dynamite ready to explode.

When they finally all sit down, Red's collar starts to itch, triggering a memory that brings him to where he is today.

When he first arrived on campus as a freshman, it wasn't a given that he'd play football. Actually, his first love growing up was baseball. He used to skip school to take the bus to watch his beloved White Sox, even though they broke his heart when they were caught cheating. He planned to focus on baseball in college until an older fraternity brother forced him to go out for football.

Red showed up for football practice with a hundred other freshmen, who, at a glance, all seemed bigger and tougher. Earl especially. Red hadn't even been on the field a minute when his wool uniform sweater was killing him, leading him to have to run those ten laps.

By the sixth lap, it was still all he could do to ignore the itch, not realizing the entire coaching staff had halted practice to watch him run. Even Zuppke eventually quit barking, his whistle accidentally falling out of his mouth. The moment Red finished his laps with more speed and grace than Zuppke had ever clocked, he was immediately rostered on the first squad of the freshman team. It was one thing to prove he could play at this level, but it's another to have to defend himself to the entire football establishment.

Apparently, the powerful men in the room hadn't rehearsed who was going to say what, so they all looked at each other, deciding who should go first. Should it be the president, athletic director, Big Ten, Ohio State, or the NCAA? Or maybe it should be one of the lawyers? They aren't sure who should cede to whom in this unprecedented situation when Zuppke finally can't take it any longer.

"Turn in your uniform," Zuppke barks at Red. "Turn it in und get the hell out of here."

Red's heart sinks. Never in his life has he seen someone more disappointed in him.

"Now, Bob, please," George Huff, Illinois' athletic director, says, "give the boy a chance. He has a right to defend himself."

Zuppke's arms are crossed. Red knows his coach. Nothing he says will change his verdict.

"Go ahead, Red," Huff says. "We've all read the papers. Versions of Warren's story have permeated across the entire country. More articles and accusations are coming out daily. We all know you to be a straight shooter. Tell us the truth now. We deserve to hear it from the horse's mouth."

Red takes a deep breath. He spent last evening rehearsing with Pyle and their lawyer. At Pyle's suggestion, Red had requested to have a lawyer present in this meeting but was denied on the grounds of amateurism. "A college man of moral repute upholds his honor by simply telling the truth," he was told. Every entity represented in the room has lawyers present, but a student-athlete is not permitted to bring one for himself.

"I've also read the papers," Red says. "My understanding is eighty-five thousand tickets have been sold for Saturday's game at Ohio State, the highest expected attendance of any game in the history of the sport."

Heads turn to the Ohio State athletic director who confirms the statement's accuracy with a nod.

"It has also been reported in those same papers that the two universities stand to generate over one hundred and fifty thousand dollars on this game alone."

Both athletic directors can't deny that to also be true, each nodding their heads.

"I play football for the University of Illinois," Red says. "Despite immense temptation, I remain today an athlete of amateur status. I have less than twenty dollars in my bank account. My father has even less. He's deep in debt thanks to my brother's surgery and the obligation to pay my tuition."

Red looks around at the faces of all the men in the room.

"I risk my life every time I step on that field," Red continues, pausing to allow that realization to sink in. "And I intend to step out there on Saturday one last time against a violent Ohio State eleven who've been practicing all week with one goal in mind: to knock me out of the game. They've said as much in those same newspapers. Their entire stated strategy is to harm me. I'm considered by most Ohio sports columnists to be a 'dead man walking.'"

The Ohio State athletic director doesn't deny it.

"My father pays my tuition. I work in the summer to generate spending money since I can't take a part-time job during football season. There is no NCAA rule against me acting in a movie or endorsing products, but I imagine the lawyers present will plug that hole soon enough."

The lawyers don't deny it.

"Everyone in this room is paid except me. And who's the one filling the stands?" Red says, letting that sink in a moment. "I turned down substantial endorsement and movie opportunities and have maintained my amateur status. By playing college football, I risk future earnings and my health – and even pay my own way to do it – for one reason and one reason only."

Red musters the courage to look over at Zuppke.

"I'm willing to risk everything for him. I'd be nothing without him. I owe it to my coach."

All eyes in the room shift to Zuppke. As Red expects, his beloved coach is so stubborn that none of what was just said has changed the coach's facial expression in the least.

"Coach, we started this together. Let's finish it together. When the game is over we can let the world debate how the NCAA treats athletes. But first, we have one last game to win together. Then, privately, you can lecture me on my future."

Zuppke's jaw remains set. He may be even redder in the face than at the start of the meeting. Finally, the president of the university takes charge.

"Each entity represented in the room must be allowed due process to conduct its own collective investigations," Illinois President Kinley says. "When we have more to report, we'll reach out. In the meantime, Red, I'm sending you home. You're suspended pending further investigation."

Red is barely listening. All he cares about is his relationship with Zuppke.

"Go home, son," the president says again. "I'm ordering you home."

CHAPTER 29

Red would love to go home more than anything, especially given Garland has recently been discharged from the hospital. He'd love to see his family, but his father advised him against stepping foot anywhere near Wheaton, given the number of reporters camped outside Lyle's apartment.

Instead, Clem opens the door to Pyle's suite at the Chicago hotel.

"Red, let me get you a water," Clem says. "And order you some room service. You gotta be starving."

"Thank you. Anything's fine," Red replies, dropping his tiny suitcase on the floor and looking around the suite while Clem picks up the phone to place an order.

Pyle is nowhere to be found, but Red is amazed to discover the entire suite has been turned into a war room with maps covering the walls. Pins stick out of every major city up and down the east and west coasts, including Chicago and St. Louis in the middle, and Boston, Miami, Seattle, and San Diego at the extreme corners.

Lying around on chairs, the floor, and tables are artwork drafts of Red's face and name on scorebooks, game programs, pennants, megaphones, and banners.

"They're all coming here Saturday night after the Ohio State game," Clem says, hanging up with room service. "The entire hotel is booked. Most NFL teams. The New York Giants, for sure. Tim Mara just called to confirm. C.C. had me take a train up yesterday to help. 'All hands on deck,' he said."

165

Red looks around the room. Piles of letters and draft contracts are scattered on every surface of the hotel suite. He flips through letters on stationary from MGM, Paramount, Fox, Warner Bros, Columbia, Universal, United Artists, and First National. Not to mention Coca-Cola, Campbell Soup, Hershey's Chocolate, Kellogg's, Proctor & Gamble, Johnson & Johnson, and Levi Strauss.

"Where's Pyle?" Red asks.

"Running around town. I don't know," Clem says. "Doing what he always does since the day I met him. Turning wild ideas into realities. He also makes time for a massage, haircut, and shave every day. He could be in any of a hundred places."

There's a knock at the hotel room door.

"That was fast," Clem says, opening the door.

Red turns to see it isn't room service. Instead, Helen is at the entryway with a concerned look on her face. She marches right into the room and heads over to the window, motioning for Clem and Red to look down on the street below.

College students, most likely from the University of Chicago, Loyola, and other local universities, are starting to form a picket line with signs that read things like "Red Bleeds Green," "Preserve Amateurism," and "Greed is Sin."

"Red, you gotta get out of here before they get better organized," Clem says, observing more and more students hopping off every bus that passes.

"I got nowhere left to go," Red says.

Clem appears to be considering options when Helen takes Red's hands and leads him to the door.

"I hope you like green bean casserole," she says. "Even if you don't, I advise you to pretend you do."

CHAPTER 30

Red drops back to pass, avoiding defender after defender, waiting for his receiver to get open. He jukes to the right, then to the left, scrambling around desperately to buy more time.

His receiver is running as fast as he can, hopping along, dragging a bum leg. Red can't hold off the defenders any longer. Five of them are now upon him, hugging his pants, laughing, weighing him down.

In a last-ditch effort, as he's being dragged to the ground, he launches a pass. He can see the ball sailing on target as he hits the dirt.

The receiver finally breaks free, spinning around, just in time for Red's missile of a pass to ricochet off his chest, bouncing high into the air. Red watches helplessly from beneath a pile of defenders as the ball is intercepted and run back past him for a touchdown.

Red pushes the gaggle of giggling seven-year-old attackers off him and makes his way over to his five-year-old receiver, Norman, who is mad as hell, having just been beaned with the ball.

"Terrible pass," young Norman says, pushing Red away from him, dragging his palsy leg back to line up to receive the kick.

"It hit you in the chest," Red pleads.

"Wobbling. A hundred miles an hour. Who taught you to throw? Terrible."

Red can't help but laugh. Funny kid. He's the smallest one out there, fighting through his disability more competitively than any teammate Red has ever known.

Red's been sacked a hundred times today while waiting for little Norman to get open. But by Norman's estimation, Red's the one to blame every time the ball bounces squarely off his chest.

Helen smiles, watching through the window from the kitchen, helping her mother, Lillian, set fourteen places at the dinner table.

"Norman is so close to catching one," Helen says.

"And Red's supposed to be the best," Lillian scoffs, pulling rolls out of the oven.

"He is the best," Helen says, having watched Red tirelessly play with the neighborhood boys all afternoon.

Red's about to call another play when a chorus of mothers from every house on the block yell, "Dinner." The boys immediately stop playing and sprint home. Being late one minute to dinner risks having their portions eaten by their fathers or siblings.

The boys sprint away without so much as a "Bye" or "Thanks for playing." Norman hobbles up Lillian's porch and barges through the front door with Red trailing behind him.

The dinner table immediately fills up with Helen's father, brothers, and the boarders who stay in every nook and cranny of the two-story house. Two extra spots are set for Helen and Red, and Norman squeezes in right between them balanced on each of their chairs.

Lillian, a no-nonsense force of a woman, makes everyone say grace and then slops green bean casserole, corn, and bread onto the plates. No sooner does food hit the plate than everyone gulps it down as if they haven't eaten all day, which is the case for many of them.

Red notices a police car pull up in front of the house. Officers jump out and make their way up the porch. The first

THE GOLDEN AGE OF RED

time Red saw that happen, he feared they were coming for him. Now, two days in, he understands the routine.

Lillian makes the officers wait in the foyer as she runs upstairs to fetch something for them. Red keeps his head down, but he can tell the officers are sneaking peeks over at him. Lillian comes back down the stairs with a case of bottles.

When Red first arrived, Lillian said he could make himself comfortable anywhere in the house, except he must stay away from the bathtub. He had no idea what that meant, at first. But this is his third day in a row watching different groups of police officers take a break around dinnertime to buy illegal gin from Lillian.

The officers pay, but not without stealing several more looks at Red.

"Got any leftover casserole, Lil?" one of them asks.

"Get going, degenerates. Do your job. You've wasted enough taxpayer money. Get," she says, ushering them back out the door.

Lillian grabs more food from the kitchen and makes another lap around the table. Red learned quickly that if you don't eat fast enough, you don't get a chance at seconds because once she makes the final lap, that's it for food until tomorrow.

He's never witnessed a family dynamic like this before: the passing of food, everyone talking over each other, the teasing, and the raucous laughter. He absolutely loves it.

The best part, though, is watching Helen with Norman. The way they interact is pure joy. Teasing and hugging each other. Helen wipes his face. Norman resists. Helen asks him if he made any big plays out there. Norman rolls his eyes and answers, "Red couldn't throw one decent pass."

Not only is he as adorable as Helen, but he shares her same wit and sense of humor. Red can't help but notice how closely their faces resemble one another.

Given this is Red's third dinner, he's managed to work himself into the routine, as well, because as fast as everyone eats, sweeping through like a tornado, they disappear just as quickly. Helen helps Norman get ready for bed, quizzing him on his alphabet. All that's left in the dining room are Red and Lillian. It's his pleasure to clear the dishes, allowing her to eat in peace.

He's always loved doing the dishes. It's a task where when you're done, you're done. People assume that's what he likes about football, too. When the game is over, it's over. Everyone moves on to something else. That's never been true for Red. Football is a game that never goes away for him. When he's done with the dishes, however, he's done.

Lillian helps him finish up the remaining plates. After working side by side with her for three days, he finally braves a question that's been lingering on his mind.

"Norman," he finally finds the courage to say to her. "He's, well, he's not yours...is he."

"There are no jobs out here in Evergreen Park for women. None," Lillian replies. "You get married or go work in the city. That's the choice. If someone were to fall in between, I pick up the pieces just like anything else in this house. Any other details ask your *friend* Helen, not me."

Red nods.

"Your *friend* Helen," she repeats. "'Ma, meet my *friend* Red,' she says, barging in here with you unannounced the other day. What's that mean anyway? 'My *friend*.' Men and women can't be *friends*. Why are you here? Really?"

"I like doing dishes," Red replies.

"You're not bad at it," Lillian admits. "According to Norman, you're much better at dishes than football."

"Observant kid."

"You don't get good at doing dishes without practice. You've had your fair share somehow, I'd say."

"That I have."

"Too bad one can't make millions doing dishes. I'd be a millionaire myself if that were so."

"I'm far from being a millionaire."

"The papers are lying then?"

"Do I look like one to you?"

She looks him over for a moment. He does not.

"What would you do with all that money anyway?" she asks.

"What would *you* do?" Red replies.

"Me? That is a ridiculous question. Asking a woman what she'd do if she were a millionaire. That's like asking me what I'd do on the moon. It's an impossibility."

"What would you do on the moon?"

"Easy answer. It's made of Swiss cheese, right? I'd eat as much of it as possible. Swiss is my favorite. I'd eat it all."

That cracks him up.

"And then what?" he asks.

"Then I'd grow lonely and freeze to death."

He can see where Helen got her wit.

"So that's what you'd do with a million dollars?" he asks. "Spend it all?"

"No. Well, yes…in a way. But not on me. Never on me. I'd get Norman's leg fixed. My husband could quit his job and start the business he's always talking about. My sons could work there. Everyone would be happy."

"And what about Helen?"

"Have you met her? I thought you were *friends*. She doesn't need anything from anyone. She'll be just fine."

"And what about yourself? Surely you'd buy something for yourself?"

"You let on like you know what running a household is like. If you really did, you'd know I couldn't begin to think about myself until everyone else is taken care of."

"But that day never comes?" Red asks.

"That day *never* comes. That's just how it works. Everybody always needs something. But there is one thing, if forced to admit. I might buy one thing."

"What's the one thing?"

"Cheese," she says. "I could eat mountains of it."

Red can't help but laugh. Eventually, she joins in before they are interrupted by a knock at the front door.

"Do me a favor and tell them to go away," Lillian says. "Salesmen always come around after dinner to sell encyclopedias and other crap. Get rid of them for me, and I have something for you when you return."

Stashed behind the bread box, she pulls out a plate covered with a towel. She lifts the towel to give Red a peek at a secret stash of apple pie.

"I'll split it with you."

"Deal," he says.

Red walks to the foyer and opens the front door to get rid of the salesman, except it isn't a salesman.

"You're a hard man to find," Warren says, standing on the porch.

Red doesn't have much time to process Warren's presence because behind him, out in the street, Red sees a convoy of Illinois State Troopers.

One by one, Lillian, Helen, Norman, and the rest of the household join Red in the foyer to see the commotion out front for themselves. The same is true for all the other homes on the street. The boys in the neighborhood and their families are also on their porches.

Warren knows Red could kill him for publishing the story of him signing with Pyle and tracking him down, but he unapologetically stands his ground.

"In my heart of hearts," Warren says, "I'm just not destined to write a national column like Rice. I'm not wired to be everyone's friend."

"What are you wired to be then?" Red asks. "A snake? A serpent?"

"I'm a journalist, not an entertainer," Warren replies. "I report without bias on what happened. The public then decides how they feel about it. I'll never regret or apologize for reporting the truth."

"The *truth* you hope will get you promoted. But it never does, does it?" Red says.

Warren doesn't deny it.

"Taylorville didn't get you promoted, and neither will this," Red says. "All you end up doing is tarnishing Zuppke and me."

"You two are far from tarnished. No matter what I publish, you two continue to shine."

All that's shining on Red at the moment are the lights from the police cars.

"Regardless," Warren continues, "this story has become bigger than both of us. Greed abounds. There's just too much money to be made. The Big Ten, NCAA, Illinois, Ohio State. The lot of them can't pass up eighty-five thousand paying fans on Saturday. Big surprise. You've been cleared to play. The governor has ordered a multi-state escort to get you to Columbus on time."

"And what if I don't want to go?" Red says.

"Now that would be a story," Warren says, getting his notebook out. "And I'd be proud to break it. Go ahead, tell us all to go to hell."

Red strongly considers doing just that before feeling a tug on his pants leg.

"You gotta play," Norman says, stepping forward. "If I could run like you, I'd already be there."

Red looks down at him and then at Helen, who is tearing up and also nodding. Red glances at Lillian.

"Rain check on that pie?" Lillian asks.

One of Helen's brothers cuts in and says, "You got pie, Ma?"

"Not for you," Lillian replies, slapping her son on the back of his head.

Red laughs. He hugs Norman, winks at Lillian, and then takes Helen's hand and pulls her off to the side.

"So, here's the thing," he says to Helen. "My life is slightly complicated at the moment."

173

"You think yours is complicated?" Helen says.

"About that. Norman?"

"None of your business."

He's taken aback, clearly not expecting that reaction.

"Unless you want it to be your business," Helen says. "Are you asking for more complication in your life?"

"Look around: police cars, newspaper reporters. You don't think I could handle it?"

"In the coat room, the day I taught you to dance...."

"The day you taught me to put on lipstick?"

"Yes, I was all puckered up, and you didn't kiss me. Why? That's about as cute as I can get."

"I wasn't sure if you actually wanted me to."

"Oh, really. It had nothing to do with that temptress who showed up a minute later?"

"Ah, yes, well, now that's complicated."

"Listen, I'll tell you about Norman when you tell me about that siren."

"So that's how we're going to leave this?"

"Unless you're going to kiss me."

Again, Red is confused about whether she's serious or not. Before he can decide, Warren interrupts them.

"Red, there's a lot of taxpayer money out here. What do you think? Maybe it's time to go? Maybe time to wrap up whatever this is? What is this, by the way?"

"Just two friends," Helen says. "And one of them is about to punch you in the face."

Warren looks at both of them for a moment before realizing she's talking about herself.

"Rain check?" Red says to Helen.

"Or coat check," she says. "You know where to find me."

Red takes her hand in his for a moment before Warren leads him off the porch toward the police escort.

"Just one thing," little Norman says, stepping down from the porch.

"What's that, buddy?" Red asks.

"You still need to learn to throw a spiral. Yours is terrible."

Everyone laughs.

"Can I quote you on that?" Warren asks Norman.

"No!" the entire porch says back to him.

"Okay, okay," Warren says. "Okay."

As the caravan pulls away, the boys in the neighborhood run alongside the car, slapping the windows, cheering Red on.

Red longingly looks back at Helen and Norman. His life is full of complications, but he'd certainly prefer a private life back on that porch over rushing back into the national spotlight.

CHAPTER 31

Illinois at Ohio State
Saturday, November 21, 1925

The horseshoe-shaped Ohio Stadium is more than a sporting arena. Even a poet like Grantland Rice struggles to select adjectives to capture today's record eighty-five thousand-person crowd who couldn't care less about the game or their allegiance to either team.

One glance reveals the mortals in attendance are not sports fans today. Ohio Stadium has been transformed on this brisk Saturday into a temple. The faithful have flocked to pay homage not to sports but to greatness. All in attendance today worship in the House of Red.

With his Illinois teammates already on the field warming up, Red enters a deserted locker room in the catacombs of the venue. The twenty-two-year-old prepares for battle in further isolation, forcing his head through the opening of a blue wool sweater. Auburn locks emerge in complement to the orange 77 stitched on the back of his uniform.

He pulls his sweater down over the thin leather shoulder pads the entire team started wearing after Garland got hurt. His sweater fastens with snaps under his crotch, like a onesie, to keep it from being ripped off his body.

He pulls on striped wool socks and steps into baggy moleskin pants that come up over his hips. He pulls the drawstring tight and fastens a leather belt before sitting down to squeeze his feet into ankle-high black boots fitted with spiked cleats. His thin leather helmet obediently lies next to him on the bench.

The anticipation of the crowd vibrates through the concrete floor. The players have taken the field for warm-ups, except for the one player that matters. The fans struggle to remain patient but appreciate that their hero has earned the right to make them wait as he laces up for the last time at the collegiate level.

The door opens to the locker room, letting in even more noise. Red glances up to see someone he was not expecting. Mrs. Zuppke winks at him before reaching back out into the hallway and pulling her stubborn husband into the room.

It's been five days since the meeting in the president's office, and Zuppke is still just as red in the face. Fannie's grip on her husband's arm appears to be the only thing preventing him from spontaneously combusting.

"Tell him, dearest," Fannie says. "Bob, you tell him now."

Red stops lacing his cleats to look up at his coach. Fannie squeezes Zuppke's arm, forcing him to comply with what she's told him to say.

"Against my better judgment, you have been cleared to play," Zuppke says.

"Bob, we all know that," she says. "Tell him."

Zuppke lets out a long sigh. She's the only person in the world who could get him to go into that locker room.

"Fannie und I love you, Granche," he sputters, saying the words she clearly scripted for him, "more than you'll ever know. Und I'm honored to coach you today."

"I love you guys, too," Red says, causing Fannie to immediately tear up, squeezing her husband's arm even more.

"It wouldn't be right not to finish what we started. Would it, Coach?"

"It depends on your plans after the game."

"We'll discuss that then."

"Yes, we will," Zuppke states.

"But I do have one stipulation," Red says. "Or I won't play."

"Und, what is that?"

"I run the offense my way."

"Oh dear, God, Fannie," Zuppke says to his wife, further signaling to Fannie that the love fest is over by shaking her hands off his arm. "I knew it. I knew it. Capone und his thugs have sunk their rotten teeth in the boy."

"Bob, please," Fannie says. "That's ridiculous. Our boy would never do that. Right, Red?"

"We play to win," Red confirms. "You know me, Coach. You know me."

"I thought I knew you until I read the papers," Zuppke shouts.

"We are going to win," Red says definitively. "But you let me run the offense my way, or I'm out of here. I'll board the first train toward a private life. I've thought it over. I run the offense. That's just how it is gonna be. That's my one condition. I've never asked anything of you in four years. This is my one thing. We play the way I want to play today and involve more guys in the scoring, or I hang up my cleats."

"Fine," Zuppke says.

"What? Really?" Red asks, expecting more a drawn-out fight.

"I was going to let you run it anyway. I only get players for four years. Und just when they get smart, they graduate. If you can't both run and modify the offense by now, then I'd be the worst teacher in the world."

Red hasn't smiled since he left Helen's family, so it feels good when a grin forms on his face. Fannie hasn't smiled in the last week. Hers feels good, as well.

"But I have one condition," Zuppke barks.

Fannie rolls her eyes.

"I know what it is, Red," she says. "I've had to listen to him talk about this Ohio State game for over a year."

"It has to do with the...," Zuppke starts to say before changing his voice to a whisper, "the defense." Even in a stadium with a noise decibel level never reached before in American sports, Zuppke feels the need to sit close to Red on the bench and whisper his prized strategy. Red nods as he finishes tying his laces. The whole time he is speaking, Zuppke motions over and over again for his wife to keep guarding the door.

CHAPTER 32

All eyes in the huddle are on Red, their quarterback and leader. Earl admires how Red grants a moment to each of them, but specifically pulls Earl to the side.

"We're going to shake things up a bit today on offense," Red says before whispering a few secrets. Afterward, he pats Earl on the shoulder and gives him a hug.

"Next to Zup," Red says, "I couldn't imagine going into this last battle without you, my friend."

It's all Earl can do to stop tears as they break from the huddle and line up strong to the right. He is so choked up that he loses focus, allowing Red to only get a few yards before both of them are violently slammed to the ground.

The whistle is blown, but Ohio State's scarlet and gray couldn't care less. Under cover of the scrum, Walter Camp's attempt to civilize the game is ignored. Earl helplessly watches as Ohio State bites and scratches Red. Out of sight of the fans and officials, the game is primal.

The Buckeyes coach, John Wilce, embarrassed by a loss to rival Michigan the week before, threatened his team in the locker room before the game. He kept his instructions simple: "Knock Red out of the game or turn in your uniforms." End of story.

Earl snaps out of it, restores his focus, and wrests guys off Red. But over and over, Ohio State players get more chances to play dirty, and they get dirtier with each possession, taking potshots at Red every chance they get.

However, with sheer will and talent, Red follows Earl's blocks, and they carry the team to the two-yard line.

It's particularly upsetting to the Ohio State players and their coach that the home crowd isn't supporting Ohio State or Illinois. The fans have cheered Red's every move since he stepped out on the field late for warm-ups.

Again, Illinois lines up strong to the right. Earl is positioned to push Red over the goal line if it comes to it. Red takes the snap and barrels toward a mob of Buckeyes that have already broken through the Illinois line. There is no way in hell they are going to allow him to score. They slam Red to the ground with such force that the largest sports crowd on record goes silent. All eighty-five thousand hear the breath escape from Red's lungs.

As Ohio State slowly climbs off Red's motionless body, taking even more potshots in the process, the crowd suddenly cheers louder than they have all day. The roar is deafening, causing the Ohio State players to look around stupefied as they slowly realize that Red had snuck the ball to Earl before getting annihilated.

Standing alone in the endzone, Earl pointedly touches the ball to the ground, races back to peel his friend off the grass, and helps a dazed Red take a knee behind center. Somehow Red takes the snap, holds the ball on the ground, and Earl sends the extra point through the goalposts.

Illinois 7. Ohio State 0.

A few plays later, Illinois gets the ball back. Red has taken an absolute pounding so far. Every play, whether Red touches the ball or not, no fewer than three Ohio State players slam him to the ground. Each time, his teammates take turns picking Red up and carrying him back to the huddle.

Illinois lines up with twenty yards to go. Red receives the snap and scrambles out to the right, drawing the entire Ohio State line with him. He's so far out to the right that he's unprotected beyond his blockers, but he doesn't take off running down the sidelines.

Just as all eleven Buckeyes close in on him, he uses his remaining strength to plant his outside foot and throw the ball back across the field before disappearing under a pile of Buckeyes. Chuck Kassel receives Red's perfect spiral pass and runs it in for a touchdown. It's the same perfect pass Chuck has thrown to Red for four seasons, but now Red has returned the favor.

Chuck and Earl run back after the touchdown to peel Red off the ground. They barely recognize his face with its two black eyes and a gash across the bridge of his nose, blood pouring from everywhere.

Earl turns to motion for Zuppke to take Red out of the game. Red stops him and resolutely stumbles to the line of scrimmage. Against Earl's better judgment, he positions Red again on one knee. Red takes the snap and holds the ball to the ground, dripping blood on it as Earl kicks the extra point.

Illinois 14. Ohio State 0.

As hard as Ohio State hits Red when he has the ball, Red hits them even harder on defense, splattering his own blood on their faces. Both teams are forced to punt until Illinois gets pinned down on its own goal line toward the end of the first half.

A misplay by Illinois' center sends the ball sputtering around their own end zone. Just as an Ohio State player is poised to recover it for a touchdown, Red jumps on the ball, covering it to take a safety. Out of sheer frustration, but out of sight of the referees, Ohio State's largest player kicks Red as hard as he can in the kidney as the clock winds down.

Halftime arrives with a score of Illinois 14, Ohio State 2.

In the locker room, the trainers struggle to determine the source of Red's bleeding. They evaluate for internal injuries while Zuppke screams, "Fix him!"

The best the trainers can come up with is cutting off a piece of rubber from some equipment in the corner and gluing it against Red's side where he was kicked. When they finish,

Red can't even reach down to fasten his own onesie. Earl offers to do it for him.

Back on the field, Illinois protects their lead, punting the ball away nearly every possession, hoping to run down the clock.

Ohio State does, however, gain yards on the success of unexpected pass plays. Passing isn't their forte, but desperation has forced a change in strategy. Normally, Red would have easily intercepted at least one of those passes, but Earl can tell his friend is struggling just to remain on his feet.

Ohio State keeps up the passing strategy, scoring a touchdown and making the extra point, putting the Buckeyes within a touchdown of winning going into the final quarter.

Illinois 14, Ohio State 9.

The fourth quarter is the same, with Illinois just punting it away and Ohio State driving, utilizing risky passing plays to gain ground.

With less than a minute left, Ohio State is threatening to score. Red is all but useless on defense. Earl can't take it anymore.

"Coach, you gotta take him out!" Earl yells desperately to the sidelines.

Zuppke waves him off.

Ohio State is setting up to score a touchdown to win. There is nothing Earl can do but take matters into his own hands by breaking through the line and sacking the quarterback.

The ball is snapped, and Earl does just that, slamming the quarterback to the ground, but not before the pass is thrown. Earl sees the ball sailing in the air, watching helplessly as Illinois and Red's legacy are about to go down in flames.

Out of nowhere, Red intercepts the pass. Not a tired Red. Or an injured Red. But a resurrected Red.

To Earl's astonishment, Red is back to perfect form, easily running the ball back past the fifty-yard line and sliding to the ground. Red protects the ball as the entire Ohio State eleven piles on top of him in hopes of ripping it away.

By the time the officials, with the help of Earl and his teammates, pull legions of crimson and gray away, all that's left at the bottom of the pile is a blue jersey with an orange 77. The face of the hero holding the ball is grinning.

The siren wails. Game over.

Illinois 14, Ohio State 9.

Red pops up. He's bloody and bruised but otherwise fine. He wraps Earl in a bear hug, interrupted by Zuppke flying off the bench and nearly tackling both of his players in celebration.

Zuppke and Red share a moment, causing Earl to realize Red's exhaustion was all a ruse. Zuppke's defensive strategy was to bait Ohio State into throwing the ball in the fourth quarter so Red could intercept it. And Red's offensive strategy was allowing his friends to score for a change.

Earl tears up watching his Illinois teammates line up to hug Red. Then, all of Ohio State's players and coaching staff line up to hug him, as well. By the time Earl gets his chance, he's not sure what to say.

Were it not for Red's grin, Earl would have assumed from the swollen eyes and blood-smeared face that he should be on his way to the hospital. Earl's not even sure how he can possibly see, yet Red's eyes light up as Earl approaches.

Before he can say anything, legions of fans rush the field, demanding to touch their god. State police run in to establish a perimeter around Red. Illinois and Ohio State players and coaches team up to protect him. As if the crowd weren't relentless enough, the media have now reached Red.

Backed up against the goalposts, Earl is trying to help, but reporters are demanding to know Red's plans now that his college playing days are over. Zuppke shoves people to the ground, fighting to get to Red, shouting at the media to back off.

"He's going to graduate," Zuppke says. "Let him be. He's done. It's over. He's going to graduate and become an ambassador for the amateur game."

Zuppke pushes the cameramen away until being caught off guard by Red, who raises his hands to settle his coach. Then Red faces the media to make a statement. Over the noisy crowd, reporters jostle for position as Red wipes enough blood off his face to form a few words that only those near him can hear.

Earl can't believe what Red has just said. Zuppke is outraged.

Their little coach, wired to fight to the death for his players, particularly for Red, whom he loves like a son, releases his grip and walks away, leaving Red unprotected to be swallowed up by the world.

CHAPTER 33

The elevator operator at the Chicago hotel does a double take as his lone passenger removes a black wig and shakes out his auburn hair.

Holding the wig in one hand and a manilla envelope in the other, Red has two black eyes and a swollen face to match. The elevator operator immediately recognizes him. Like the rest of the nation, he's seen that same brooding face plastered all over the papers for the past week.

Getting to Chicago required Red to climb down the fire escape of his hotel room in Columbus, run across train tracks, and hop onto a moving train. The last stage of his escape required him to don the wig until making his way up the elevator to Pyle's suite.

Now that he's safely in the hotel, he thinks back to what happened after the game. He fought the crowds to hail a taxi only to have Zuppke and Fannie hop in alongside him before it took off.

"Where to?" the cab driver asked.

"Just drive in circles around town," Zuppke commanded, handing the driver some cash.

Pinned in the backseat, Red had no choice but to endure his coach's wrath.

"You're turning professional?" Zuppke barks. "That's what you say to the media without talking to me? You're quitting school. You've had signed contracts all along. You lied."

"I didn't lie, and I've not yet signed a professional contract," Red says. "But, I'm intending to do so in Chicago. I'm scheduled to be there in a few hours."

"Perfect," Zuppke says to his wife. "We still have time to talk the boy out of it."

"I don't understand," Red argues. "You get paid to coach. Why can't I cash in?"

"You can. You'll be the ambassador to football. Like Camp did, you'll have syndicated columns. Endorsements. You could probably have your own magazine dedicated to the college game. You could make out like a bandit if you want. Just stay away from the pros. Protect amateurism."

"But you don't hate professional baseball? What is it about football?"

"Baseball has integrity. They don't poach college players," Zuppke explains. "They formally sign them to minor league contracts after graduation. The NFL is barely functioning. They'll never have a minor league system. Instead, they use und abuse the college game—a sport universities invented."

Zuppke uses the back of the driver's seat like a chalkboard, laying out his explanation with imaginary chalk.

"If they sign Red Grange, then next they'll sign Wildcat Wilson, Big Dog Ernie Nevers, und The Four Horsemen. Even Lester out of Tulane. Und what's to stop them from signing them right in the middle of a college season? A college player has a good week und the next they are playing professionally. That's how it works in a minor league system. I don't coach semi-pros. I'm not wired for it. I teach college students who graduate with an outstanding degree that has more longevity than any professional career."

The hand of Zuppke that holds the invisible chalk is now pointed right at Red.

"You quit school und sign und you'll kill college football. You'll go down in history as the player who ruined it. Instead, be the hero. Be the player who saved it."

Fannie couldn't agree more, holding her husband's arm in full support.

"Look, coach, you made a grand argument," Red says, "but you're not the one with a banged-up brother. You're not the one with a father buried in hospital bills. You're not the one with less than $20 in his bank account. You're not the one who has to scrounge up tuition to finish college. And you're not the one who suddenly finds himself more famous than Babe Ruth."

"Und you're not the one facing betrayal," Zuppke replies. "I taught you everything I know. Fannie und I love you like a son. You've turned it all against us."

For the next hour, the cab driver circled while Zuppke's once articulate lecture transformed into profanity-ridden ramblings about honor, discipline, tradition, respect, etc. On top of that, Red had to listen to Fannie sob as Zuppke barked at the cab driver to keep circling.

But eventually, the cab ride ended, and that is behind Red now as he exits the elevator, walks down the hotel hallway, and knocks at Pyle's suite. While he's waiting for someone to answer, he notices a door open up down the hall. Out steps Giants owner, Tim Mara, straightening his tie.

Mara hasn't even looked up yet to notice Red when a slender arm reaches out of the room to wipe some lipstick off his cheek. The woman can't quite get enough leverage, so she holds the door open with one foot and briefly leans into the hallway. She is wearing a negligee and grinning because she has to use extra force to rub the lipstick off.

It's a smile Red has never seen before, but one he once longed to see. He used to dream of seeing it. He'd begged to see it. But this is the first time.

Polly finally gets the lipstick off Mara's face. He still hasn't looked down the hall at Red, but Polly does. Her smile never drops despite spying him. She doesn't express embarrassment or remorse.

Whenever Red thinks back on this moment, he recalls only one word to describe her face: professional. A fate he's soon destined to join.

Clem opens the suite and shoos Red in, shutting the door behind him. The last time Red was in the suite, it was set up like a war room. Now, the war has arrived. Lawyers scurry from one end of the room to the other. A dozen girls from the hotel and nearby speakeasy answer phones and shuffle papers. Others constantly refill coffee. The suite is so busy not one person pays any attention to Red.

It takes Pyle a moment to notice him before telling someone on the phone to hold a minute so he can run over and greet his star client at the door.

"You look absolutely terrible," Pyle says. "Clem, get him some ice or something. Dear God, my boy. Look at your nose. Your eyes. I hope it was worth it, playing that last game, sacrificing yourself just so your teammates could score."

Clem runs off to make an ice pack as Red hands Pyle the manilla envelope he's holding.

"What's this?" Pyle asks, opening it and flipping through the papers inside.

"Warren gave it to me," Red says. "He dug all this up on you."

Pyle barely flips through before closing it.

"Deny, deny, deny," Pyle says. "None of it matters. You know that, right? They are going to say all kinds of crazy things about me. And about you. It's just getting started. Who cares? Deny, deny, deny."

"Every editorial I read in the papers asks, 'Why does Red need an agent? Babe Ruth doesn't have an agent. No athlete has ever had an agent,'" Red says. "Tim Mara is even quoted as saying, 'Why give someone ten percent? Why not just use a lawyer for the transactions? What's the point of a college degree if you need so much help?'"

"Look around," Pyle says. "This isn't a transaction. It's an empire. It's my vision mixed with your once-in-a-generation talent. It's a lifetime of all my connections coming together for you, my boy. It's a partnership."

"Except you didn't talk me into ten percent all those months ago when I was at my most vulnerable. You talked me into something different."

Pyle doesn't deny it.

"Sixty-forty," Red says. "You talked me into sixty you, forty me."

Pyle has a million things he could say but smartly holds his tongue to let Red finish.

"Fifty-fifty would be nuts," Red says. "But sixty-forty is insane."

Pyle's winning smile appears.

"I might cry," Pyle says. "My word, you are a fast learner. No wonder Zuppke loves you so much. I accept. Fifty-fifty. I'll have our agreement revised. That's wonderful negotiating."

"And, another thing," Red says. "No deal with the Giants. No to New York."

"Woah," Pyle says. "Woah, my boy. No one else besides Mara has real money. Or vision. We need Mara. We're not ready to form our own team yet."

"Get a deal done with George Halas and The Bears, or I walk."

"You walk? What's that mean? Halas isn't even at the hotel. He gave up. He went home."

"Get him back here," Red demands. "If I'm going to risk my neck playing pro ball, I will need some orange and blue around me. I'll get killed out there without someone who played for Zup beside me. If I'm hurt, none of this will matter."

"You barge in here, renegotiate our deal, and now you're asking me at the eleventh hour to get Halas back to the table? A man who has no money?" Pyle argues.

"And I want a deal with Halas worth double Mara's offer."

"Double? Double the fifty grand guaranteed?"

"I did my job," Red says resolutely. "Now you do your job. I could get fifty grand on my own with Mara. Double it by the morning, one hundred grand, or I disappear. I vanish into thin air. You and the world will never see Red Grange again."

"'Never see Red Grange again?'" Pyle repeats, not believing him.

"You don't think I'm capable?" Red says. "That's always been my preferred option. Always."

"But you ask the impossible of me. And overnight."

"People have been asking the impossible of me since I was twelve years old," Red emphasizes. "You want fifty percent? Show me you deserve it. Show me I have a business partner who can play at my level. Everything we are considering here tonight is stupid. It's never been done before. If I'm going to be stupid, then I at least want stupid money. Otherwise, I vanish."

Pyle looks Red over. Red's face is calm and relaxed. Pyle's winning smile quickly returns.

"Get some sleep. Rest up," Pyle tells him, turning to find Clem. "Clem, get the boy a sandwich. Set him up in the spare room. Shut it nice and tight. I want it as quiet as possible. And get a girl to work on his face. Some makeup should do it."

"I got a girl," Red says, picturing Helen downstairs behind her counter.

"You do? Oh, okay," Pyle says, winking at Red before turning back to Clem. "And get me Halas' number, Clem. His home number. Or, get me a cab, and I'll go over there if I need to. Red, I fight for you. What kind of sandwich do you want?"

Red doesn't answer. Pyle turns back around to find Red is gone. He's vanished. Pyle opens the door to the hallway and looks to the left toward the elevator. Nothing. He turns the other way, barely in time to see the door to the stairs closing.

"Clem? God love him. Clem?"

Clem pokes his head out in the hallway.

191

"Clem, it's showtime!" Pyle exclaims. "Our boy just turned pro."

THE THIRD QUARTER
◦◦ Bleeding Red ◦◦

CHAPTER 34

Twenty-five years earlier…

Standing just off stage, holding a baby girl, twenty-year-old Pyle mutters, "Showtime," signaling ten-year-old Clem to dim the torches.

"Here comes Mommy," Pyle whispers to the baby as Dot Fischer steps out on the makeshift outdoor stage to perform a sonnet.

When Dot was a chubby little girl, Pyle had no doubt her father considered her a cute way to warm up the audience for the traveling Fischer Theater Company. Now that she's twenty, Pyle can tell by the faces of the audience that she'll never be the Fischer girl they want to see.

This is the company's first performance since her father died, and Pyle runs the show now. He's already renamed the theater company and has many other changes in store, including breaking it to Dot that this will be her last sonnet.

Dot finishes and accepts polite applause. She steps off stage and takes the baby from Pyle so he can quickly find his mark behind the curtain.

"Daddy's turn," Dot whispers.

Young Clem uses all his strength to pull open the curtain, revealing Pyle and ten other male actors set to perform *The Three Musketeers* before an enthusiastic crowd just outside of Eugene, Oregon.

The audience loves the sword fighting, the humor, and the French-plumed costumes. Pyle commands the stage, playing the lead role of D'Artagnan and dueling Cardinal Richelieu and his evil henchmen.

While Pyle clinks swords in pretend battle, he reminds himself that firing Harry Pollard, who plays Cardinal Richelieu, is also on his to-do list and for one simple reason: Harry is just too good-looking.

As the duel progresses, Pyle can tell women in the audience are beginning to root for handsome Harry despite his playing the villain.

Regardless, Pyle knows their infatuation with Harry won't last long. The audience isn't there to see any of the men on stage. They are patiently waiting for the namesake of the newly titled Margarita Fischer Theater Company.

After renaming the company, the second thing Pyle did was rewrite the play to give the ingénue character Milady de Winter the best lines, while putting a sword in her hand and making D'Artagnan her love interest.

None of the other actors, including Pyle, matter any longer as Dot's slightly younger sister, Margarita, takes the stage in a whirlwind of sass and beauty that exceeds the advertising posted around town the last few weeks announcing the arrival of her extraordinary talent.

Margarita's stage presence is so striking that, within moments, the crowd is mesmerized by the combination of her exotic beauty, contagious laugh, sparkling eyes, physical humor, impeccable timing, and radiant charm. She mesmerizes Pyle, too, and it's not uncommon for the spellbound Pyle to occasionally forget his lines whenever standing opposite her.

Just two years earlier, fired from his job as a traveling salesman, he had been stranded in the Pacific Northwest. He was supposed to be riding the rails, selling time clocks to small businesses. Instead, he'd been caught selling to other travelers the stack of train passes his company had given him.

He got drunk one night and stumbled into a traveling theater show, easily finding a seat for the half-empty performance. Despite only being a bit player at the time, Margarita's stage presence so enraptured Pyle that he talked her father into allowing him to travel one town ahead and manage advance publicity and ticket sales in exchange for a percentage of the gate.

"If I can increase sales," Pyle pitched to the father, "what do you have to lose?"

Pyle did increase sales by making one tiny adjustment: he put Margarita front and center in the marketing. Sure enough, it worked. Ticket sales took off, and the number of shows in each city expanded, which, in turn, led to an increase in her role in the show. More and more butts filled the seats, followed by a shotgun wedding several months later to Margarita's sister, Dot, and Pyle had a new job and a new family.

After another captivating performance as a modernized Milady de Winter, Margarita takes her final bow. The audience leaps to its feet, demanding more.

"Isn't she a marvel?" Pyle says to the crowd, attempting to calm them. "Simply show your ticket stub for a nickel off any other performance this week until tickets run out. Thank you and good night."

However, that offer isn't good enough. The crowd wants more Margarita right now. Pyle continues to quiet them, but to no avail, until there is no choice but to have Margarita return to the stage.

Though not rehearsed, she motions to Pyle that she has a plan. With no musical accompaniment, he watches in amazement as Margarita simply sings "Auld Lang Syne."

From the moment she renders the opening line, "Should auld acquaintance be forgot," the crowd quiets. In no time, they transition to tears as every verse and chorus resonates more than the last until the crescendo of:

*We'll drink a cup of kindness yet,
For the sake of auld lang syne.*

Pyle's eyes water. The way to make money in theater is not to give a sold-out performance but to give multiple shows in a row in the same city, which is exactly what begins to happen after these changes he's made. Money rolls in.

A few months later, Pyle discovers an amazing new technology called "the motion picture." It's not long before he films a test reel of Margarita and sends copies off to the silent studios forming in California and Chicago.

While waiting for a response, he counts the money from one successful show after another, ignoring Dot's accusations of him harboring an "unhealthy obsession" with watching Margarita's test reel.

With tickets already sold out for the week, he wakes up one morning to discover shocking news—Margarita and handsome Harry have run off, taking Dot and the baby with them.

As the news leaks throughout the day, the other actors in the company disappear one by one, leaving just Pyle and Clem backstage that evening with an impatient sold-out crowd demanding the show start.

"Surely you know the lines?" Pyle says to a nervous young Clem. "You've seen the show hundreds of times."

"I do, but I can't," Clem cries. "I can't."

"After all I've done for you? Taking you in. In my hour of need, you can't help me?"

Clem loves Pyle more than anything, but stage fright is real. Clem just can't do it. Pyle insists, forcing Clem into costume and wig. Clem, shaking in fear, breaks free, rips off the costume, and runs away into the darkness.

Ten minutes later, a frustrated Pyle has no choice but to mutter "Showtime" under his breath, pulling open the curtain himself and launching into *The Three Musketeers* as a one-man show.

He switches costumes and wigs with each line, makes two swords fight each other, and changes the pitch of his voice up and down for each character, reserving the highest pitch he can muster for Margarita's lines while mimicking her timing and movements. His performance is a perfect imitation, which is made easy by having watched her film reel thousands of times.

After a few minutes, he's feeling confident about how everything is going until he feels a June bug dive past him. Dodging insects is part of the occupation when performing outdoor evening theater under torchlight. But he feels more and more of them flying past, each growing larger.

Insects are one thing, but bats are another. When they circle, the audience panics and stops paying attention to the show. Pyle instinctively looks off-stage for Clem, whom he relies on for everything.

Pyle is deciding what to do when one of the bats hits him square in the chest and explodes. Blood is everywhere. Then he's hit again…and again…and again. Except it doesn't smell like blood.

Clem watches in horror from a tree line in the distance as the crowd throws tomato after tomato at Pyle, jeering and shouting profanities. Discussions of gathering tar and feathers start to trickle through the aisles. Even young children are pelting Pyle with anything they can get their hands on, including their shoes.

Pyle knows he needs to exit the stage, but he's unsure which way to go, given the crowd is starting to move in on him. He's debating between stage left or right. Before he can decide, the crowd is forced to part to make way for a horse galloping right down the center aisle, knocking chairs in all directions, and careening toward the stage.

Cowering in fear, Pyle covers his face with his hands as the rider halts in front of him. Pyle peeks through his fingers to discover a rider he's never been happier to see. Young Clem reaches out his hand, imploring Pyle to hop on and join him in their escape.

Twenty-five years later…

"And that was my lowest moment in show business," Pyle tells a female reporter from *The New Yorker* magazine.

He's sitting behind a desk in a dimly lit office in the bowels of a concrete building just two weeks since Red played his last college game against Ohio State.

"Film actress Margarita Fischer?" the reporter asks. "She's your sister-in-law?"

"Yes, indeed," he confirms. "For the last twenty-five years, I've bounced around recruiting a new theater troupe, then making films, then building a small theater, then selling pipe organs to theaters, and then building movie palaces. For a short stint, somewhere in there, I may or may not have been forced to take a break and sell insurance. But whenever a new Margarita Fischer movie came out, I held no ill will. I've always been first in line to watch every single picture she's ever made."

He reflects privately for a moment, recalling her films and feeling his blood boil every time he has to witness "Harry Pollard Presents" in the opening title sequences. Reading handsome Harry's name haunts him, not to mention thoughts of those two getting married and living it up in their Los Angeles mansion.

Sitting through the films is worth it, however, because his daughter, Katherine, has bit parts in every one of the movies, allowing Pyle to watch her grow up. Of course, her mother, Dot, can always be found lurking somewhere in the pictures, too.

"What do you have to say to readers who have labeled you as the biggest threat to college football?" the reporter asks.

Pyle thinks about the question for a moment.

"Tell your readers I admit I am a threat, but not to college football. I'm a threat to the NCAA and all other organizations that take advantage of amateur athletes. I'm a threat to the practice of indentured servitude. Not only do college athletes play for free while the NCAA rakes in millions, but the athletes are forced to pay their own tuition for the right to do so. What the NCAA does is not only highway robbery, but it goes directly against the 13th Amendment. We fought a war to abolish slavery, didn't we? I'm not afraid to lead another charge. But I'm not a threat to college football, and neither is Red. I'm a threat to the NCAA. I'm a threat to men who profit off free labor."

She ponders his statements for a moment, reading over her notes.

"So, would you go so far as to suggest that colleges pay the athletes?" she asks.

"I would," he replies. "The least they could do is offer free tuition and a generous living stipend."

She furiously scribbles notes as Pyle looks her over.

"What can I say? My gift is not only spotting talent, but also helping them realize their full potential," he remarks, raising his eyebrows at her. "You ever consider acting or modeling? With those cheekbones, I could line up a screen test for you."

She stops scribbling and looks up at him with a mix of flattery and disdain. Before she can answer, a sweaty Clem barges into the room, holding out his hand to rescue him just like Pyle claims he did all those years ago.

"You're going to miss it," Clem says, pulling Pyle up from his chair, grabbing Pyle's hat and coat off the borrowed desk, and leading him out into the underground passageway with the reporter trailing behind.

Clem helps Pyle dress while leading him toward the sunlight at the end of the tunnel. The crowd noise begins to overwhelm them. Just before stepping out into the light, Pyle has another thought for the reporter.

"My friends at MGM are seated in the front row," he says. "We're going to a club tonight. I'll get you the password and save you a spot."

He gives her a wink before turning toward Clem.

"How about you join me on stage today, my friend? What do you say? Today's the day to conquer that fear."

The simple suggestion of stepping into the limelight causes Clem to freeze. Panic spreads across his face.

"I'm going to get you out there someday," Pyle says, calming Clem with a pat on his shoulder. "At least do one thing for me. Tell our lovely new friend here what time it is."

That Clem can do. Relaxing a little, he says to the reporter, "It's showtime."

"Indeed it is, my friend. The biggest one yet." Pyle replies before stepping into the sun which illuminates the green feather in his hat.

Pyle, standing on the sidelines of a freshly painted football field, squints as he looks up at the record seventy thousand fans crowded into the Polo Grounds stadium in New York City.

The only thing more glorious than seeing seventy thousand paying customers would be if he could have figured out a way to charge the thousands of freeloaders he spies sneaking free looks from Coogan's Bluff overlooking the stadium. It will bug Pyle forever knowing the record gate for an NFL game could have been even bigger.

He's so lost in that thought he almost doesn't step aside quickly enough to make room for the entire New York Giants football team sprinting past him, charging out onto the field for warm-ups. The crowd leaps to their feet the moment they see their home team in royal blue sweaters with red lettering.

"All aboard the gravy train," Tim Mara shouts, jogging past Pyle, following his Giants onto the field.

"Toot toot," Pyle responds.

He watches Mara basking in the attention, waving to his wife and children, who proudly cheer in the stands.

Suddenly, the roar of the crowd cranks up tenfold. Pyle turns back to the tunnel to see the visiting team jogging out in a train of orange sweaters with blue lettering.

The fans scan the visiting Chicago Bears, searching for a certain player, except they all look alike in their leather helmets and wool uniforms.

Pyle can't find the player everyone is searching for, either. Just then, an orange sweater running by pats him on the shoulder.

"Gravy train," George Halas says, grinning and suited up to join his team in battle on the field.

"Choo choo," Pyle replies.

Halas was the last Bears player to run out. Pyle, along with the fans, still can't find Number 77 anywhere on the field. Red is a master at vanishing, but Pyle thinks twice before panicking, peering back into the tunnel.

Sure enough, Red is inside the tunnel giving Clem a big hug in front of *The New Yorker* reporter. Pyle laughs, watching the starstruck reporter lose her footing.

Red catches her before she hits the ground and politely helps her regain her balance. He gives Clem another pat on the shoulder and puts on his helmet. He's about to step into the light when Pyle stops him.

"Wait a sec," Pyle says, slowing Red down. "You forgot again."

"Right," Red says, remembering to take off his helmet.

The moment Red steps into the sun with his auburn hair glistening in the light of day, Pyle fears the stands at the Polo Grounds might collapse. The massive crowd loses its mind as it tracks his hair galloping across the field in a Bears uniform.

"Red!"

"Go Red!"

"It's Red!"

Red acknowledges the crowd with a wave, which he's done dozens of times in the House of Red, except these worshippers are different. This time, half the revenue will end up in his pocket.

Two weeks ago, when Red demanded Pyle double the offer but with Halas, they ran into the small problem of Halas not having that kind of money. Pyle knew immediately what to do. He simply needed to strike the same deal he'd made with Margarita's father.

"You're drawing a few thousand at best to Bears games," Pyle pitched to Halas in the middle of the night. "If Red can increase sales, what do you have to lose by splitting the gate?"

Two weeks after their conversation, Red has since dropped out of college and has already dazzled four record professional football crowds: two in Chicago, one in St. Louis, and, just yesterday, another in Philadelphia.

Today, New York City is his fifth game as a Bear in two weeks. Fourteen more are scheduled over the next eight weeks for a barnstorming tour up and down the East and West Coasts. Many of the games are scheduled on back-to-back days. Tickets are flying out of box offices for every single one of them.

For today's single game, Red will make more money than Babe Ruth makes in an entire season playing baseball. In fact, Babe Ruth is right now sitting at the fifty-yard line, doing that math himself.

This is the first professional football game with national press in the history of the sport. Up in the crowded press box with Grantland Rice and all of the greats sits Warren, who is fortunate to have the Chicago Bears added to his beat. He has his stat sheet ready to calculate not just yards per carry, but the amount of money Red will make each step he takes on the field.

Pyle jogs out, wearing his designer three-piece suit, surrounded by screaming sports fans whom he only views as dollar signs.

As he jogs, the feather in his hat flickers in the wind. His real Italian leather shoes are getting caked in mud, *but who cares?* Plenty more where those came from.

To make it easier to move, he unbuttons his suit coat, allowing the jeweled "C.C." on his belt buckle to sparkle in the sunlight.

"Okay, tell the girls what the C.C. stands for," Charlie Chaplin asked him in his theater office the night he discovered Red.

After some coaxing, Pyle revealed, "Well, I've been accused of the C.C. standing for Charming Charley, Casanova Chas, Clever Chico, and Couch & Cuddle. There are a few more naughtier ones, ladies, but I doubt you can handle them."

"Hmmm," Chaplin said. "I've always known it to stand for something else."

While running onto the field, C.C. "Cash and Carry" Pyle takes the national stage, balancing his jeweled cane in one hand and using his other hand to adjust the brightest green tie in sports.

CHAPTER 35

Chicago Bears at New York Giants
Sunday, December 6, 1925

In Red's first college game, he remembers glancing around at the faces of clean-cut young men in the huddle, who were excited to compete, playing for the pride of their school. In the professional huddle, however, he feels more like the new guy gearing up for a knife fight at a state penitentiary.

"Rookie, this ain't Illinois, this ain't college, and Zup ain't in the building," were the first things the Bears star quarterback, Joey Sternaman, said to Red in his first pro game in Chicago a week after dropping out of college.

The faces in the Bears huddle are those of mercenaries who play for two reasons: money and violence. No matter the score or outcome, they make between fifty and two hundred dollars a game for crushing other human beings.

"They have zero loyalty to you or Halas," Joey explained. "For an extra ten bucks, they'd switch to the other team at halftime. This ain't the Red Show. They couldn't care less. And they get paid to tackle, not to block for you."

Red discovered very quickly just how good professionals are at defense. The average NFL team scores less than one touchdown per game. These guys are athletic and brutal. Any team in the NFL could beat the best college teams with their defense alone. On offense, not so much, given they are lucky to practice once a week and don't have much motivation to block.

Red expected Halas to call the plays since he has the advantage of being in the huddle. Instead, Joey runs the offense. Halas trusts Joey because of who trained him. Years ago, Joey called the plays under Zuppke's mentorship at Illinois. That is until Zuppke disowned him over the Taylorville scandal.

Red respected Joey's leadership and unselfishly took orders. He barely touched the ball during his first two professional games, despite Chicago fans' chant of "Give Red the ball!"

Two games in, and Red had yet to score at the professional level. He did throw a touchdown pass to Laurie Walquist—another banished Illinois player—but that didn't matter to the fans. These were the first football games most of them had ever attended. Based on what they'd read in the papers, they expected to see Red score every time he touched the ball.

In the third game, an exhibition in St. Louis, Pyle pressured Red to break loose and give the crowd what they wanted. He scored four touchdowns, lighting up sports pages across the country, demonstrating he could be just as exceptional in the pro game as he was in college.

In their most recent game, just yesterday in Philadelphia, his offensive line had reminded him the Bears are not the Red Show by stepping aside a few times and allowing the other team to murder him. The Bears still won, but Red received the message loud and clear that Joey remains their leader. To survive at the pro level, he plans to revert to just being "one of the guys," which, ironically, is all he's ever wanted.

To the Giants players, however, Red is not just "one of the guys." He's a rookie on the other team selling out stadiums, getting the lion's share of the gate, and making more money today than they will make in their lifetimes. The salt in the wound is witnessing their sold-out home crowd rooting for the hotshot on the other team, mixed with the fact that this kid is undoubtedly talented.

In no time, the Bears score two touchdowns using Joey's offense, which he now calls "Decoy Red." It's a simple strategy. Hand the ball to Red a few times and don't block for him. Red gets killed. Then, fake the ball to Red, and he still gets killed, but this time Joey scores.

Halas supports this offense because, in the end, the Bears will likely win; Joey, his star, remains happy; and Red pays his dues. The fans? Well, they get to see Red play in a Bears jersey. All in all, from Halas' point of view, mission accomplished. Pyle, on the other hand, is only interested in Red Grange touchdowns. Same with the fans.

The Giants players rarely look up at the scoreboard. They do rush for one touchdown, making it Bears 12, Giants 7, but their incentives have nothing to do with the score. They put money in a jar before the game, competing with each other for who can take the best potshot at Red.

While Red is flat on the ground after a play, Joe Williams punches him in the back of the head. After another play, Tommy Tomlin stomps on Red's left arm with his cleat. After each cheap shot, the Giants players celebrate as if those guys had won the lottery.

Halftime: Bears 12, Giants 7.

In the locker room, the Bears trainer examines Red's arm while asking him what day it is.

"Never ask a player on tour what day it is," Pyle says, butting into the locker room and interrupting the examination. "I don't even know what day it is. He's fine."

Halas, banged up himself, watches the interaction. Red sits blank-faced while the trainer looks closer at his stomped arm.

"I'd say the tendons are torn," the trainer says to Halas. "He needs to sit out the rest of the game, if not the rest of the tour."

"You're not a doctor," Pyle yells at the trainer. "He's fine. Put some tape around it. Dope him. My boy is tougher than that."

Halas stands and walks toward the door.

"Pyle, come out in the hallway for just a second," Halas says.

Just as Pyle steps out of the locker room, Halas slams the door behind him and locks him out. Pyle uselessly slaps the door a few times before marching down the hallway, yelling for Mara, yelling for Clem, trying to figure out where the Giants locker room is located.

"Mara, you begged me for these games," Pyle shouts, banging on doors in the hallway. "One in New York, one in Chicago, and more on the tour. You're going to ruin this for everyone, encouraging potshots. What the hell is wrong with you?"

Back on the field in the second half, Halas sits Red out despite seventy thousand fans demanding he go back in.

"We want Red! We want Red! We want Red!" echoes through all of Manhattan.

On the bench, Red, despite being doped and taped and pressured by Pyle to get back in the game, doesn't fully regain consciousness until the fourth quarter begins.

"We want Red!" vibrates through his head, which perfectly translates to the same melody of the three words Red's been saying to himself.

Three more years.

He's been telling himself all along he just needs to survive football for three more years. *Three more years* until he vanishes off the face of the earth. *Three more years* to honor his agreement with Pyle. *Three more years* until he can play golf, fish, or do whatever the hell he wants for the rest of his life.

Three more years of Cash and Carry.

The instant Red stands up, the chants stop, and the crowd goes wild.

Red talks Halas into putting him back into the game, which they're still leading 12-7, with the Giants driving for the win with hardly any time left on the clock.

Red still has no idea what day it is. He's not even certain what city he's in. But he knows one thing: Joey is in charge of the offense, not the defense. Halas allows Red to play back in the safety position, giving him the freedom to roam the field.

Just three weeks ago, before his last college game against Ohio State, Zuppke had Fannie guard the door while whispering a defensive strategy in Red's ear.

"When the opponent is losing, they get desperate," Zuppke said. "Let them complete a few passes. Have the patience of a viper. A viper! Sit back, wait, und when the time is right...."

Red strikes.

For most people in the stands, this is the first football game they have ever attended. They've read about Red, "the football god," for years. The opportunity to see him play in person was too good to miss. Except, up until this point in the game, they haven't seen him do *anything*.

By *anything*, they mean score. They don't appreciate his tackles on defense or his blocking. They don't appreciate his passing or being used as a decoy, taking brutal hits and freeing up Joey. If Red doesn't score a touchdown, then he didn't do *anything* in their minds.

The crowd erupts as the viper in orange, wearing number 77, strikes. Red intercepts the pass one-handed, tucks it under his nearly useless stomped left arm, scans the field, and plots a path to the end zone.

At Illinois, he could count on blockers. In the NFL, he's on his own. He makes the first two Giants miss by simply swiveling his hips. The next few require a stiff arm. He takes another Giant down with his shoulder. A Zuppke cutback trips up a few more. The next few, he simply outruns.

All that's left is the Giants' best player, Hinkey Haines, who had the misfortune of throwing the pass Red just intercepted. Haines has an angle on Red with enough momentum not just to tackle him but to win the money in that pot.

Red knew his run would end this way when he plotted it. Even he can't, on his own, elude all eleven professional Giants players. He braces for the hit, which he imagines might cause his throbbing left arm to shatter.

Out of nowhere, Halas flies in and throws a rare yet calculated NFL-team-owner block, taking out Haines, causing both of them to tumble away and open a clear path for Red to steam into the endzone.

After the Red Grange touchdown and an extra point, the final score is Bears 19, Giants 7. The House of Red is restored. The fans have a memory of a lifetime, and the national press corps is already talking their editors into booking them hotels and trains for the rest of the tour.

Red has played five professional football games in eleven days. Five more games are scheduled in the next nine days on the East Coast and nine more await after that on the West Coast. That's sixteen pro games over eight weeks on the heels of Red's brutal senior college season.

His left arm hangs uselessly, and his head throbs. Even so, before he leaves the field, Red recalls something Pyle begged him to do after the last few games and he'd forgotten. In appreciation of the sold-out New York City stadium, Red takes off his helmet, revealing his trademark auburn locks.

He has the press box and euphoric crowd to thank, not just for putting the NFL on the map today as a major sport, but for their generous donations to the Red Grange retirement fund.

CHAPTER 36

Pyle peeks out from behind the curtain into a packed Madison Avenue hotel ballroom. Chairs are arranged in rows facing posters of Red's face on easels flanking a podium. Each time a row is filled with men in expensive suits, Pyle motions to Clem to add more chairs.

Behind the curtain, a team of doctors examine Red's swollen and bruised arm. After a private discussion, the most senior physician pulls Pyle to the side.

"The tendons are most certainly torn," the doctor says. "If he doesn't rest it, he's at risk of a blood clot forming that might cause him to lose the limb. Even worse, if the clot makes its way to his heart or brain, it could kill him."

"I see," Pyle says, watching Red struggling to put on his shirt, tie, and suit coat. "What have you told him?"

"Nothing. Just as you instructed."

"Okay, thank you," Pyle says. "Clear out. I'll break it to him."

Pyle peeks back out into the ballroom to find Clem has placed all the chairs, forcing some men to stand in the back of the room. Pyle straightens his greenest tie yet, grabs his jeweled cane, and takes center stage.

"Welcome, gentlemen, welcome," he says. "How about that Giants-Bears game yesterday? Enjoy your seats? Did I promise you a Red Grange touchdown, or what? The boy never disappoints, does he?"

The men in the room express their agreement with loud cheering.

"We're in new territory here. The way we're going to run today's auction is to grant exclusivity to each individual merchandise category to the highest bidder. We'll start with the opportunity for one of you lucky advertising executives to win the exclusive rights to Red Grange socks. Then we'll make our way through the other categories—clothing, sporting equipment, food, candy, automobiles, etc.—finishing with movie rights."

The men in the room nod in agreement.

"Okay," Pyle says, flipping through a clipboard of papers he's holding, "let's start with socks. Who will give me...."

"Where's Red?" someone shouts.

Others join in, asking the same question.

"The opportunity for Red Grange to endorse your products is a world-class investment," Pyle says. "You know what he looks like. You know what he stands for. You know his fame and reach. How can you go wrong with Red lending his image to endorse your brands?"

"How bad's he hurt?"

"Can he even play?"

No matter what Pyle says, he's losing the crowd. Until their eyes light up as Red steps out from behind the curtain, waving with both hands and taking bows to the cheers of the audience.

After an ovation that lasts several minutes, Red gives a final wave and begins to head back to the curtain.

"Can you play?" men shout.

"How bad are you hurt?"

"Is the tour still on?"

Red pauses for a moment, turns back around, and makes eye contact with Pyle. Without hesitation, Pyle gives Red a thumbs up.

In turn, Red gives the audience a thumbs up with his right hand, joined by a more labored thumbs up with his left hand.

That's enough for the crowd, who erupt again in cheers as Red disappears behind the curtain.

"Okay, let's get back to the auction," Pyle says, looking over his clipboard. "Where was I? Right...okay...socks. We'll start with Red Grange socks. Who will give me...."

Before he can finish, a guy wearing the cheapest suit in the room yells out, "Fifty dollars."

Pyle pauses on stage and stares the man down for a moment before stepping away from the podium and approaching him.

"Sir, an offer like that has earned you a special privilege today," Pyle says. "Follow me a moment, if you will, please."

Pyle takes the man's arm and walks him toward the door.

"Clem, do me a favor?"

Clem comes bounding over and takes the man's arm from Pyle.

"Clem, please show this fine man not only into the hallway but out to the alleyway."

Before the man in the cheap suit knows what's happened, Clem has carried him out of the hotel and tossed him into the trash cans in the alley.

"Now, where was I," Pyle says, stepping back to the podium with his papers. "For each advertising category, I will set the minimum bid. Back to exclusivity for Red Grange socks. Who will give me one thousand dollars?"

Hands fly up.

They continue to go up all afternoon for Red Grange socks, footballs, shoes, candy bars, sweaters, swimsuits, soft drinks, coffee, dolls, cereal, malted milk, books, and even a recipe for meatloaf.

Pyle strikes a deal for cigarettes, as well, which causes Red to step back out from behind the curtain for a moment to engage in a private conversation before Pyle turns back to the audience.

"I'm reminded Red doesn't smoke," Pyle says to the disappointed looks of cigarette executives. "However, he is willing to have the advertisement read, 'but my friends do, and they love Lucky Strikes.'"

The Lucky Strike team talks it over for a moment and replies with an enthusiastic thumbs up.

The event culminates with photographers taking a photo of Red, Pyle, and Arrow Movie Studios executives standing in front of a large check made out for three hundred thousand dollars to start filming a movie in February in California as soon as the tour ends on the West Coast.

Pyle positions himself by Red's side, blocking Red from any well-wishing slaps on his left arm. If the Bears players are too stupid to block for him, Pyle thinks, at least, he will.

CHAPTER 37

A day later, on Tuesday, Red plays in Washington, D.C. Wednesday, he plays in Boston, and Thursday, in Pittsburgh. Warren and others have written stories suggesting that Red doesn't look like himself on the field.

That Friday, when his father, brother, and Earl catch up to him in Detroit, they find Red delirious in his hotel room. His left arm is swollen to twice its size. At first glance, Garland mistook it for a leg. Due to the pain, Red hasn't slept in days.

Red's father, Lyle, is enraged. In this state, he could fend off the entire Bears team alone, not to mention Pyle. However, the rest of the Bears are also so banged up from the grueling schedule that they couldn't put up much of a fight if they wanted to.

With help from the hotel concierge, Lyle finds a local doctor who provides proper treatment, putting Red's arm into a splint and medicating him for a proper night's rest.

Lyle and Garland sit on one side of a fancy hotel suite across from Pyle and Halas. Garland is still doped up, his own arm still in a sling from his shoulder surgery. Earl paces the room, fists clenched, barely holding back his rage.

"Tomorrow's Detroit game is sold out," Pyle says. "Thirty thousand tickets. Same with the next day's game in Chicago against the Giants."

"So what?" Lyle asks.

"Lyle, look," Pyle explains, "Red has me depositing all his money in the bank. You're on the account. He's saving it all until he's done playing. Except, that is, for the money he instructed you to withdraw so you could retire, pay off your debts, buy a house, buy a sports car for Garland, and have enough tuition money for Garland once he is healthy enough to re-enroll."

Lyle shrugs.

"What would you all have us do? Announce Red can't play? Offer refunds?" Pyle asks. "We're set to take in a hundred thousand dollars at the gate over the next two days."

Earl can't take it anymore and starts yelling directly at Pyle, "You're gonna kill him, and just to make you all rich."

"Now wait a minute, son," Pyle says before Halas holds out his hand to demand that Pyle shut his mouth.

"I have an idea for the Detroit game tomorrow," Halas explains. "And an even better idea for the game in Chicago the day after."

Two days later...
New York Giants at Chicago Bears
Sunday, December 13, 1925

Earl stands on the field in a Bears uniform, listening to "Amazing Grace" performed by a brass band. Maybe the Bears don't care about blocking for Red, but Earl always has. He's proud to quit college to defend his friend.

Halas stands next to Earl in line with the other players, smirking at a pissed-off Tim Mara in the stands. Mara traveled all the way from New York City for only twelve thousand paying customers. Halas also enjoyed watching Pyle break it to Mara that because of his players' potshots in their previous meeting, the Giants are being excluded from playing in additional games for the rest of the tour.

Halas couldn't care less about today's reduced crowd size. Twelve thousand is still significantly more than attended any Bears games in prior years. Chicago definitely loves Red, but this crowd proves they are also showing signs of supporting the other Bears, too.

As the band finishes, Lyle and Garland stand next to Pyle in the stands, patting each other on the backs, huge grins on their faces. They join the crowd in an exuberant cheer, applauding a beautiful sight materializing on the field before them.

Out walks Red with his arm in a sling. He's wearing a suit and tie under a beautiful new five-hundred-dollar fur coat, accepting an ovation from Chicago fans who knew in advance he couldn't play but decided it was worth the price of admission just to see him decked out in raccoon. The same thing had happened the day before in Detroit.

Dear God, Halas thinks to himself, realizing the Golden Lad, as he's begun to call Red, can draw record crowds just by walking a lap around the field, enough to allow them one day to boast, "I saw the great Red Grange."

Halas shifts into warrior mode. His squad is particularly fired up, especially since Halas dropped a one hundred dollar bill himself into the Bears potshot jar for this re-match against the Giants.

CHAPTER 38

"You know what would draw two hundred thousand fans?" Helen asks, wearing her hotel uniform while massaging Red's bare shoulders.

Red's never felt more relaxed, lying in a warm bathtub in a Chicago hotel suite, his muscles on display, a strategically placed washcloth providing a modicum of modesty.

"What would draw record fans?" he asks.

"If we transported this bathtub to the middle of Times Square," she answers.

Laughing still hurts his much-improved arm, but being back home in Chicago and with her is worth it.

"You know, C.C. Pyle would be upset," she says.

"Why's that?

"Because I'm getting a free view."

Again, the laughter hurts.

"Speaking of which, Mr. Grange, how long will we have the pleasure of your company in our fine hotel before Mr. Pyle ships you out again?"

"Our next game is Christmas Day in Miami. A week and a half from now."

"Miami? Sounds terribly boring. And after that?"

"We go to Tampa, Jacksonville, New Orleans, Los Angeles, San Diego, San Francisco, Portland, and Washington. We wrap up January 31st."

She's been trying to follow along by counting the stops on her fingers.

219

"That's like nine games in five weeks or something."

"Instead of playing NFL teams, C.C.'s agreed to line up local exhibition teams for these. He's out on the road already, recruiting other high-profile All-Americans to quit school and play against us."

"Like The Four Horsemen? Wildcat Wilson? The Big Dog? Those are such great nicknames."

"You know them? You follow football, huh?"

"Norman says those names all the time. When they play in the neighborhood, the boys pretend to be them."

"Who is Norman's favorite?"

"Wildcat Wilson. He's the most handsome. That wavy blond hair."

Red just shakes his head.

"Followed by The Big Dog. Followed by the Four Horsemen. Lester something from Tulane. Then, The Ghost. At least, you're in there somewhere."

"Lovely."

"I'm teasing. You know every kid in Chicago longs for The Galloping Ghost. So does every girl in this hotel."

"Is that right? Every girl?"

She changes the subject.

"So, February 1st is when we'll next have the pleasure of your company back in Chicago, Mr. Grange?"

"First, I have to film that movie in California."

"Speaking of which, how's the lipstick going? Your teammates helping you? The guys taking turns? A little red on Red action on the road?"

"Stop making me laugh," he pleads, fighting through the pain. "But, seriously, I could use a lipstick refresher."

"I thought you'd never ask," she says, stopping the massage, grabbing her purse, and pulling out a lipstick container. She sits on the edge of the tub.

"I've been thinking a lot about this," she says, "and I have a new technique I'd like you to watch carefully. No fingers this time."

Holding the container, and without a mirror, she perfectly applies red lipstick to her lips with zero residue on her fingers.

"Woah, that's way too fast," he says. "I can't do that."

"You don't have to. I put extra on," she says, closing her eyes. "You see, this is my new technique. It's less complicated."

With her eyes closed, she puckers her lips.

He smiles, shaking his head.

"I'm not falling for that again."

"What, too complicated for you?" she says, opening her eyes.

"Just the right amount," he replies, gently pulling her toward him.

CHAPTER 39

Teachers experience a unique phenomenon each school year when just as students begin to show the most promise, they up and graduate.

Fannie Zuppke lives that same phenomenon each winter. Whether her husband's team had a good or bad record, the end-of-season banquet is always bittersweet as they say goodbye to the seniors.

The worst is when she looks over at the senior table and sees that two chairs are missing. In the year of the Taylorville scandal, multiple chairs were missing, which was heartbreaking. This year, however, these two empty chairs hurt even more.

"Fannie, how do I reflect on the season without Granche and Earl? How is that even possible," Zuppke said to her in the middle of the night just the other day.

Her strategy was first to let him jot down all of his angriest feelings. Then, with her encouragement, he ripped that draft up and started over with her help. She's satisfied with how they eventually worded it, taking the high road on the issue of having two students drop out of school to make a buck.

It's been particularly challenging around Champaign, lately. Twenty thousand fans carried Red in triumph down Main Street just over a month ago. Today, in protest, the residents have removed all posters or evidence of Red, and students want nothing to do with Pyle's theater. Almost as fast as this town grew to worship Red, they now revile him.

The revised version of Zuppke's speech is immediately under threat when, unexpectedly, Fannie notices Red and Earl stroll into the room, both of them in fancy new suits, Red's topped by the raccoon coat that costs as much as a year's tuition at Illinois.

She glances nervously at her husband, who is showing off his latest series of paintings to alumni when he notices the party crashers. His fists clench, and his cheeks turn so red she's worried he'll explode.

Fannie tries to hurry across the room to her husband, but she can't reach him in time. Athletic Director George Huff, at the podium, asks the room to take their seats and calls Zuppke up to say a few words. Prohibition has been disappointing to Fannie on so many levels, but especially at this moment because if there was ever a time she needed a drink, it is now.

As her husband steps up to the podium, she's relieved to see him pull his prepared speech from his pocket, smooth out the crease, and start with the opening line they had rehearsed.

"I'll always remember this year's team as my November Boys," he says to great cheers from the room, referring to the fact that they were 1-3 going into the Penn game and won every subsequent game, finishing 5-3 with the win at Ohio State.

He appears on his way to continue with the script, which has wonderful things to say about the season, each of the seniors, his coaching staff, and the amazing crop of freshmen he believes have the potential to win a national championship, and it's going great until he suddenly pauses. For a moment, he's lost in thought. Then he rips the speech to shreds.

Fannie reaches for an imaginary cocktail.

"There's a disturbing trend in college football that, unfortunately, appears to be originating right here at Illinois. Und under my watch," he continues. "It was one thing to have men who earned their college degrees degrade themselves by playing in the NFL. But students dropping out of school und not graduating? Students choosing blood money over a college degree? Students turning their backs on a great institution like the University of Illinois? That is entirely another form of degradation."

Fannie looks to where Red and Earl are sitting, expecting to see Red's empty chair wobbling. Instead, even more terrifying, she watches Red and Earl slowly rise from their seats and make their way to the door.

"To the actual college students in the room," he continues, "follow them out. Go ahead, follow your heroes. I don't want you here if you admire them. If you're planning to follow in their footsteps, then weasel on out of here. Right now. Go ahead. Get the hell off my team."

Fannie watches as Red and Earl reach the exit and take one last look back at their beloved coach before giving her a farewell nod. Warren takes notice of their expressions and scribbles furiously in his notebook.

Red and Earl, in Fannie's estimation, no longer seem confident or resolute. Instead, they appear heartbroken. She will never have her own children, and the closest she'll ever come is the auburn-haired wonder boy who slowly vanishes out the door.

CHAPTER 40

Earl was born to be a professional football player. With a proud, confident grin on his face, he stands at a train platform in Chicago, waving goodbye to hundreds of Bears fans and signing autographs before embarking on an adventure to introduce the NFL to the rest of the nation.

"Welcome to the Dog Pound," Pyle says to the entire Bears team, sliding open the doors of two custom Pullman train cars bound for Miami. "Hand your luggage to Clem, who is graciously serving as our porter for the trip, and let's begin the tour."

Earl steps into the first train car, and he can't believe his eyes.

"It's not just a massage parlor and training room, but it also converts into sleeping quarters," Pyle demonstrates, pulling out mattressed sleeping bunks. "No more slouching on seats, drooling on the windows, leaning on the guy next to you, whispering sweet nothings in his ear. What do you think?"

They love it. No NFL team has ever been treated like this before. All athletes know a good night's sleep makes a world of difference to their performance when every game is on the road.

"Now, I think you'll especially enjoy this next part," Pyle says, motioning for the team to follow him into the adjacent car.

Earl steps through the walkway to discover the second car decked out like a fraternity house, complete with card tables, bar stools, plush velvet seats, a stained glass window etched with the Bears logo, and a phonograph machine with stacks and stacks of jazz records.

"It takes just the right amount of hip action, but watch this," Pyle says, bumping up against a panel on the wall, opening a secret liquor stash that folds out into a full bar.

The guys start making "Ruff! Ruff!" sounds, breaking in the Dog Pound.

The minute the team says goodbye to their wives and girlfriends and the train takes off is the moment Earl really falls in love with being a professional athlete.

Oh, the tales players tell. Bar fights. Night club arrests. Brothel escapes. And much, much worse. Earl can't get enough of the stories, and being the new guy, he gives the veterans fresh ears to hear them.

The only person who loves the pro football lifestyle even more is Garland. Since he is out of school recovering, Lyle has sent him along to look after Red and ensure Pyle doesn't take advantage of him should his injury persist. However, Red expects to spend more time keeping Garland from adding to the legends than Garland will spend protecting him.

Earl is so caught up in his new lifestyle and meeting the guys that he often forgets who made the trip possible. In the back of the train car, Red sits by himself, holding a phonograph on his lap, and listening to jazz while looking out the window.

The accommodations aren't the only improvement. Pyle also learned from the East Coast leg of the tour how to select the competition. Most of the games they've played to date were previously scheduled Bears games against NFL teams. On this leg of the tour, the competition will be exhibition teams made up of hand-picked offseason pro players. Potshots will be a thing of the past thanks to one person: George Trafton, universally recognized to be the meanest and toughest player on the planet. Halas signed him not only to play football but also to be an enforcer to assist Earl in protecting Red.

Earl picks up from conversation that Trafton lasted one season under Knute Rockne at Notre Dame, playing alongside George "The Gipper" Gipp. They were undefeated that year, thanks to Trafton's brutal play. He set a personal record of knocking four guys out cold in a single quarter.

Trafton's departure from Notre Dame wasn't a result of his schoolwork, though he never went to class. Nor was it his temper or his propensity to fistfight—both were encouraged. And it wasn't because Rockne brought him in as a ringer at age 22. Playing pro football for money on the side was what quickly led to Trafton's downfall.

"Which I find hilarious," Trafton tells Earl, "because I made a lot more money boxing in side alleys, and the NCAA never knew about that."

With Earl and Trafton looking out for Red, Red's game stats and the fans' satisfaction level improve dramatically.

In Miami, Red scores the only touchdown against a gaggle of players safely handpicked from other NFL teams. Later that evening, Earl and Trafton get drunk, have a disagreement, and punch each other silly. The next morning, neither remembers what happened and assumes their bruises are from the game.

In Tampa, Red breaks loose for a seventy-yard run thanks to Earl and Trafton working together, and Red throws a key block to help Joey get a touchdown, beating a former all-star team led by 41-year-old Jim Thorpe. Earl and Trafton again wake up the next morning hungover with unexplained bruises.

In Jacksonville, Red throws a touchdown pass and again makes a key block to make a long run for Joey possible. Even Halas catches a pass for extra yards. Earl enjoys seeing Red with a rare smile at the end of the game, given that they beat a team assembled around All-American Ernie "Big Dog" Nevers, who quit Stanford to play this game. That evening,

Earl and Trafton each meet a girl at a nightclub, avoiding any additional bruises.

In New Orleans, Earl and Trafton team up to block a punt, setting up a Bears touchdown. They also set Red up to score another on a long run against a team led by Lester Latenschlager, who quit Tulane to compete in this game.

There was a slight issue at halftime when Lester almost refused to play the second half, claiming Pyle hadn't paid him the promised six thousand dollars in full. It was reported that Pyle worked it out with Lester's father, and the game resumed.

After the game, Earl read a story written by Warren that the three hundred thousand dollar Arrow Studios check was a hoax. Arrow Studios, Warren uncovered, wrote an advance check for only ten thousand. The studio chief admitted the larger amount was part of a publicity stunt, its amount nothing more than an "anticipation of royalties." Within a few days, Arrow Studios goes bankrupt. Pyle's response is three-fold: deny, deny, deny.

To add insult to injury, a national reporter publishes a story calling Red the "loneliest young man in America," chronicling how his teammates have partied up and down the Southeast while Red stares out the window listening to music.

Earl suspects Pyle would have given Trafton and him permission to throw that reporter off the train if Pyle had been around, but he is already off to Los Angeles, traveling ahead of the team, putting the final touches on the marquee game of the tour.

On the final night in New Orleans, Earl is thinking of a way to get Red to quit staring out the window and live life in the present. Earl has heard all his teammates' best stories multiple times when he stumbles into an opportunity to create a story of his own.

Red is lost in thought before the train takes off, only to slowly realize the Bears players have all formed a semi-circle around him. He looks up to see Earl escorting a scantily dressed, voluptuous young woman down the aisle.

"Red, meet Miss Betty," Earl says, trying to contain his excitement along with the rest of the guys. "She was hanging around outside. She says that if you give her an autograph, she'll show us all something we'll never forget."

Betty nods, confirming this is indeed the case, as Trafton shouts, "Ruff! Ruff!"

Even Halas is a part of the action now, enjoying the show with the rest of his team. Clem and Garland peek in, as well.

Earl knows Red is prone to vanishing in a situation like this, but Red still hasn't yet figured out how to escape a train car. Everyone waits for Red's reaction.

"Okay, fine," Red finally says, acknowledging that peer pressure is one thing, but something quite different when applied by an entire NFL team.

Earl and Trafton shake with excitement as Betty slowly moves her hands to the bottom of her cleavage, unfastening more buttons.

The guys whoop and holler, Trafton's voice rising above the others. Earl thinks Red might be about to smile. Just as Betty is about to unfasten the last button, she surprises everyone by pulling legal documents out from under her brassiere and delivering them to Red.

"You've been served," she says.

CHAPTER 41

The Los Angeles hotel suite is bristling with people mingling and drinking, but Red doesn't care, barging in and scanning the room for Pyle's stupid winning smile.

Red weaves and pivots through the room despite everyone beginning to recognize him. He slides out of the way of cocktails, ducks under long cigarette holders, and swivels past wild hand gestures of people accentuating their stories. A final spin move narrowly avoids a tray of hors d'oeuvres, allowing Red to shove the legal papers right in Pyle's face.

"You don't even own the Virginia Theater?" Red says to Pyle. "And you're behind on your rent? Not to mention the Arrow Studios check was a hoax?"

The crowd quiets now, watching a livid Red Grange awaiting C.C. Pyle's response.

"Red, I'd like you to meet Charlie Chaplin," Pyle says, motioning to the person he's been speaking with.

Sure enough, Charlie Chaplin is indeed standing right next to them. Red quickly thinks back on the path he just made through the room, realizing that Chaplin isn't the only face he recognizes.

"Also, meet Douglas Fairbanks, Jr.," Pyle says, "and Mary Pickford, Jack Warner, Alfred Hitchcock. You know Grantland Rice. And, brace yourself, the lovely Marion Davies."

Red can't help but lose his footing when he sees her face.

"My apologies to all the other starlets in the room," Pyle says, "but it's been well-reported by my friend Grantland Rice that Miss Davies is Red's long-time movie crush."

Grantland confirms this to be true with a nod of his pipe. Red has only ever seen Marion Davies in black and white on the screen and in photographs. Chaplin has to reach out and steady him. Red will never understand how anyone could be that beautiful.

"And, meet William Randolph Hearst," Pyle says, "who was kind enough to let Marion out of his castle, so she can return the favor by watching you play in the Coliseum tomorrow."

"The editors of my papers keep insisting we expand our coverage," Hearst says. "Pro football has captured the public's interest, they say. You're costing me a lot of ink since you quit college."

"I'm not sure what to say," Red replies.

"Say, you're welcome," Pyle says. "Hearst makes a fortune with every touchdown you score. If only he had to pay a license for each one just to print your name."

"Pyle, you'd love that, wouldn't you?" Chaplin says to laughter from the crowd.

"The First Amendment upsets me almost as much as the Eighteenth," Pyle admits.

"But at least Prohibition has a chance for repeal," Chaplin says, holding up his drink to cheers from the crowd.

"But, Red," Pyle says, "the real person you must meet is the one who, along with yourself, brought all these fine people out to this private reception, the person you are set to battle in the Coliseum tomorrow. Red Grange, meet Wildcat Wilson."

The crowd parts, revealing an athlete across the room standing arm in arm with his strikingly attractive date. Red and Wilson are the same age and nearly identical in build. Like Red, Wilson had toned his physique with manual labor, though his was earned working summers as a longshoreman. They share a strong jawline, determined eyes, and pronounced

231

cheekbones. The two of them could almost pass for twins were it not for their biggest difference: Wilson is blond.

Red is visibly distracted, not by Wilson's resemblance, but by his alluring date whom Red knows all too well. Suddenly, camera flashes go off. In short order, Wildcat Wilson and Red Grange are photographed with each other and, soon, with each celebrity in the room.

After a while, Red pulls Pyle aside.

"Is anything about you true?" Red asks pointedly while trying to keep his voice down. "Was it all lies?"

"What's got into you, my boy?" Pyle says, trying to calm him down. "We're in the public eye. We're going to be targets, that's all. Those bills will all be sorted out shortly. Never pay a bill right away. Always wait until you're forced. That's just good business. Besides, the tour is going splendidly. Don't you worry. You play football. I got the rest."

"You got the rest? Do you see the woman with Wilson?" Red says, pointing over at her. "Do you even know who she works for?"

Pyle isn't really paying attention to him. Instead, Pyle waves someone over for Red to meet.

"Red, say hello to Joe Kennedy," Pyle says, changing the subject as Red and Joe shake hands. "And meet his son, Jack. He's eight years old. He's a big fan of yours."

Red would prefer to finish the conversation, but he's a sucker for kids. He kneels down and talks to young JFK, who is holding a football. Red overhears Pyle leaning in closer to Joe.

"What do you say?" Pyle says. "Is your FBO studio interested in making a picture? Or do we go with Warner? We're making our decision after tomorrow's game."

"You really embarrassed the industry with your Arrow Studios stunt," Joe says. "But I'm leaving this one up to my boy Jack. He's the football fan, not me. Walter Camp's rule book is too thick for me. I prefer baseball."

Red signs young Jack's ball before working with him on his football stance and how to properly extend a stiff arm. Red even asks some of the celebrities in the room to step aside so he has room to throw Jack a few passes. The whole time he's throwing, Red imagines shutting Pyle up with a spiral to the face.

As the event goes on, Wildcat Wilson and Red pose for even more photos. Pyle joins in, too. Despite all the world-famous faces in the room, all eyes are on the two handsome All-Americans set to battle tomorrow.

Except for Red. Even while he was playing with Jack and fantasizing about smacking Pyle, his eyes were locked on someone else in the room: Wilson's attractive date, Polly.

CHAPTER 42

Chicago Bears at Los Angeles Tigers
Wednesday, January 6, 1926

Seventy-five thousand pairs of eyes at the Los Angeles Coliseum lock in on Number 77 in orange and Number 33 in blue.

Except, of course, when they get distracted and sneak peeks at Marion Davies and Charlie Chaplin in the front row. Or stare at any of the other dozen A-list actors in the stadium. Or ogle the latest fashion trends of floral skirts and bow ties. Or become engrossed with any of the hundreds of wannabe starlets begging photographers to take their photos.

For Wilson and Red, it's all about watching each other's eyes. Wilson trusts his hastily-named Tigers exhibition team comprised of former USC, Cal, and Stanford stars to handle Joey, Laurie, and the Bears' other scoring threats. His entire focus is on Red's eyes, anticipating any changes in direction.

Red is also entirely focused on Wilson's eyes for a different reason. He's anticipating the off chance Wilson might glance in the stands, revealing where Polly is sitting.

At a press conference before the game, Red had one moment to lean over and privately ask Wilson a question.

"How did you meet Polly?"
"Who's Polly?"
"The woman you are with."

"You mean Anne? She had car trouble. Why? She's a looker, isn't she?"

That was all Red needed for now. Except, he would like to know where she is sitting and who she might be sitting near.

Neither team scores in the first quarter, mostly because Red and Wilson refuse to take their eyes off each other.

In the second quarter, Halas instructs Earl, along with his new inseparable pal and occasional sparring partner, Trafton, to hunt like a pair of wolves whenever Wilson carries the ball. They hone in on him. A few plays later, Earl slows Wilson down while Trafton slams his leather head into the ball, resulting in a fumble at midfield that the Bears recover.

After resetting on offense, Laurie passes to Red for a few yards. Then Laurie runs the ball for a few more. Then Joey carries the ball. Halas, Trafton, and Earl each throw solid blocks along the way. The Bears are now one yard from scoring.

Even when Red is in his huddle, he watches Wilson's eyes. *Will he not look in the stands even once?*

And then Wilson, for just a moment, glances a few rows beyond Marion Davies. Red follows that line of sight.

Bingo. Polly and, interestingly, her brother.

Red almost falls over when he recognizes who else she is sitting next to.

"Red Walter Camp Thirteen," Joey calls.

Hearing Walter Camp's name reminds Red he's playing football. It also reminds him of a story Zuppke told him about how Camp insisted there be only eleven men on a football team. Previous to that, football was played with dozens on any given side. Camp worked hard in committee to pare it down to eleven.

"The compromise, however, was that, on occasion, allowing for a twelfth und thirteenth player," Zuppke said, referring to the two goal posts buried into the ground directly in play on top of the goal line. "It's in the rules. Use them."

Red recalls that story while peeking back up in the stands. He swears he sees Zuppke and Fannie mixed in with the crowd, but his eyes must be playing tricks on him.

"Red, you with us?" Joey says again. "Let's give the audience what they want. Red Walter Camp Thirteen."

Red nods and the Bears line up on the one-yard line, threatening to score. The ball is hiked to Joey, who fakes a handoff left to Laurie. Then Joey takes two more steps to the left with the ball, using Laurie as a blocker. The defense follows Joey, except for Wilson. Wilson only follows Red.

Then Joey tosses the ball underhand to his right to Red. Red also fakes left with his eyes, forcing Wilson to hesitate a slight moment before Red dives to his right, directly at a goal post. At the last moment, Red spins further right to avoid the post, causing Wilson to bang into it.

There's a strong chance in the next annual rules meeting, and now that Walter Camp has died, that the goalposts will be moved back out of play. In the meantime, "Red Walter Camp on Two" is a beautiful tribute and call.

Also beautiful is that in order to avoid hitting the goal post, Red's spin at the last moment caused his helmet to fly off.

Thus, there is no question despite the melee of bodies as to which Bears player scored. Seventy-five thousand fans jump to their feet, paying tribute to Number 77's auburn hair. Pyle couldn't have planned that better himself.

The rest of the game is a back-and-forth affair, with the exception of a field goal by Joey, another touchdown by Red, and a late touchdown by the Tigers.

Final score: Bears 17, Tigers 7.

As Red walks off the field, he sneaks one last look at Polly. Sure enough, plain as day, she's still there, laughing with her brother on one side and, on her other side, luring yet another young All-American: Ernie "Big Dog" Nevers.

CHAPTER 43

A week later, the Bears locker room in San Francisco is quiet—dead quiet—despite twenty-five thousand fans anxiously waiting in the stands.

The Bears still have two fancy train cars, but the second isn't for sleeping any longer. Pyle had to convert it into a medical ward, giving their trainer flashbacks from the war. Playing so many games in a row has taken its toll. The day after Los Angeles, the Bears played a game in San Diego. All twenty guys on the team are reporting some form of injury.

However, this time around, the healthiest of all of them physically is Red, thanks to Earl and Trafton looking out for him on the field. Mentally, though, Red doesn't appear as sound. Pyle can't remember the last time he smiled. He doesn't even grin in photos anymore.

Pyle doesn't understand why. The Los Angeles matchup went so well that Pyle contracted "Wildcat Wilson and His College All-Stars," who all quit school to play against Red Grange and the Chicago Bears in San Francisco, Portland, and Seattle to close out the tour.

Before each game, Pyle gives Wilson a fat paycheck and a fresh set of college all-stars. Wilson, at least, is ecstatic.

Pyle walks into the Bears locker room with a huge smile. "We got a great crowd, boys," he says. "Perfect weather. A beautiful San Francisco day."

No one even looks up at him as he counts the number of guys in the room with his fingers. There are just twelve players. The guys that can at least walk have suited up, including Red, Joey, Laurie, Trafton, Earl, and Halas, who shouldn't have, but he's pushing through injury, anyway. Clem is doing his best to assist, running around the locker room, taping guys up, and helping them stretch.

Pyle sits down on the bench next to Halas, who is working on tying his cleats, showing strain on his face by simply bending over.

"Are you sure you can play with one sub?" Pyle whispers to him.

"None of us are sure of much of anything any longer," Halas replies.

Pyle thinks for a moment when an idea suddenly hits him. He grabs a Walter Camp rule book and flips through it, becoming increasingly pleased as he finds nothing to stop him from fielding a Black player.

A few minutes later, Clem has been fully outfitted in a Bears uniform.

Clem is already sweating and pulling at the itchy wool sweater as Trafton and Earl try to teach him the basics of being a lineman in the two minutes they have left before taking the field.

Earl begins with situational strategies when Trafton cuts him off.

"This ain't college. We ain't got time for dive blocks, cut blocks, and pass sets," Trafton says. "What you're going to do, Clem, is line up in front of your man and not let him push you around. Simple as that. Stand up now. Get in front of me. Let's try."

Clem reluctantly lines up against the toughest player in the NFL.

"Now, hit me. Push into me. Knock me down," Trafton says.

Clem gives Trafton the slightest of shoves, and, in return, Trafton hits Clem so hard he flies backward, flips over the bench, and slams up against the lockers.

Pyle, Halas, Red, and just about everyone in the locker room attempt to step in to protect Clem and get him back on his feet, but Trafton fights them all off, shouting for Clem to get up on his own.

"They are going to do worse to him out there," Trafton yells, pushing the others away from Clem. "Get back up. Get your ass up, Clem."

Clem does just that. He picks himself up, steps over the fallen bench, and lines up against Trafton. Clem stretches his neck and assumes an attack position. Years of scampering around all day, carrying heavy things, setting stuff up, and breaking stuff down shows in the muscle definition of his chest, arms, and legs.

Before Trafton tells him to try again, Clem drives into Trafton hard, getting the best of him and pushing Trafton back a few steps up against the other set of lockers.

Cheers ring out. Caught up in the intensity, it takes Clem a moment to let up on Trafton. When he does, Trafton has the biggest grin on his face.

"Hot damn, Clem," Trafton says. "Excellent. Except, see how your elbows are out like that? If you don't tuck them...."

In a quick motion, Trafton bends Clem's arms in an unnatural direction. Trafton is a moment away from snapping both of Clem's arms in half when he lets up at the last second. No one in the room would have put it past Trafton to have gone through with it.

"Keep those elbows tucked in, and you just might survive out there," Trafton says, smiling and patting Clem on the shoulder. "Let's go knock some heads."

A minute later, the Bears are lined up in the tunnel, ready to take the field. Clem stands just ahead of Trafton and Earl. The team slaps Clem's shoulders, attempting to pump him up.

Pyle is in the back, watching an increasingly nervous Clem move closer and closer to the sunlight. Just as Clem nears the light, he stops. His panic holds up the line.

Trafton and Earl try to push Clem out, but he won't have it. Holding his ground. Trafton and Earl push harder when, in a flash, Clem turns and breaks through the toughest two guys on the Bears, sending Trafton into the wall on one side of the tunnel and Earl into the other. All that stands in Clem's way is Pyle.

Pyle has promoted sixteen professional games in the last six weeks, averaging a game every three days. He's recruited the top college players in the country, overlooking who could be the best of them all, right under his nose the entire time. Pyle watches the determination build in Clem's face as Clem takes an athletic stance and prepares to charge.

Despite the risk of forfeiting and refunding everyone's money, even Pyle isn't dumb enough to try to stop Clem. Pyle simply steps off to the side, allowing Clem free passage to flee into the tunnel.

Halas stands in awe, having watched this entire scene play out.

"Here's what we're going to do," Pyle says to Halas, thinking quickly. "I'll grab a guy or two off the other team and get them in Bears uniforms. No one will ever be the wiser."

"And I know what I need to do," Halas says. "I need to find more guys like Clem and sign them."

CHAPTER 44

At the annual NFL owners meeting a few weeks later in Detroit, Commissioner Joe Carr asks himself why he ever took this job. Herding cats is one thing. Corralling testosterone is another. Mixing in greed has made the concoction combustible.

Unprecedented events are happening in pro football. Carr longs for the days of old when his biggest issue was getting pro teams to quit recruiting active college players to play under the guise of an alias. Even Knute Rockne took cash to play in the offseason when he was a college player at Notre Dame. Yet, the Taylorville scandal forced Rockne to disavow the practice at Zuppke's urging.

It took years for Carr to clean that up. However, recently, he had to modify a loophole in the rules to prevent pro teams from paying high school players. He took care of that, too. He assumed the biggest issue at this year's meeting would be much simpler: dealing with who actually won the 1925 season.

At the moment, it is unclear which team is the champion. The Pottsville Maroons technically had the best record in the league, except they were fined for playing an exhibition game against a team called the Notre Dame Former All-Stars in Philadelphia, violating the territorial rights of the Frankford Yellow Jackets. Carr would prefer a big game at the end of the season to determine the winner.

241

He had hoped to start with that issue and then move on to his master plan of relocating NFL teams to major cities. That's the legacy for which he'd love to be remembered, but something much more urgent has arisen.

"Absolutely not," Mara says to his fellow NFL owners. "Absolutely not. Never."

"I ask that the rest of the owners consider what I'm proposing," Pyle says, sitting next to Red and looking around at Halas and the other nineteen team owners. "I have secured a five-year lease for Yankees Stadium. Red and I intend to enter the New York Yankees football team into the NFL for the upcoming 1926 season. Red drew over three hundred and fifty thousand fans on our recent tour that finished up last month in Seattle. The only question you should be asking yourselves, including the Giants, is what date you'll fit into our schedule. Which of you doesn't want half the gate to play Red and The Yankees?"

All of the owners would, except one.

"I remind you that I have the exclusive rights to New York City," Mara says, flashing his agreement. "That's why I bought the Giants. That's the only reason. For exclusivity. Pyle, put your team anywhere else, and the Giants will be the first to schedule a game with you. Otherwise, absolutely not. Never in New York."

"You are all businessmen," Pyle says to the room. "The biggest market needs the biggest player. If the NFL had Babe Ruth, this league would be bigger than baseball and any other sport in America combined. Football draws the largest crowds. We've proved it on the tour. End of story."

Mara stands and points at Pyle. "The agreement I hold in my hand is the end of the story."

"You're supposed to be a bookie," Pyle shouts back, now also standing. "Your argument has bad odds to go along with your teams' filthy play."

Mara starts to climb over the table. Pyle climbs over even faster to meet Mara in the middle until Red and the other large men in the room hold them both back.

Carr knows all the other owners, even Halas, welcome the idea of the Yankees in the NFL. Every possible compromise is posed to Mara by the other owners, but he won't budge. Every time they call a vote, Mara exercises his legal veto right to prevent a Yankees football franchise.

Carr thinks to himself, *I'd rather step out in the alley. Maybe rustle up some cats. That sounds more fun.*

Later in the hotel...

A few of the NFL owners corner Red.

"Play in Newark. Play in New Jersey. Play in Brooklyn," they plead. "Play for Halas even in Chicago. Halas says he'll continue to give you a cut of the gate. You have to help us make this work. The league needs you."

"I'm with Pyle on this," Red says. "No player can play forever, but a team lives on. It's a long-term income strategy for us. New York is the tops. It's just good business."

The owners can't argue with that, but they can plead their case to Commissioner Carr to overrule Mara, which they run off to do. What Red didn't say is that it has been his and Pyle's plan the entire time to have their own team.

All Red wants to do is finish the movie he's committed to shooting in California and get back home to Chicago. He's about to head up to his room when he gets tapped on the back once again.

"Und the Coliseum game in Los Angeles," a familiar voice says to him.

Red turns around and can hardly believe his eyes. Zuppke is standing right in front of him with Illinois Athletic Director George Huff.

"I was there. Fannie, too," Zuppke continues. "I saw you, Halas, Joey, Earl, und my other boys play. All of whom betrayed me. Eight of my former Illinois boys were on that field."

"I thought I saw you," Red says, smiling. "But I can't believe you are here."

"I'm here to propose a truce," Zuppke explains.

"With me?"

"No. A truce with the godforsaken professional piece of shit NFL league you've associated yourself with."

"What kind of truce?"

"That's between Commissioner Carr und me," Zuppke says. "But I will tell you something about the game I saw in Los Angeles."

"I think I know what you're going to say."

"Where's the blocking, for Christ's sake?" Zuppke barks, throwing his body and knocking Red back into the wall. "Didn't I teach you boys anything? Anything at all?"

Red asks himself that very same question every day.

CHAPTER 45

Losing 3-0 with one minute to play, Parmalee University finally has the ball back with their season on the line. Bundled fans huddle together in the packed stands, battling blizzard conditions in support of their beloved team.

Sally is so nervous she can barely watch, fingers over her face, daring only on occasion to allow her eyes to peek through.

Pal, her dog and best friend, wags his tail next to her. He jumps as high as his little legs allow, trying desperately to view the game.

Parmalee's coach paces back and forth, struggling with the knowledge that the one boy who can win this game is on his bench. He desperately looks up in the stands at the university's president, who cedes the decision to the man next to him—the boy's father.

The wealthy father is resolute, shaking his head. He holds a one hundred thousand dollar endowment check in his hand and refuses to turn it over if his boy steps one foot on the field. He mouths words.

Title Card: "College is about education, not playing children's games."

The coach bows his head in surrender.

Biff, the best player on the other team, is destroying Parmalee, tackling players left and right. The season is surely over with each tick of the game clock.

The boy on the bench is conflicted. His team needs him. His school needs him. His coach needs him. His father is glaring at him. He's at a loss for what to do until he feels a tiny nip at his leg. He looks down.

It's Pal!

Pal tugs and tugs and then motions for the boy to look up into the stands. He sees Sally, the girl of his dreams. She's smiling, mouthing words.

Title Card: "Play for me. Forget your father. Forget the money. Play for me."

That's enough for the boy.

To hell with his father. To hell with the president of the university. To hell with the money. He plays for something bigger. He plays for love.

The crowd goes crazy as the boy stands and puts himself in the game.

Sally cheers the loudest, followed by Pal, barking and jumping on the sidelines and leading the crowd to its feet.

There's only time for one more play. Parmalee University has twenty yards to go. They draw up the play, and the boy lines up against Biff.

Biff wears number 33. The boy wears 77.

The ball is hiked. The Parmalee quarterback drops back to pass. He throws the ball as far as he can before disappearing under the crash of the opposing team.

Numbers 33 and 77 are sprinting, side by side, bumping into each other, battling for position under the ball. Pal runs alongside them on the sidelines, barking, struggling to keep up.

Sally mouths words.

Title Card: "Go, Red. Go, 77."

The coach mouths words.

Title Card: "Catch it, Red."

The university president desperately waves him off.

Title Card: "No, Red."

Red Wade takes the briefest of moments while battling with Biff to glance up at his father in the stands.

His wealthy father, John Wade, never fully understood this silly game, that is, until now.

Despite his previous threats and demands, the father hands the one hundred thousand dollar check over to the university's president and mouths words.

Title Card: "I've done you a great injustice, Red. You're wanted out there. There's not a second to lose. Go on, son. Fight! Fight!"

As the final seconds tick off the clock, his father's support is all Red needs.

Red Wade digs in and gains a step on Biff, leaping up for the ball.

Pal has kept up with him, barking and wagging his tail from the sideline.

A smile forms on the coach's face.

The university president grips his new endowment check.

Defeat begins to envelop Biff.

Red Wade's father beams with pride.

Sally's eyes fill with tears.

Just as Red flies into the end zone and the ball is landing safely in his grip...the dog, having run out on the field, trips him.

Red Grange and Wildcat Wilson slam into the ground without the ball. They both look down to see the little dog's jaw locked onto Red's pants.

"Cut! Cut!" the director, Sam Wood, yells. "That damn dog. Reset everyone. Dammit. Reset all the cameras."

Red and Wilson burst out laughing. They look ridiculous lying there, both wearing lipstick with makeup smeared all over their faces, wearing their famous jersey numbers. It's especially funny to them now that the dog does what it was supposed to: lick Red's face once he hits the ground.

The lead actress, Mary McAllister, who plays Sally, just turned 18. This is her thirty-sixth film. She's heard adults on movie sets say they hate working with kids. But dogs, in her opinion, are far worse.

The crowd is frustrated, too. They were suckered here today by an advertisement C.C. Pyle ran in the *Los Angeles Times* reading, "See Red Grange play Wildcat Wilson. Free admission to those wearing a winter coat," despite the eighty-degree California sun.

On the sidelines, Pyle pats little Jack Kennedy on the back. Jack loves this film. It has his hero, Red Grange; football action; and a cute dog. He's in heaven. Pyle then leans over to Jack's father.

"So, Joe, is the game of football growing on you?" Pyle asks.

"I admit, it might be," Joe replies.

As the production crew resets to run the scene over again, Red has barely gotten back up when a mob of reporters and cameramen break onto the set and rush up to him.

"Red! Red!" they shout until the loudest of them crowds out the others. "Did you hear? Did you hear the NFL Commissioner's decision? He sided with Tim Mara and the Giants. The Yankees will not be permitted into the NFL. Mara is boasting that your Yankees team has been outlawed."

Pyle inserts himself into the mob, shielding Red from the reporters.

"Red's aware," Pyle says. "We learned late last night."

"So what team is he going to play for next year?" a reporter asks.

"Why, the football Yankees, of course," Pyle replies to the confusion of the reporters. "We're forming a competing league to the NFL this fall. The Yankees will be our anchor team in New York City, and the other teams will be in major markets as well. That's our only comment on our new league at this time. Except, I like how Mara called us 'outlaws.' Catchy. Now, let's get off the field so Sam Wood can keep shooting *One Minute to Play*, a major motion picture arriving this fall in time for our new Outlaw League to take the field."

Pyle ushers the media off the field. The reporters ask more questions until one voice drowns out the others.

"What about the NFL's new Red Grange Rule? Will you honor it in your league, too?" a reporter asks.

"Is that what the press is calling it? The Red Grange Rule?" he says, smiling. "I love it. Yes, I suspect we'll also agree to refrain from signing college players until after they graduate."

As Red walks back to re-film the scene, he realizes that if that rule had been in place, he'd be wearing a winter coat in Champaign right now, finishing his last semester of college. Zuppke, the genius, brokered this new rule at the owners meeting as part of his "truce". They don't call Zuppke a genius for nothing, Red thinks to himself. Only a mind like his could find a way for both college and professional football to flourish.

The NCAA's lawyers also cleared up another ambiguity by amending its bylaws. Amateur athletes now risk losing eligibility by profiting from their athletic fame.

Red will always miss playing for the little man. He's also going to miss suiting up in orange and blue and playing for Halas and the other guys on the Bears. He's even going to miss the budding rivalry with the Giants.

But why would Mara allow a competing league to form? Why start a war?

At that moment, Red realizes Mara must have somehow known the original plan to form their own league after the Yankees complete a successful year in the NFL. He must have known they were planning to start not just a new team but something bigger. It's the only explanation for why he would risk starting a war.

Bookies always know the odds, but he would have to have perfect information to be that confident.

Or a spy.

Red's mind goes back to when he stepped off the elevator after the Ohio State game and saw Polly with Mara. Then he recalls that when Wilson signed with Pyle for more games and this movie, Wilson told Red, "She left. Gone. Vanished."

All along, Mara has been trying to sign as many All-Americans as possible for the Giants.

Red suddenly stops walking. Not just because he's put all this together, but for a different reason. As much as audiences are going to love Pal, the damn dog is back to nipping at his pants.

CHAPTER 46

Outside the hotel in Chicago, before Red will even allow Helen to take a seat, she has to listen to all the features of his new toy: a Stutz Bearcat roadster.

"First, I like to point out its short wheelbase," Red says. "One hundred and twenty inches."

"Compact. Agile," she replies.

"Raised center hood. Longitudinal ridges. Sloping sides."

"Some call it a doghouse hood," she adds. "Standard. Smart."

Red gives her a side glance, realizing she may know a thing or two.

"High radiator," he says.

"Adding a touch of elegance while channeling even more airflow to the engine."

"Cylindrical fuel tank."

"Located in the rear. Easy access. Functional yet visually interesting to the design," she adds.

"Monocle windshield."

"Offering some protection, yet promoting the pleasure of windblown hair."

"Wire wheels."

"Charm, in contrast to the curves of the bodywork."

"Orange."

"Custom. Oskee-wow-wow! Go, Illini! Factory colors are red, yellow, or blue."

"Open cockpit."

"Exposed bucket seats invite adventure, creating thrilling connections to the open road."

"Does it have an engine?" he asks.

"I'm glad you asked," she replies. "Sixty horsepower. Multi-valve. Four per cylinder. Robust construction. Strong performance. An eight-cylinder model is rumored to be in production. Four is plenty for now. It's probably all you can handle."

"Okay, okay," Red says to her. "That's enough. What's going on here? You memorized the brochure, I take it? You know everything about this car."

"Not everything."

"What don't you know?"

"I don't know how it drives."

She hops into the driver's seat, puts on goggles, and revs the engine.

He's too dumbfounded to move.

"You going to get in? Or do you need me to get out and help you?" she says.

Red holds on for dear life as Helen races through the streets of Chicago. The only help she needs from him are directions to where they are going as she accelerates into every turn, tests the suspension on straightaways, passes Model-Ts, and floors it every chance she gets.

Riding in the passenger seat instead of driving allows Red to enjoy the landscape shifting from busy city to rolling countryside. There's no point in conversation. Neither of them would be able to hear each other over the engine and the wind if they tried. Besides, opening one's mouth, even a millimeter, invites insects.

Already having one full professional season completed, not to mention having finished principal photography on a film, Red's recently lived a lifetime of memories. Watching Helen master this car, however, tops them all.

Red's father and brother are working on three new cars in the driveway of a two-story mansion just outside of Wheaton.

All four garage doors are open to a building connected to the house that isn't just the garage but a recently outfitted autobody and repair shop.

Lyle and Garland look up, hearing the Bearcat come screaming up the drive and skidding to a halt just a few feet in front of them. They've seen Red come roaring in several times already since his return from California, but never this aggressively. As shocking as the length of the skid is to them, it's even more so when they discover Red in the passenger seat, white-knuckled.

An adorable brunette pops out of the driver's seat and lifts her goggles, exposing the only natural color on her mostly dirt-covered face.

"Mr. Grange, you guys have a powder room in this place? Or is it just one big bachelor pad?" Helen asks.

Lyle walks her into the house, but not before he sneaks a look back at Garland and mouths, "I like her."

Garland does too. Red's still sitting in the car.

"That's the coat check girl?" Garland asks him.

"I'm not positive any longer," Red says, finally mustering the courage to release the handles.

Helen cleans up and helps Lyle fry chicken and mash some potatoes in their brand-new kitchen, which is stocked full of pots, pans, and utensils that Helen can tell have never been used. Lyle has a cook and housekeeper scheduled to start next week.

The kitchen and garage remodels aren't the only modifications they've made to the house since Red's been on tour. Lyle and Garland also turned the entire first floor into a bachelor parlor, complete with a full bar, poker tables, leather couches, and a pool table.

When it's time for dinner, Helen makes the guys go back into the washroom twice to get the grease off their hands before joining her at the table. Then she forces them to say grace before they dig in.

"So, Helen, Red told us you have a kid," Garland says, one bite into the meal.

Everyone nearly spits out their food.

"We're just gonna dive right in then. Okay, I see how it works in this family, here we go," Helen replies. "I was sixteen when my son brought joy to my life and to the world. He's a prince. His name is Norman."

If Garland wasn't still recovering from his surgery, Lyle and Red would both send him flying across the room for his rudeness.

"And Red told me something about you, Garland. He told me the Bears gave you a nickname," she says, looking directly at him. "Pinky. Which I understand to mean, 'Not quite Red.'"

Lyle really does spit out his food this time. Red has never seen his father laugh so hard, all three hundred pounds of him convulsing.

"Oh, before I forget," Helen says, "I brought dessert."

As soon as she leaves the room, both Red and Lyle reach over and punch Garland on his good arm. Helen comes back, holding her handbag.

"Just so you know, I'm capable of making all types of pies, cakes, and the like. But the one feature Red's new Bearcat doesn't have is a trunk. So I brought these."

Helen reaches into her bag and hands each of the men a candy bar. The guys crack up seeing Red on the wrapper, holding a football and avoiding a tackle.

Helen quotes the radio commercial: "'Red Grange Candy Bars. Only 5 cents each. Perfect for social gatherings of all sizes.'"

"'Milk chocolate,'" Garland adds, continuing the commercial. "'Plus nuts.'"

"'Not just a confection,'" Lyle continues, "'but a souvenir.'"

"'Another fine product from Shotwell's in...,'" Helen says, waiting for the guys to join her.

"'Chicago, Illinois,'" they all finish to great laughter at Red's expense.

Red rolls his eyes. "Very funny."

"I think they're delicious," Helen says, taking a bite. "All the girls at the hotel buy them, but not just for the chocolate. They pin the wrappers up on their walls."

"Is that right?" Lyle says.

"Well, look at Red's hips there in the photo," Garland cuts in. "Look at that swivel."

Garland gyrates his hips until Lyle stares him down.

"Well, they're going to need to sell train loads of these to pay for that crazy football league Pyle is organizing," Lyle says. "Seriously, Harold, that is the riskiest damn thing I ever heard. A New York Yankees football team? Taking on the NFL? You just made this money. You better not lose it all propping up your new league. And I like that Halas fellow. Why not just ask him for a piece of the Bears?"

"Halas wouldn't accept an ownership deal, Dad," Red says. "Believe me, I tried. I really like him. And I love his team."

"He probably didn't want to be in business with C.C. Pyle," Lyle replies, to which Red doesn't answer.

"So you're moving to New York then?" Helen asks, bringing the mood down even further.

"I live here," Red answers. "Mostly, I live in hotels, but Chicago is my home. I even lined up my old ice route for the summer."

Helen can't believe it.

"You're going to drive your Stutz Bearcat to work at the ice house?" she says.

"I'm not posed like that on that candy bar for fun," Red says. "I'm avoiding getting killed. I need the ice truck to stay fit. Garland's going to join me. We're going to get ole Pinky back in shape. I have two more years of football. I'd prefer not to be dead when this is all over."

"Or broke," Lyle adds.

CHAPTER 47

Children, on their parents' shoulders, point up at the two-story tall marquee of their sweatered hero. Number 77 towers over Broadway in moleskin pants and a leather helmet.

Flashbulbs at the ready, paparazzi and autograph seekers jostle for position. Men with slicked-back pomade hair, clouded in cigarette smoke, fight to hold their spots against velvet ropes. Their dates, shimmering in silk, adjust cloche hats and peer down the street, vying for a view.

A collective hush falls over the scene as a sleek black limousine rolls up, slowly gliding to a stop. The car door opens. The paparazzi erupt in a frenzy of clicks and flashes. The crowd holds its breath.

Out steps movie star Mary McAllister, a goddess draped in sequins and fur. With practiced grace, she radiates glamor and fame, ignoring the disappointment of the fans' faces, especially the children looking past her, hoping for someone else.

Maintaining a professional yet forced smile, she anticipates the crowd's imminent transformation from politeness to hysteria, questioning why she ever agreed to be in this picture. At that moment, gasps of awe and excited screams fill the air. Mary McAllister might as well have vanished as the auburn hair of the real star appears.

Across the street, up in a conference room, looking down on the scene, the owners of all nine new American Football League teams assemble around a large circular table. Pyle holds court with Red's glorious face shining on the marquee across the street behind him.

"The problem with the NFL isn't just that they lack vision. Or that they lack a star," he says. "It's where they play."

Placards placed on the tables in front of each AFL owner read: "New York," "Chicago," "Boston," "Philadelphia," "Los Angeles," "Brooklyn," "Newark," "Cleveland," and, for some reason, "Rock Island."

"Outside of the Giants and Bears," Pyle says, "I couldn't even find most of the NFL cities on a map."

The men in the room break into laughter.

"We have the greatest player to ever play football on our New York Yankees team."

Cheers ring out around the table.

"We have Wildcat Wilson on our Los Angeles team."

More cheers.

"The Four Horsemen, or two of them anyway, along with Earl Britton, on our Brooklyn team."

More cheers.

"Joey Sternamen," Pyle says, motioning to Joey sitting at the table, "has defected from the Bears and the NFL to be the owner, coach, and star of our Chicago Bulls."

More cheers, which Joey graciously accepts.

"We got all the big stars, except, of course, The Big Dog, Ernie Nevers," Pyle says to boos from the room. "Tim Mara and his cronies outmaneuvered us there. But we'll get The Big Dog next year and our pick of the litter when the NFL folds."

Louder cheers ring out. The men clink drinks. They are living the dream.

Suddenly, a flash of lightning blinds everyone in the room, followed by a boom of thunder so strong it rattles the windows down Broadway.

"Let's hustle over to the movie theater before we drown," Pyle says. "I've got a seat reserved for each of you. You're gonna love this picture. They're already calling our boy the next Rudy Valentino. It's all coming together, my friends."

The new league hustles to cross busy Broadway, getting soaked head to toe, every single one of them.

CHAPTER 48

(Upbeat intro music plays and then fades.)

Good evening, sports fans, and welcome once again to the National Sports Syndicated Report! I'm your host, Grantland Rice! We're brought to you tonight by our friends at Ovaltine—the delicious and nutritional drink, making young athletes strong and their mothers proud!

(Sound of powder being stirred into milk, with a tap of a spoon on the side of a glass.)

Rush down today to your local grocer and grab a tin of Ovaltine! Don't delay! Remember, you can tell when someone's been on the Ovaltine!

(Sound of galloping men on the field, tackling each other, hitting the ground, cheering crowd, whistles.)

Now, snap your jerseys tight and hold onto your helmets here tonight because we're diving headfirst into the gridiron's greatest grudge match.

(Ding! Ding!)

Ladies and Gentlemen, in one corner the reigning champ, the NFL—the National Football League.

(Sound of a crowd cheering.)

In the other corner, the audacious upstarts, the outlaws, the AFL—the American Football League!

(Sound of a crowd cheering.)

Let's set the stage, shall we? The 1926 season's final whistle has blown here in December, and the dust has settled, revealing a battlefield littered with fallen giants and wounded patriots.

Every team in both leagues has tasted a form of defeat, their banners stained with the inevitable sweat and financial woes of two heavyweights going toe to toe, trading blow after blow, both too stubborn to fall.

Yet, the greatest enemy this past fall was neither pugilist. It was neither the NFL nor the AFL. Something more sinister plagued arenas.

(Spooky sounds.)

What was it?

(Dramatic pause.)

Rain. That's right, the weather.

(Sound of lightning, thunder, and heavy rain.)

Every Sunday, the skies opened up. Torrential downpours flooded the battlefields and dammed the stands. Noah, himself, would have drowned.

(Cries of "Oh no.")

Attendance decreased, then dwindled, then vanished.

(Somber music plays, transitioning into morning birds chirping.)

The skies cleared each Monday, only to reveal another team or two on either side had folded, merged, or worse.

(Soft playing of *Taps* on a trumpet.)

Rest in peace to these NFL franchises: Akron, Brooklyn, Canton, Columbus, Hammond, Hartford, Louisville, Milwaukee, and Racine.

Rest in peace to the AFL's: Philadelphia, Los Angeles, Cleveland, Boston, Newark, Brooklyn, and, how'd they get in there in the first place, Rock Island.

Not to mention the tragic loss of Joey Sternamen and his Chicago Bulls, forced into…

(Shouts of "No!")

…bankruptcy. Poor Joey gambled and lost his entire savings.

(Cries of anguish and despair, silence, and then sounds of a whistle.)

A ceasefire has been called. Both sides walk white flags to the center of the field. Smoke clears from the cannons.

What's left, you say? Who is still alive? Only a few shining beacons.

(Sound of a hush forming over a crowd.)

In the hallowed halls of the NFL, the Chicago Bears remain gallant, their roar echoing through the land, no longer just a team but now a brand of football to stand the test of time.

(Soft strokes of triumphant trumpets.)

Alongside the Bears, their NFL brother, a battered Giants team, lives on, having the distinction of winning the most games but losing the most coin.

Of twenty-two teams that started the NFL season...only ten remain.

(Soft strokes of a harp, silence.)

And still standing in the scrappy, upstart AFL? Nine brave warriors braved the storm, but eight tragically fell, leaving but one.

(Silent pause.)

Is it the Yankees, you ask? Is it Red? Does our hero still walk among the living? Has he perished? Surely not? Tell us. Tell us!

(Suspenseful music.)

He's alive! Red's alive! Stronger than ever.

(Cheers of relief.)

The New York Yankees, led by the Galloping Ghost himself, live on.

(Sounds of triumph.)

Our hero stands as tall as his movie marquees, a warrior barely scratched. His legend prevails, having conquered attendance records in every city despite the rain. Not to mention, his movie was a box-office smash. Who didn't love Pal, the dog?

(Sounds of a small dog barking.)

Red's only blemish: bare coffers. You see, dear friends, the eight fallen AFL teams were financed by him and his agent, C.C. Pyle.

(Cries of "oh no," anguish and despair, silence, and then sounds of a whistle.)

What's left to do now, you ask? Where do we stand?

By all accounts, the experts agree we're right back to where we started, down to two men: the Giants' Tim Mara, guarding his domain with the ferocity of a lion, and the sorcerer C.C. Pyle, weaving dark magic, ensnaring a spellbound Red Grange.

Both men, however, now face the reality of bank accounts thinner than a well-worn playbook.

(Sound of coins trickling, a mournful horn playing.)

With Fall behind us, trench lines have been dug, advanced, retreated, re-dug, and returned back to where they started. What we have is an old-fashioned stalemate.

NFL Commissioner Joe Carr, desperate to avoid further carnage, has called for a parley, begging the two stubborn pugilists, Mara and Pyle, who wouldn't shake hands holding ice tongs, to come to the negotiating table.

(Sound of a gavel striking, a calling of order.)

Can these adversaries forge a treaty? Can reason prevail over the primal urge for victory? Or will the flames of this conflict continue to flicker, leaving empty stadiums, shattered dreams, and insolvency in its wake?

(Pregnant pause.)

You'll have to tune in next week, dear listeners, for another chapter in this grand gladiatorial spectacle.

Remember, as you head out to face your Monday morning battles, fuel your inner warrior with a refreshing glass of Ovaltine! Isn't it time you woke up to Ovaltine?

This was the National Sports Syndicated Report. I'm Grantland Rice, signing off until next time.

Good night, and good sports!

(Outro music, a blend of string quartet and classical piano, slight roar of fans, fades out.)

CHAPTER 49

NFL Commissioner Joseph Carr attempts to lighten the mood at the negotiations by setting an ornate wooden clock on the table in front of him.

Even Mara and Pyle smile at the reference to the Treaty of Versailles, which was negotiated at the French Foreign Ministry's office in the Salle de l'Horloge, otherwise known as the Clock Room.

"I solicited help from nearly everyone I know to construct the peace treaty I'm holding in my hand," Carr says. "I've consulted with all the remaining NFL team owners, along with the Mayor of New York, the Commissioner of baseball, the owners of the Polo Grounds and Yankee Stadium, and even the President of the United States."

That elicits chuckles because the President of the United States part isn't true; everyone knows Coolidge is not a football fan. But they believe the rest. Carr passes out a multipage proposal to both sides.

"As you'll see, the Giants and the Yankees will never play a game on the same weekend in New York," Carr says. "Mara, you'll never be at risk of having competing games going on at the same time across town from each other. And, Pyle, you'll play each other twice, once at the Polo Grounds and once at Yankee Stadium. Meaning, you'll each have a home game against the other. Once the regular season is over, you can play each other as much as you like."

Carr appears pleased with himself, looking over the faces of Pyle and Mara, awaiting their response as they each flip through the proposal.

"Unlike the Treaty of Versailles, we feel this proposal is elegant, simple, and fair to both parties," Carr says. "It ends the war, but not the Giants-Yankees rivalry. Our hope is this matchup outlasts all of our lifetimes, leading to sold-out stadiums for your heirs."

Pyle and Mara have each finished reviewing the document.

"I trust you both agree?" Carr says, gripping the clock, praying the hands are about to tick forward toward a resolution.

Neither Pyle nor Mara desires to be the first to speak. After what seems like the longest timeout in sports history, Pyle finally reveals his winning smile.

"Let's play ball," he says.

Mara, on the other hand, turns toward Carr with a frown.

"Where's my compensation for allowing a second team within my territorial rights?" he asks. "I see nothing."

The other owners sigh.

"Tim, come on," Carr says. "This is a fair deal. And one that is good for the league."

"I don't represent the league," Mara replies. "That's your job. My job is to continue the success of the Giants, who, I might add, just won the NFL Championship in only our second season."

"Not if you had played the Yankees," Pyle interjects.

"I offered to play you," Mara says. "NFL versus AFL. It would have been bigger than the Rose Bowl."

"Scheduling conflicts," Pyle replies.

"Bullshit," Mara says. "You wanted an advance because you were out of cash to pay your players."

"Gentlemen, gentlemen," Carr says, gripping the clock with two hands. "For the betterment of the sports world, the fans, and the players, let's consider my proposal."

"What's to stop me from running off and starting my own league?" Mara replies. "The Giants are the premiere team now."

"What's to stop me from scheduling independent teams to play the Yankees every Sunday this fall in New York," Pyle says. "Without Red Grange, you'd have nothing."

"Without Red Grange, you are nothing," Mara says. "My sources tell me that your contract with him has an expiration date on it. You only have one more year. Maybe he'd prefer to be a Giant after that?"

Carr notices Pyle's hands closing into fists.

"Timothy," the commissioner says directly to Mara, "the owners have discussed it. I fear they might pick the Yankees over the Giants if you start another war."

Now Mara's fists clench.

"However, the owners also want me to uphold your territorial rights because the others wouldn't want to lose their rights either," the commissioner continues. "Thus, I have prepared an alternate agreement."

He passes out a surprise set of documents. The Germans got a bad deal at Versailles; however, Carr prays an idea suggested by a brilliant little German will end this war.

He watches as Pyle and Mara each run their fingers over a new concept where Mara would technically own the Yankees franchise, but Pyle would control it.

Or, as Zuppke called it, "a long-term *leaze*."

CHAPTER 50

Red balances a picnic basket on his lap, holding on for dear life in the passenger seat of his Stutz Bearcat.

When he's not thinking about Helen's aggressive driving, he has time to reflect on the last few months leading to the start of what he expects to be his third and final professional season. His additional games against Wildcat Wilson in California were a success. Completing principal photography on his new "Racing Romeo" was an adventure, and he loved working with Garland on the ice route all summer, building Garland's strength to return to school to play for Zuppke.

He snaps back to reality as Helen skids to a halt in a secluded spot near Chicago's Swan Pond Waterfall Overlook. After laying out a blanket and lunch, Helen admits, "Yes, my mother packed this picnic for us."

Red has assumed as much, given the hints of Lillian all over it—green bean casserole, mashed potatoes, and two slices of apple pie.

"Did she pack these too?" Red asks, noticing a pile of newspaper clippings at the bottom of the basket.

Helen doesn't respond, eating her food as Red flips through the clippings from the past year. It doesn't take but a few of them for Red to recognize a theme.

The clippings are of him photographed with just about every actress who has ever starred in a movie. He's also featured at dinners with tennis player Suzanne Lenglen and other female athletes while he was on tour. There's one of him

267

practicing the Charleston with Marion Davies. Another of him balancing swimsuit models on both of his shoulders. There's even a photo of him shirtless, hammering a shoe on a horse.

Circled, however, are dozens of gossip columns outlining his rumored relationships, including lawsuits in which he's mentioned as the cause of divorce, fines for speeding, a story of Garland being sued over an auto accident, and another about him and three other teammates being arrested for disturbing the peace in a hotel room.

There's also a series of photos of Red next to piles of large mailbags with a caption that reads, "Red Grange receives 200,000 letters a year. Most of them from admiring women."

The clippings culminate with the most concerning one of all, an article about his rumored engagement to Mary McAllister, the lead actress in his movie. It even includes guesses about the wedding dresses she's considering and the flavor of the wedding cake.

Helen continues eating her lunch as Red reads through the stack.

"I'm trained to deny, deny, deny," he says. "But I must admit to something."

She looks up at him with a mouthful of food, motioning as if to say, "Let's hear it."

"I'm in love with that horse," he says. "She's a fine filly. Smooth. Shoes real nice."

Helen makes a face as if to say, "Very funny."

"And I think Mary's and my wedding cake flavor should be something special, you know," Red says. "Chocolate, maybe. Better yet, red velvet. Get it, red? Red velvet."

Dumb joke, but a slight smile creeps across Helen's face.

"But I support her dress ideas," Red continues. "The ones she picked out are all very California. Traditional yet modern. Practical lace. Your take?"

"I think she would look gorgeous in anything."

"There's just one problem with our *fake engagement* created by *publicists* baiting *paparazzi* to sell movie tickets," he says. "In real life, Mary McAllister hates dogs. I loved Pal. I even negotiated for him to be prominent on the movie poster for my next film, *Racing Romeo*. Wait until you see it. I appear to be in love with the girl, but if you look closely, I'm really making eyes at the dog."

"Lovely, I can't wait to watch another movie of you kissing girls while longing for animals."

She always cracks him up.

"Tell your mother I brought something to ambush you with as well," he says, digging around in his suit pockets until pulling out a jewelry box. "It's just a bracelet and a necklace to start."

He opens the box and takes out a beautiful, expensive aquamarine pendant and matching bracelet with rows of stones woven into a pattern complementing six radiant circles. The pendant's silver setting cradles the queen of all aquamarines.

"One more year," he says, placing them on her. "I just need to get the Yankees off the ground this season in the merged NFL, and I will have completed my agreement with Pyle. And then, that's that."

She inspects the jewelry, hiding the fact that she's never seen anything like it outside of the fanciest stores in Chicago.

"Why do you need a year?" she asks. "You're always planning. 'I need to wait for this.' 'I need to wait for that.' Why not live life? What are you waiting for? You're always lost in the future. What's so wrong with the present?"

Red suddenly realizes that he never considers what he's achieved versus what he hasn't.

"You're right," he says. "What's wrong with me? I've been fixated on the future for years. That needs to change. It has to change."

"Speaking of the present," she says, motioning to the jewelry. "You picked this out all by yourself?"

"I did. I went to a store and everything. What do you think?"

He searches her face for a reaction. At first, she plays coy, then she pushes him down on the blanket and pins him to the ground.

"I love it," she says, giving him a huge kiss, aggressively smearing lipstick all over his mouth and face.

He playfully pushes her away to wipe it off.

"By the way, I found out in the movies they have girls to put lipstick on for me," he says.

"I bet they do," she says, teasingly punching him in the gut before pinning him back down again. "And after the season ends, Mr. Grange, gossip columnists demand to know what's next? What's after that? Any other fine fillies catch your eye?"

"After that?" he says. "After next season? You just told me to focus on the present."

"Good point," she replies, pinning him down even harder.

CHAPTER 51

New York Yankees at Chicago Bears
Sunday, October 16, 1927

A few months later, Lyle and Garland save two seats at the recently named Wrigley Field in Chicago as they watch the Bears warm up on the field in front of a sell-out crowd of thirty thousand fans on a brisk Sunday, two years after Red played his last college game.

Up in the press box, Warren was tasked with the seating chart. He broke tradition by assigning local reporters like himself to the front and relegating Grantland Rice and all the other national guys to the back.

"Make yourself comfortable in the rear," he enjoys saying to the out-of-town reporters. "Chicago is my town."

Warren arranges his usual station with typewriter, notebooks, binoculars, and pencils, minus one thing—his ashtray. He gave up his aspirations to write at the national level. Turns out he's a journalist at heart, not an entertainer. Thus, he no longer smokes, finding it much easier to keep stats and notes without the risk of burning his crotch and polluting his soul.

Lyle's and Garland's faces light up as they stand to make room for their two guests—the Zuppkes.

"You must be in heaven," Fannie Zuppke says to Lyle. "You got to watch Garland play college ball yesterday and now Harold today."

"And both undefeated," Lyle says. "Zup, could this be another national championship run?"

"Until the season is over," Zuppke says, "I never make predictions."

It takes Lyle a moment to recognize the humor in that response. All thirty thousand fans suddenly leap to their feet the moment the Yankees take the field. Moments later, fingers begin pointing as the crowd spots Number 77 with his trademark auburn hair dressed in red, white, and blue.

Red diverts from his Yankees team for a moment to shake hands with Halas, who is also in uniform.

"Welcome home," Halas says. "Look around, it must feel good to still be the Golden Lad."

"Nah, they root for the Bears," Red says. "So do I."

Suddenly, orange-sweatered arms wrap around him from behind and lift him into the air. For a moment, Red's worried he's about to be body slammed into the ground until bruiser George Trafton, laughing hysterically, releases him.

"No Earl?" Trafton says, looking around. "Who's going to save you from me?"

"The Yankees couldn't afford him," Red says. "I played him in Dayton the other day. He told me only one game matters this year. When he plays you in a few weeks."

"I can handle Earl," Trafton says. "If you had shown up with Clem, I'd be worried."

"He's here somewhere," Red says, motioning back into the tunnel.

"By the way, Wildcat says hello from Providence," Trafton says. "And The Big Dog says howdy from Duluth. It's an old friend every week these days. No need for the draft they've been discussing. With so few teams, everyone has an All-American now."

Just then, another Bears player gives Red a hug.

"Welcome back," Joey says.

"I always liked you in orange," Red says to him.

"Halas here gave me a spot after the Bulls folded," Joey says. "That's the good news. The bad news is he also demoted me."

Joey points to Paddy Driscoll warming up for the Bears. Halas couldn't pass up on arguably the best passer and punter in the game in the reshuffling of players after the NFL contracted. The upside of the smaller league is all the teams have better players.

"I'm going to let you in on a little secret for our game plan today," Halas says.

"Let me guess?" Red says. "Same as the other teams. You passed a jar around to knock me out?"

"No," Halas says. "Right, Trafton?"

"I may forget here and there," Trafton says, "but right. Right, coach. Clean ball today."

"Our game plan is very simple," Halas says to Red. "Make Zuppke proud."

"That's going to have to be a lifetime goal for me," Red replies, looking over at his family, Zup, and Fannie in the stands.

Over in the tunnel...

"Just this one time, old friend," Pyle says, pleading with Clem. "It doesn't get more beautiful than this. Join me on the field. What do you say?"

Clem takes a long look at the fresh sod, capacity crowd, and the field littered with more success than he ever dreamed possible for Pyle.

"Just give me a moment," Clem says. "I'm thinking about it. I'm working up the will."

Pyle understands. He straightens his suit, regrips his cane, and adjusts his green tie.

"We did it, my friend. We did it," Pyle says, stepping out into the sunlight.

Clem watches Pyle run out onto the field, waving to the fans. Clem musters his courage to put a single foot out into the light, but he still can't do it, choosing to stay hidden in the shadows.

In another corner the field...

The maintenance gate bends until it violently snaps, allowing five thousand gatecrashers to flood the sidelines

Despite pleas from Halas, Pyle, the police, and the announcements on the loudspeaker, the free-loading fans won't budge. Eventually, at least, Wrigley Field workers get the gate back up, preventing more people out on the street from flooding in.

"We need a bigger stadium," Halas finally says to Pyle and the officers. "But, what the hell. We used to play with fans around the field all the time. We can handle it."

"We should at least charge them," Pyle pleads.

"Walk around and collect," Halas replies. "I'd love to see you try."

Once the police push the crowd back enough to play, the game goes according to Halas' plan. Paddy Driscoll, who played at Northwestern against Illinois just as Zuppke was entering the college coaching ranks, razzle dazzles the fans. Zuppke always loved watching him play, especially considering that Paddy weighs less than 150 pounds—inspiring little guys everywhere.

Late in the fourth quarter, the scoreboard reads Bears 12, Yankees 0.

The Yankees have been struggling to figure out if they should play as a team like the Bears or if they should give in and become a one-man Red Grange show. Red, of course, prefers the play-as-a-team route. When the game is on the line, however, the team strategy goes out the window.

The ball is hiked to Red, who tosses an underhand lateral to Eddie Tryon, a great player out of Colgate. Eddie takes a few steps to his right before stopping, planting his outside foot, and throwing a beautiful pass high in the air as far as he can to a completely empty downfield.

The first in the crowd to his feet is young Norman, along with his mother, Helen, watching Number 77, a blur of red, white, and blue, sprinting to meet the ball. Lyle, Garland, Zuppke, and Fannie are not far behind, rising to witness another feat of greatness.

Pyle, along with the Yankees' reserve players, breaks protocol and stands up from the bench, risking a penalty. Clem leans out of the tunnel, just to the brink of sunlight, peering through the gatecrashers, and watches the ball soar toward his corner of the field.

Red knows he's going to catch it. He's tracking the ball just fine, giving him enough time to reflect on all the choices he's made and risks he's taken leading to this moment. He has but one regret.

He thinks back to the evening just before he and Pyle entered the speakeasy two years ago. Garland was lying in pain in the hospital and his father was upset with him. He and Pyle waited in line at the florist for the little old lady to complete her purchase.

As he was looking out at the movie marquee announcing *The Freshmen*, he saw Pyle, out of the corner of his eye, stop for a moment to smell the roses.

Red never does that. He's always worried about one more year of this or one more year of that. One more big game. One more season. One more something before his life can begin.

At this moment, tracking the ball, it dawns on him that his life can begin whenever he wants it to begin, despite whatever contract he's under or whatever demands his family, sponsors, or fans place on him.

What am I waiting for?

Red leaps into the air and catches the ball. He's going to score this touchdown, kick the extra point, get the ball back,

win this game, and take Helen and Norman, his family, and the Zuppkes out to dinner. What the hell, Pyle and Clem, too.
It's time to live life.

As his foot comes down onto the turf, the bruising bulk of George Trafton crashes into him. Red's cleat catches the fresh sod, twisting his ankle as Trafton falls over his leg, redirecting his knee to an opposite angle nature never intended.

Before their bodies hit the ground, the gasps of thirty thousand fans transform from glee into despair. Red and Trafton, entangled, careen out of bounds, scattering gatecrashers and smacking against the unforgiving retaining wall.

Red has few memories after that moment, mostly just flashes of images. He recalls not being able to stand. He recalls Trafton's despondent face, profusely apologizing, tears in the killer's eyes. He recalls Halas pushing gatecrashers aside, clearing a path. He recalls the look of pure white on Pyle's face, especially in contrast to his green tie.

Most memorable, however, is Clem's determined face, braving the sunlight, effortlessly scooping Red off the ground and carrying him back inside the tunnel.

THE FOURTH QUARTER
∽ Being Red ∾

CHAPTER 52

Pyle steps out of a hospital elevator on his way to Red's room only to be mobbed by a throng of reporters and cameramen yelling out questions: "What did the doctors say?" "Will Red ever play again?" "Will Red ever walk again?"

Pyle holds out his hands to quiet them.

"Nothing, and I repeat nothing," Pyle proclaims, further commanding the attention of the reporters. "Nothing can stop a juggernaut like Red Grange. He'll be fine. Mark my words. We'll have him back on the field in Green Bay next week."

The reporters are ecstatic to hear the news, jotting down Pyle's quote.

"You mean on the field next week wearing crutches," Warren clarifies, causing the media to turn and cede him the floor. "I have a doctor on record from yesterday afternoon when Red was admitted who looked over the x-rays and told me playing next week is impossible. Red's season is over as well as his career. He'll be lucky to ever walk again."

Pyle maintains his trademark smile while staring down Warren.

"With all due respect to a young emergency room doctor relegated to work on a Sunday," Pyle replies, "the best sports doctors in America are en route now to give second, third, fourth, or as many as it takes, opinions. Even Babe Ruth is sending his personal physician from New York."

"Won't your Yankees football team fold without Red?" Warren asks. "Isn't Red all you have? Won't you go bankrupt without him?"

Pyle's face appears to waver just a smidge, yet he recovers his perfect smile.

"Red will be on the field next week in Green Bay," Pyle replies. "Buy a ticket and see for yourself."

Warren remains dubious as Pyle pushes past the reporters to the door of Red's private room. Before Pyle can open the door, Helen grabs his arm.

"They won't let me in to see him," she pleads. "They say only family can enter."

Pyle takes a good look at her, trying to register her face, and notices her eyes are puffy from worry.

"I'm Helen Morrissey," she says. "Ask Lyle. Ask Garland. They know me. I have something important to give Red."

She hands a sealed envelope to Pyle.

"Please," she says. "Will you give it to him? The nurses won't. It's important."

"Of course, my dear. Of course. Yes, Helen. Of course," Pyle says, taking the envelope and patting her on the shoulder. "Go home now. Let Red rest. I'll have him contact you as soon as he can."

She appears relieved as Pyle enters Red's room. As soon as the door shuts, Pyle's smile disappears, and he tosses the envelope into the first wastebasket he can find.

CHAPTER 53

Legion Ascot Speedway
Saturday, March 3, 1928

Red sits alone at a picnic table in sunny Santa Monica in a roped-off area of the speedway. Unshaven and wearing a wrinkled suit, all he wants is to eat his ham sandwich in peace, but Pyle's jeweled cane haunts him, leaning against the table, mocking him, glistening in the sun.

As he forces a bite of his sandwich, two hundred of the craziest of characters pass by him, but Red doesn't glance up. Among them are a long-bearded Moses, an Italian singer, wealthy college boys, a Native American wearing a white scarf over his head, an Alaskan mailman, has-been movie stars, elite European athletes, hikers, swimmers, walkers, wrestlers, marathoners, eccentrics, charlatans, and even a Hindu philosopher.

Lined up in a row behind Red is a train of automobiles, including a mobile radio transmitter, a land yacht that can hold twenty VIPs, an infirmary bus, a red sports car, and rows of trucks loaded with carnival tents, rides, freak show performers, and unsavory souls.

Five months ago, Red was playing professional football before a sold-out crowd in Chicago. Today, he's sitting under a banner that reads "C.C. Pyle's Trans-American Footrace," and next to Red's sandwich is a button with a ribbon he's to wear that reads "Grand Marshal."

He was forced to play in the Green Bay game. Handing his crutches to Clem in the tunnel and hopping out on one foot into the huddle for one play before leaving the game was the most deceitful thing he's ever done in his life.

With Red useless in that game and several more, the fans began to catch on that he was only in the starting lineup to sucker them into buying tickets. His father implored him to quit Pyle and come home, even at the risk of a lawsuit. He has remained out of obligation, becoming increasingly complicit in Pyle's desperate schemes to keep the Yankees football team afloat.

Worse than being barely able to walk, or much less run, is having not heard from Helen despite giving Pyle multiple letters to mail for him. Her abandoning him the day he became injured has been the worst pain to endure.

Snapping Red out of his malaise, three women brashly step over the rope line and approach him at the picnic table. Two of them appear to be Pyle's age, twenty-plus years older than Red. The other is a young woman about his age. All seem vaguely familiar to him, especially the boldest of the three, an expensively dressed older woman who sits uninvited in front of him at the table.

"I'm assuming you know who I am?" she says.

Red gets a better look at her, and it suddenly dawns on him.

"Margarita Fischer," he says, looking her over and then realizing the other two are Pyle's ex-wife, Dot, and daughter, Katherine.

"I asked around about you," Margarita says. "Joe Kennedy, Sam Wood, Charlie Chaplin, Marion Davies, Mary McAllister, and even Tim Mara. All of them agree that you might indeed be the nicest, humblest young man on earth. I said to them, 'I understand that's his press persona, but come on. What's he's really like?' And every one of them insists it's true. They swear it. Even Mara."

"Look," Red replies, "if you're here for a shakedown, I'm the wrong guy. C.C.'s the wrong guy, too. All the money we have left is tied up in this footrace to New York City."

"Our years of trying to get C.C. Pyle to pay his fair share are behind us," Margarita says. "The same for his second wife. Not to mention, his third wife and kids. Did you know he's still married? They live in Chicago. Not to mention all the other women along the way. They've all given up, too."

Red's expression never wavers. He's been aware of this ever since reading the contents of the manilla folder Warren handed him after he played his final college game.

"I've supported my sister and my niece this whole time and will continue to do so. That's not why we're here."

Red goes back to eating his sandwich.

"Listen to me, young man," Margarita says. "We feel it's our responsibility to tell you the same thing we told all his wives and girlfriends, even though none of them listened."

Red continues eating his sandwich, looking out at the insane scene before him on the racetrack, watching crazy contestants start to line up.

"We're here to tell you to get out," Margarita says. "Get the hell out. Walk away."

"No, don't walk away," Pyle's daughter clarifies. "Run."

"As fast as you can," Pyle's ex-wife implores.

All three of their faces demand his attention, begging him to heed their warning.

Red finishes his last bite, uses the table as leverage to stand, and steadies himself.

Katherine, Dot, and Margarita Fischer watch unshaven Red Grange, relying on Pyle's jeweled cane, limp off to obediently take his place in the line of cars.

They take in the scene as the motley crew of runners, assembling alongside the train of automobiles, embark on a 3,500-mile race designed to inaugurate the new Route 66, traversing it backward, starting in Santa Monica and culminating with the final laps to be run inside Madison Square Garden.

Nothing surprises Margarita any longer, but this latest promotion is madness, even for C.C. Pyle. These runners have assembled for the promise of fifty thousand dollars in prize money that Pyle admits he doesn't have but plans to accumulate by organizing carnivals in each town they sleep in along the way. The runners' times are to be tracked for each day's leg of the race and added up at the end. The racers will be averaging forty miles a day for eighty-four days.

Margarita watches Red limp to his seat in the red sports car and rest Pyle's ridiculous cane across his lap. She realizes she didn't need to bother warning him. If the young man could run, he would.

CHAPTER 54

*Chicago's Oriental Theater
Tuesday, October 16, 1928*

Couples on a matinee date casually settle into their seats at the Oriental, Chicago's largest movie palace, one year after Red's knee blew out.

Sharing popcorn and soda, they bide their time sitting through a twenty-minute vaudeville pre-show, waiting for the main event, *The Docks of New York,* starring George Bancroft.

The curtain goes up, revealing a painted vaudeville set with a backdrop of a college campus. Girls in college outfits scurry on stage, holding their dance cards for the big homecoming dance that evening.

"Mine's full," one says. "So is mine," another says. "Ours too," the rest say.

All of them are proud of themselves, except one sad girl, who steps forward, facing the audience with her card in her hand.

"I have one spot left," she reveals. "I'm saving it for the shyest boy at school. He just has to believe in himself, and I know the coach will put him in the homecoming game."

Just then, Red Grange is pushed out on the stage.

Theater ushers hold up signs reading "Applause," and polite cheers from the half-empty audience follow.

With zero energy, Red limps out, and reading off cue cards, he mutters through his obligatory lines, accenting all

285

the wrong syllables, and often reading stage direction out loud.

"Greatness begins with believing in yourself," he mutters. "You gotta believe you can run with the thoroughbreds before you even lace 'em up. I just need one snap, one chance to show the coach I'm worth my sweater. 'Come On, Red,' I tell myself. 'Come on'."

The organist kicks off a playful Charleston beat as the college girls break into dance. Pom-poms morph into feather boas, twirling with a wink. Cheerleading chants transform into sassy lyrics belted with playful defiance. Each flick of a tassel exudes an irresistible blend of athleticism and sensuality, playing off the original title song composed for this production, *Come On, Red*.

When the dance number finishes, stagehands push Red back onto the stage to read more lines.

"The game is on. I'm left out of the stadium. Every roar I hear from the stands is a punch to the gut. I yearn to be out on the battlefield, helmet strapped tight, teeth gritted as I razzle and dazzle past lumberin' giants…. But…but…fate, she hath dealt me a bum knee."

The cue card guy shakes his head.

"A bum hand," Red corrects. "I'm ignored by the coach. Sidelined. Look sad."

The cue card guy hates his job.

Regardless, it's harder to look any sadder than Red already does when the main girl from the opening runs out onto the stage.

"Red! Red! There you are," she says, sighing with relief. "There's been a mistake. It's the fourth quarter. The coach turned to look for you. You didn't get the message. The coach knew if anyone could find you, it would be me. I've been looking everywhere. There's but one minute to play. Come on, Red! Come on!"

The organ kicks in as she takes Red's hand and drags him across the stage. He struggles to keep up, favoring his good leg. The other actresses dance around him, holding out football pants for him to step into, a sweater to pull over his head, cleats to slide on, and, in the final moment, as the song crescendos, the main girl slips on his helmet.

Before she can give him a good luck kiss, the other dancers throw him into the game. A ball is placed in Red's hand.

The lights in the theater flash, heightening the drama. The girls bump him around. He's supposed to stiff-arm them, but he never times it right, missing. With nearly every movement, he looks like he's about to tumble over. The dancers, who are professionals, are acutely aware. They swing in at just the right time to keep him upright and moving.

The crowd noise plays as they get him to the goal line. He's reminded by a dancer to stretch out his arms as the final clock winds down. He's won the game.

Again, stagehands hold up applause signs.

In the middle of the celebration, the main girl desperately fights her way in, searching for Red, holding out her dance card.

Red fumbles with the card and begins to sign it before tossing it away. Instead, he holds her tightly in his arms, a kiss is imminent as the dancers complete their final routine, surrounding them, celebrating the win.

Just as he's about to kiss her, Pal, the dog, runs out across the stage, pausing to ham for the audience before getting a hold of Red's pant leg. The main girl scoops the dog into her arms and pretends to scold it, which gets the dog the loudest reaction from the audience.

Right before Red can finally kiss the girl, the dog gets in the way, licking his face.

Stagehands hold the applause signs even higher, but they don't need to. The audience loves it.

The actors each take their bows, with Red receiving the second loudest applause at the end, after the dog. Once the applause dies down, the other actors leave Red alone on stage to read another cue card.

"And now," Red says, choking on the words to come, "I will take your questions."

The real nightmare begins as the questions flow in.

"Red, how's the knee?"

"What was in your mind after scoring those four touchdowns against Michigan?"

"What is Mary McAllister like?"

"What's Garland up to after winning the national championship with Zuppke?"

"What do you think of Babe Ruth's sixty homeruns last season?"

"Did C.C. Pyle ever pay out the race winners?"

"Does Pyle still own the Yankees, or does Mara now?"

"Will you ever walk again without a cane?"

"What's the naughtiest thing you ever received in a letter from a fan?"

Since March, when the race took off, he has performed "Come On, Red" in more cities across the country than he knew existed, answering the same questions over and over.

At least, in Panama, he knew when the trip would be over. He's now beyond the terms of his three-year agreement with Pyle, with no end in sight, forced to answer these questions and act in this show or lose his home.

On top of this drudgery, once he leaves the stage in just a moment, he'll be hustled across town to perform the same show at the Paradise Theater before that audience watches *The Tempest* starring John Barrymore. The two theaters have generously staggered their start times, allowing his vaudeville troupe to go back and forth across town for a total of eight glorious shows a day.

Thankfully, Red calls on the last hand raised he'll have to deal with at this show. The spotlight shines into the audience before resting on a familiar face.

"Very kind of you to *finally* call on me, Mr. Grange," Helen says, now illuminated.

"Hi ya, kid," he instinctively replies, always enraptured by her adorable face before matching her seriousness. "And very kind of you to *finally* call on me."

"Is that so? Well, I do have a question for you, if you are brave enough to answer?"

"Answering questions is my new occupation."

A few chuckles rise from the audience.

"So, if I ask you a question you'll actually respond and not disappear for a year?" Helen says.

At this point, the crowd sits up, turning their heads back and forth between Helen and Red, realizing they must know each other.

"It's pretty hard for me to disappear, given I perform eight shows a day."

"Here's my question," Helen says, "but it's a doozy. I'm not sure if you can handle it."

Even the dancers and stage managers are now peering out from behind the curtains to watch their conversation.

"Let's hear it," Red says.

"My question is what type of woman would it take for the great Red Grange to settle down, get married, escape the limelight, and start a real life?" she asks.

Red stares back at her, locking his eyes on hers while the entire theater awaits the answer.

"It's a simple question," she confirms. "What type of woman would it take?"

"The type…," Red struggles. "The type…I thought my type was…*you*…."

"That's all the time we have for questions," the stage manager interrupts, signaling the band to start playing and closing the curtain promptly on Red.

Behind the curtain, Red motions to the stage manager.

"Bring her back to my dressing room, please," he says, walking down the hallway.

No sooner is he settled in the room than he hears a knock at the door. Nothing good has happened in an entire year. He can feel his face immediately flush in anticipation that his luck may finally be about to change.

As the door opens, he tries to play it cool until he sees not Helen but Polly enter his dressing room.

"Let's make this quick," Polly says. "I'm owed for my services. I've come to collect."

Were it not for Red's cane he would have stumbled to the floor.

"I'm sorry. What?" he responds.

Her brother also enters the room. He seems even larger than when Red carried him up the stairs.

"Don't play dumb, kid," the brother says. "We did our job. We delivered Wildcat Wilson, 'Big Dog' Ernie Nevers, Lester whatever-his-name-is, and all the All-Americans who played in the barnstorming tour and joined the NFL. We did our part in the league's success. We're way overdue payment."

Red is dumbfounded, having to take a seat as Polly and her brother hover over him.

"We've tried a few times to collect, but he keeps giving us the slip," Polly says. "So we've come to you."

Mara, Red realizes.

"What do they have to do with me?" Red asks. "I don't know what you're talking about."

"Let's be professionals here," Polly says.

"Professionals?" Red replies. "You and your brother barge in here and…."

"Brother?" the brother says, laughing hysterically. "I'm her husband."

The news hits Red hard, almost worse than when he blew out his knee. Before he can further process the chaos, his door opens again, and his driver barges in with the dog, Pal.

"Red, we have to go to the next theater," the driver says. "We're already running late."

Pal dashes in and grabs Red by the pant leg. Pal tugs him toward the door to the bewilderment of Polly and her husband.

However, as Red reaches the doorway, Polly grabs his cane to stop him. She leans in closely.

"You have eight shows a day," she says. "You're pretty easy to find. I suggest we settle this without having to resort to...."

"To what?" Red says, standing his ground and steadying his cane.

"Easy," she replies. "Without having to resort to publicly taking you to court. You're a lot easier to sue than Pyle."

Now Red is even more confused.

"Pyle?" he says. "But I thought Mara?"

She laughs and plants a big kiss on his lips. Red takes one more look at Polly and her husband, finally realizing both of them have been working for Pyle all this time.

Red is so preoccupied with the truth about Polly and her "brother," not to mention the threat of a public lawsuit, that he doesn't notice Helen, who the whole time has been standing next to the stage manager down the hallway, heartbroken from having witnessed his and Polly's kiss.

CHAPTER 55

Red hobbles into his hotel suite after stumbling through his remaining shows. Finally ready to reflect on the humiliations and realizations of the day, he's startled to find someone sitting in his room.

"Well, I'll be…," Babe Ruth says, grinning ear to ear. "The Great Red Grange."

Red can hardly believe his eyes.

"Dear Lord, son, sit down before you fall over," Red's father, Lyle, calls from the other corner of the room. Red is as shocked to see his father as he is to see Babe.

"I sent Mr. Ruth a telegram a few weeks ago," Lyle explains, helping Red into a chair next to Babe, "and now that the Yankees won the World Series in four straight, it fit his schedule to help me with a favor."

Red has barely heard a word said thus far in the conversation. He's still coming to terms with Babe Ruth, not to mention his own father, sitting right in front of him.

"Look, son," Lyle says. "I'm worried about you. Nobody likes to listen to their old man. So I signaled the bullpen and brought in a lefty."

Babe laughs. Red is still processing as Babe's face grows serious, leaning in to talk to him.

"You know I saw ya play at the Bears-Giants game when you first turned pro," Babe says. "You drew a big ol' crowd. No way I'd miss it. You put the NFL on the map."

That game seems like a lifetime ago to Red.

"In my first big league game," Babe continues, "I fizzled. But not you. In fact, I was so jealous the entire time watching you. I was in the stands before the game, and all the photographers were taking my photo. Then you step out on the field and that's it for me. Chopped liver."

Babe and Lyle again break into laughter. The thought of Babe Ruth playing second fiddle to him also seems surreal.

"I've been in the big leagues since 1914. You were just a little kid, I bet. Well, I've learned a few things since then," Babe says. "Stuff like liquor, women, fame, and money. I don't know. I guess I thought I was invincible. I thought none of it would ever run out. It all came so easy."

"You hit sixty home runs last year and fifty-four this year," Red says. "I'd say it's still coming easy."

"I'm on a good run, for sure," Babe replies. "But do you remember 1925? Your senior year in college you were 'bigger than the Babe' while I was out 'sick' all season. Remember that?"

Of course, Red remembers that.

"I was down and out. Now, you're smarter than me. College boy. Clean cut. You don't drink. You're humble. You're all about the team. You're the one who should be givin' me advice. 'Cept, that is, for one thing."

"What's that?" Red asks.

"I negotiate my own playing contracts."

"I see," Red says. "And that's why my dad asked you here."

"Break it off with C.C. Pyle," Babe says. "Clean break."

Red lets out a long sigh.

"If only it were that easy," Red says. "I'm in it thick. Thicker than I'd like to admit. I'm broke."

"Look," Babe says. "I don't know what Pyle has on you. But I feel like you are forgetting something important."

"What's that?"

"You're forgetting who you are, is all," Babe says. "Who the hell is C.C. Pyle? Come on, son, know your worth. You know who you are?"

Red longs for that answer.

"You're Red Grange."

CHAPTER 56

But he doesn't feel like Red Grange. He'd love to confront Pyle. He'd love to break free of the chains of his contract. Except, he can't find Pyle. No one can find him since the unsuccessful footrace ended. Red assumes he's probably off masterminding another hair-brained scheme.

Instead, over the next few weeks, Red gets in the car along with Pal every time it arrives and is driven to his stupid performances, where he continues to make a fool out of himself to pay the bills.

After every show, he answers the same questions, longing for Helen's hand to shoot up. He's sent her a letter every day since she came to see him. Letters he stamped and mailed himself, but he's still awaiting a response.

After fumbling through another lackluster performance, he pets Pal in his dressing room backstage. The two of them have grown inseparable as of late. He sits down to pen another letter when a younger man about his age in a three-piece suit enters his dressing room.

"Mr. Grange, I'm on your legal team," he says. "The judge has demanded you show in court. We had hoped to plead for you, but he's being a stickler and threatened an arrest warrant if we don't produce you immediately."

Red has feared this for weeks.

"This matter requires your immediate attention," the young lawyer says. "A married woman is claiming you owe her money."

At the courthouse...

Their car is mobbed the moment the young lawyer and Red arrive. As instructed, Red steps out, smiling the whole time, waving, signing autographs, and answering the same questions he's always asked by fans about football and such.

Once inside, Red's main lawyer, Howard Brundage, takes him aside.

"It's very simple," Howard says. "Smile the entire time in the courtroom. On the way in, shake hands and sign autographs, but never under any circumstance say anything or look to your right at the accuser. The judge only demands you show up in person. Nothing else. Got it?"

"Got it," Red nods.

The moment Howard opens the door to the courtroom, those lucky enough to have ring-side seats cheer as Red walks in, immediately asking for autographs. Red signs every single one, slowly making his way to the front of the room.

Halfway down the aisle, he runs into a familiar face.

"Do I get an autograph?" Warren asks.

"You really want one?"

"Most days, yes. Today, no. No, I do not," he replies.

Red makes his way up to the front and finds a seat next to Howard, doing everything as instructed without once looking over to his right.

The judge bangs his gavel.

"A minute later, and I would have sent the sheriff out to arrest you, Mr. Grange," the judge says sternly before shifting to a friendly smile. "But that's your specialty, isn't it, Red? You always beat the buzzer."

Everyone in the courtroom belly laughs, including Red and his lawyer.

"I traveled to Philly to watch you play the Penn game," the judge says. "It was a thing of beauty. When you came out of the game, I wanted to go down to the sidelines myself and help get that blanket over your shoulders."

The courtroom is a mix of cheers and laughs. Red isn't supposed to look to his right, but he can tell the prosecutor is smiling and laughing, too.

"Your honor," Howard says. "We've produced the defendant. Now, I think you will agree it is only fair that the defense be granted a continuance of at least a few weeks, if not months."

The judge nods.

"We've only recently received the accusations," Howard continues. "We feel more time is warranted to dispute these frivolous, untrue, and baseless charges that not only threaten the reputation of our beloved Mr. Grange but also may attract further frivolous lawsuits against a man of his public profile, stature, and high repute."

"I agree," the judge says. "I suggest a continuance of...."

"Your honor," a woman says, sitting near the prosecutor. "Your honor, if I may say just a few words."

"And you are?" the judge asks.

"Mrs. Mary B. Quinn," she says. "I'm the personal lawyer for the plaintiff. Your honor, please, just a few words."

"A few," the judge says sternly.

Mrs. Quinn stands.

"Thank you, your honor. We have witnesses to prove that my client personally knows Mr. Grange," she says.

"Everyone in Chicago knows him," Howard says to laughs from the courtroom, including the judge.

"And we have proof they met at her place of business," she says.

"Big deal," Howard says. "But an even bigger deal is that we can prove your client is married. Not to mention naming the baby the most ridiculous name—Princess Haroldine Grange. Who in their right mind would name a baby that?"

The crowd erupts in laughter.

A baby? Red thinks to himself. *Did he say baby?*

"I've heard enough," the judge says. "I think a continuance is fair. I'm granting...."

"One last thing," Mrs. Quinn says.

"I said I've heard enough," the judge says again.

"This is something to *see*, not *hear*," she says, turning to her client. "Show them."

Red still hasn't looked over, but he can hear the defendant stand up.

"Go ahead," Mrs. Quinn says. "Take off the baby's bonnet."

The moment the defendant does, a collective gasp fills the courtroom, followed by silence, followed by Red sensing that all eyes in the courtroom are now on him.

He feels no choice but to turn his head to discover Helen, wearing her aquamarine jewelry, holding an adorable five-month-old baby girl with bright red hair.

CHAPTER 57

Red pounds on the front door of Helen's family home. He catches a glimpse of his own reflection in the window and doesn't recognize himself. He looks like a madman.

To calm down, he peers back out at the empty yard where he once played football with Norman and the boys in the neighborhood. He wonders if they even play football anymore. It wouldn't surprise him if they all play baseball now, pretending to be Babe Ruth. The Babe's an imperfect hero, but, at least, he's smart enough to avoid public lawsuits.

An auto comes screaming down the street and skids to a halt near his. Out jumps Helen's aunt and attorney, Mrs. Quinn, who beelines for Red on the front porch.

"You've got some nerve," Quinn says. "I told Helen to call the police, but instead, she insisted I come over."

"She's inside?" Red asks, tempted to pound even harder.

"Touch that door again, and I'll call the police," she says. "What are you doing here? You know you can't talk to her. You're not even supposed to talk to me without your attorney present."

"Mine's off demanding a new judge."

"A typical tactic to delay everything for weeks, if not months, even though that judge loves you. All judges will love the 'Great Red Grange.' By the time this is sorted out, your little vaudeville show will have moved on from Chicago to God knows how many more cities. And he'll work to find a judge who won't make you come into court next time. We assumed that would be your strategy, to drag this on forever."

"Well, I was blindsided. 'Haroldine Grange?' I assume that was your idea. To name that baby for publicity's sake?"

"Her real name is Princess," Quinn says. "Yes, we made that the legal name to finally get your attention. All you had to do was respond to her note or letters."

"What note or letters? I never received...anything," Red says, finally realizing as he grips Pyle's ornate cane who is actually at fault for that. "But she's married. Helen is married?"

"That's none of your business," Quinn says.

"It appears it might be," he replies. "Is he a redhead?"

"Stop right there."

"I need this answer," Red says. "My team is going to find out, regardless."

"The truth is, well, embarrassing," Quinn says.

"More embarrassing than what I just went through? More than this story being in every newspaper across the nation?"

Mrs. Quinn takes a deep breath before deciding to answer him.

"Helen's husband, Leo, disappeared. He's a long-haul truck driver. One day, they were married, and the next day, he was gone."

Red processes this information as Quinn continues.

"Helen thought he was dead. Then she got word he was spotted alive and around town. So, her brothers tracked him down, and it turns out...."

Quinn appears to be debating if she's doing the right thing by telling him.

"Turns out what?" Red demands.

"It turns out that the whole time he was married to Helen, he was also married to someone else. He had a second family. Even kids, living but a mile away."

Red finds himself stumbling yet again, leaning on his cane for support.

"Her brothers beat him silly when they figured it out. You're lucky they are not here today to do the same to you. Helen couldn't afford a divorce. Also, Leo being double married made it even more complicated. Not to mention the embarrassment of it all."

"What color is his hair?"

"Black as a raven, but it doesn't matter. She hasn't seen him in years."

Red, at least, now has his answers.

"As soon as she started to show, the hotel fired her. Lillian was already taking care of Norman. Now she was faced with taking care of Princess, too. Enough was enough. Lillian hired me. Helen fought us. That is until she came to see you at the theater. Something happened there…something about witnessing you kiss a woman backstage…and she changed her mind."

The cane isn't enough. Red has no choice but to lean against the porch railing.

"I just…I just…don't know anymore. I'm just lost," he says. "Nothing went to plan."

"We'll take a settlement," Quinn says. "It's twelve hundred if the court finds you guilty. A minimum of eight hundred to settle. With our evidence, we'll ask for something in between."

Red grips the railing, trying to make sense of so much information.

"All the proceedings can be private," Quinn continues. "You can maintain your public image. Your lawyer knows all this. You don't have to admit to anything. The process for paternity suits is well-defined. It can appear as if it all went away with no admission of guilt."

Red takes a deep breath, thinking through his options.

"Really, you have to think about it? Even for a moment? You're forming yet another plan in that thick skull of yours?" Quinn says pointedly. "Helen doesn't get the luxury of being a man and 'forming a plan.' What about her future? She'll never be afforded that luxury. You get to confer with lawyers, contemplate options, file for delays, and try to find a way out of it and get on with your life. You know what she gets to do? Starting right now?"

Quinn answers her own question.

"She gets to raise two kids by herself. That's her life."

CHAPTER 58

Red, still using Pyle's ornate cane, limps up the familiar steps to a tiny Champaign apartment and knocks on the door. While he's waiting, he can hear food cooking on the stove.

Fannie unlocks the door and runs back to the stove without even looking at him.

"Bob, the captains are here," she says. "They're early."

Red steps into the apartment. No one is there to greet him, so he closes the door and admires new landscape paintings by Zuppke lying on what should be the dining room table.

Zuppke's paintings are of scenes in the Southwest and Colorado, except for one. Red takes a closer look at the painting, which captures a young Illinois football player sitting on the bench, elbows on his knees, dejected, resting his head in his hands, longing for his coach to call upon him.

"You were not like that," Zuppke says, having entered the room. "You were a rarity. One in a million. Once in a generation. You were just proud to be on the team. I could have never put you in a single game, und you would have never said a word about it. You would have just sat there, rooting for your teammates, enjoying their glory."

"But you did put me in," Red says, "and look where it got us."

"Where did it get us?"

"Have you read about my situation in the newspapers?"

"Listen, Granche, in my opinion, you will always be the best to play the college game. You are the greatest. I'm sorry to say it, und I know you never wanted it und blame me for it, but it is true. I couldn't keep you on the bench. It would have been a disservice to the world, und it would have been a disservice to you."

Red shakes his head, disagreeing, setting the painting back on the table.

"But there is something even the greatest player in the world can't do. Or his coach. Do you know what that is?" Zuppke says.

"What's that?"

"Change the past."

Zuppke lets that sink in.

"No one can change the past. Thus, there's no point in dwelling on it," he continues. "Last year, we were the national champions. This year we were undefeated going into last week's Michigan game. We lost. My captains are about to show up. What are we talking about this evening? That loss? The fact it already ruined this season? No. None of it matters now. There is nothing we can do about it. We move on."

Zuppke points to the painting of the dejected player on the bench.

"Get in the game. Right now. You don't like prancing around on that stage? Stop doing it. Your knee hurts? Exercise it. Play golf. Walk on it. Re-train it. You have responsibilities to that girl? To that baby? If you do, own up und be a man."

Zuppke grabs Red by the arm, walks him to the front door, and opens it.

"If I could go back in time, do you know what I would do?" Zuppke says. "I'd do exactly what I'm doing right now, which is tell you to suit up und get in the game. I wouldn't change a thing."

Zuppke guides Red through the door and is about to slam it when he thinks of one more thing. He reaches down and grabs the cane out of Red's hand.

"Maybe I'd change one thing," Zuppke says, breaking C.C. Pyle's cane over his knee and handing the two broken pieces back to Red before closing the door.

CHAPTER 59

Several months later, Red knocks on an office door. He hears a familiar voice shout, "Just a minute," allowing Red to collect his thoughts.

He had barely made it down the steps from Zuppke's apartment without a cane. But he did. The next day, he quit the vaudeville show. The producers no longer had a need for Pal, so Red adopted the dog.

They started by going on short walks to give them both something to do. Soon, they went for longer walks. Then, they walked nine holes of golf. Followed by eighteen. When Red got good at walking, he tried jogging. Pal ran alongside him.

Without fail, his knee would swell up to what felt like the size of a basketball. Over time, it swelled to a football, then to a baseball, and eventually to just a golf ball.

He progressed from jogging to running to sprinting. He even got his original job back. In the mornings, he'd climb stairs with hundred-pound ice blocks. The regular customers grew to love Pal even more than Red.

After the route, they would golf in the afternoon, and he'd wrap his knee overnight. The next day, the routine started over.

Then Red went back to the sandlot where Garland and he grew up playing football. The first few weeks he was no match for a gang of ten-year-olds. A few weeks later, they couldn't catch him.

Zuppke was even kind enough to put him up in Champaign, allowing Red to attend college practices in exchange for some coaching. Running straightaways, he was back to being fast. Though not quick enough to break open on long runs, he was agile enough to excel on defense.

His father took over all of his finances and affairs. They sold off some cars and his fancy fur coat. They soundly invested the remaining cash in the roaring stock market.

Each evening he'd ice his leg. Pal would jump in his lap while he wrote to Helen. His letters were never answered, but it didn't matter. He'd settled the lawsuit and vowed to write her a letter every day whether or not she would speak to him.

His days of being a superstar are gone. It's not lost on him that all those years of wishing he could be average have come true.

"Come in," George Halas says, swinging open the door to the office inside the Bears locker room.

Without hesitation, Halas embraces Red and motions for him to sit down. Red crosses the room with a noticeable limp the doctors say will never fully go away.

"Here you are," Halas says, motioning for Red to sit before sliding into the chair behind his desk. "The Galloping Ghost."

"Not sure about the galloping part," Red says.

"That's not what Zuppke tells me. I can't get him to shut up about you. He comes to Bears games on Sundays and afterward tells me all the things I'm doing wrong."

"Blocking?"

"And much more. Then he corners me about signing you."

Red smiles in appreciation.

"Let's cut to it," Halas says. "Zuppke says you are ready. What about you? You really think you're ready to play again?"

"I'm ready."

"And I'm negotiating with you this time, not Pyle?"

"Not Pyle," Red firmly confirms. "His first footrace across America was a bust. Last I heard, he was organizing one back the other way. I still don't know where he is for certain. As you know, Mara took back ownership of The Yankees team. Leaving me…well…without a job."

Halas nods. He's aware.

"So what's your negotiation strategy today?" he says, becoming more serious. "I heard The Babe is in your corner now. Or, are you going to rip a page from Pyle's playbook, shake me down for a percentage of the gate, tell me how lucky I am to have you back?"

"No. None of that," Red says. "I just want to play football."

"And why is that? Cause you need a job?"

"I do need a job, but I want to play because…well… because I've come to terms with the fact that playing football might be the only thing I'm actually qualified to do. Not to mention, there's some evidence that I'm pretty good at it."

"Come on, you can do better than that."

"Okay," Red says. "I also want to play because I miss the game. If I'm being honest, I love it. I do. I've done some serious soul-searching, and I absolutely love the game of football. I just want to get back to playing it, and not trying to own it."

Halas smiles.

"Now that we can work with," he says, passing a folded piece of paper across the desk to Red.

Red opens it and reviews the offer.

"That's not a starting point," Halas clarifies. "That's the best deal you are going to get."

Red nods, still looking it over. This offer isn't anywhere near what Pyle negotiated years ago, but Red didn't expect it to be.

"Allow me just one tiny thing," Red says, watching Halas immediately cross his arms. "But it isn't related to my offer. It has to do with someone else. A rookie I think you'd be a fool not to consider."

Minneapolis Red Jackets at Chicago Bears
Sunday, October 27, 1929

Halas takes himself and another player out of the game in the fourth quarter to debut his newest two players.

The capacity crowd rises to its feet to welcome Number 77 back to Chicago. Red thanks them with a wave before tucking his still trademarked auburn hair under his helmet as he and the rookie jog out to join the Bears.

Familiar faces surround Red in the huddle. Trafton, Paddy Driscoll, and Joey nod to him, welcoming his return.

Paddy barks out the play call, "R to P on 2.".

Red can't hide the surprise on his face, given he expected to be called upon only to block.

"Always give the audience what they want," Joey says to him with a wink.

The Bears line up for Red to take the snap, which he does. He takes two steps back, playing quarterback, holding onto the ball, and waiting for the play to develop. He has the new rookie receiver in mind, but the kid isn't open yet. Red needs more time, but two Red Jackets have broken through the line.

In the old days, Red would simply swivel his hips to send them screaming by him, but those days are gone. Instead, he braces to take a sack and protect the football when Joey flies in out of nowhere, taking out one of the defenders.

Trafton not only takes out the other defender but knocks the poor guy out of the game. He has vowed publicly, for as long as he's allowed to play with Red, never to allow harm to come to him again.

Free to throw, Red plants his foot and sails a pass high in the air to the back corner of the end zone where the rookie is sprinting.

For the past year, Red has thought only about what Zuppke said to him: "You can't change the past."

What he is fortunate to be able to do, however, is watch that ball he just threw land right in the hands of the Bears rookie—Pinky, as the team calls him—and witness his brother Garland score a touchdown.

Most players run back to thank their team for blocking and the quarterback for throwing a perfect pass. Not Garland. When he scores a touchdown, he starts a new tradition of hamming it up for the fans. They love it, and so do his teammates, who tackle him in celebration.

No one in the stands cheers louder than Lyle, Fannie, and Zuppke. Paddy's "R to P" call is the first brother-to-brother touchdown pass delivered in the history of the NFL.

"You can't change the past," Red thinks to himself. "Instead, enjoy the present."

Speaking of which....

CHAPTER 60

Red packs up his Stutz Bearcat outside the stadium after the game. He's decided enough with writing letters to Helen. He can do better.

He has Pal loaded up in the car and is about to drive to Helen's family home when a burgundy Wills Sainte Claire Roadster, which has seen better days, comes sputtering around the corner toward him, crapping out right behind his car, smoke billowing from the engine.

Red knows that car well. He knows its passengers even better.

"Oh good, I caught you, my boy," Pyle says, taking off his goggles and looking as dapper as ever with his green tie and feather to match.

"You know anything about this engine?" he says, getting out and opening the hood.

Unfortunately, Red does, but Pyle doesn't wait for an answer and starts messing with the engine himself. Red observes Clem trapped in the passenger seat (and in life).

Red can tell Pyle is tinkering with the wrong valve, and the last thing Red wants is for that car or Pyle to be blocking him any longer than necessary.

Without saying a word, Red walks over and adjusts the valves as Pyle backs away.

"A quick update, okay? Here's where we stand," Pyle says. "Payroll was getting too high on the Yankees. I gave it back to Mara. The footrace back from New York to Santa Monica didn't quite work out as planned."

"Neither did the first one," Red says under his breath, tweaking the broken valve.

"Take a break from that engine a second," Pyle says. "Clem, hand me the blueprints."

Clem hands the papers to Pyle, who rolls them out on the side of the car. "Look at this."

Red reluctantly glances at the blueprints, trying to make sense of it.

"Genius, right? A domed stadium," Pyle says. "The roof opens for good weather and retracts for bad weather. No more rainouts! And look at the escalators. They flow up at the start of the game and down at the end. Fans of all shapes and sizes can attend. And look at the hand cranks at each seat. Fans can crank up a binocular glass or crank it down. There's not a bad view in the house!"

Pyle goes on and on and on, referencing all the features of the stadium, saying something about a landing pad on the roof, barely noticing Red has gone back to working on the engine.

"And the playing surface can be football or baseball or, get this, hockey. I've already got franchise owners interested in San Diego, Los Angeles, San Francisco, and Sacramento. What better market than California for hockey? 'Come inside, it's cool. Bring your mother, too.' Catchy, don't you think? We'll expand to Florida next."

Red gets the engine back to revving and shuts the hood.

"I have Pollyanne out there doing advance work for me, her husband, too. They are lining up hockey recruits from Canada and Europe," Pyle says, continuing on and on. "I just need to get back out there, but I've run into a slight hiccup. I just need some travel money...."

"Pollyanne?" Red asks.

"Yes, we settled up with all the cash I had left. I just need some train fare. I got credit lined up in Los Angeles, but I'm short the cash for two tickets is all for Clem and me. And I know our agreement expired, and you got your new Bears deal without me, but I'll cut you in on the hockey. It will shore us up on some things I owe you. Fresh start. I'll reach out once I get it all arranged. I know where to find you now. I just have to look at the Bears schedule. How about that? Back where you started. Wearing the navy and orange."

"C.C.," Red says, pointedly enough to get Pyle to take a break from his jabbering. "Just stop. Stop! I got your engine working. That's the best you're going to get from me."

"Red, my boy, listen. I can tell you're taking the Polly thing personally. No one ever made an omelet without breaking some eggs along the way. It's just business. It's all part of show business. It's just how it's done. Wildcat Wilson. A few All-Americans. It's just a part of the game."

"I don't care about her," Red says. "It's Helen. She gave you a note. You never gave it to me."

"Who the hell is Helen?" Pyle says, getting back in the car and testing the engine. "Dear Lord, boy, it's running better than ever. You have a gift. So, just like twenty dollars. Maybe fifty, if you have it. It will send me on my way. If not for me, do it for Clem."

Clem looks sheepishly at Red. Other than himself, Red has never felt worse for another human being.

Red reaches into his pocket, takes out his wallet, and moves in close enough to Clem that only the two of them can hear each other given the roar of the engine.

"Listen to me," Red says, handing a wad of cash to Clem. "I'm giving this to you and not him. There's enough here to get you a ticket to go in the opposite direction of him, and then some extra for a fresh start."

Pyle can't hear them, but he watches the transaction happen and glances at the thickness of the bills.

"That's way more than I need," Pyle shouts over the sounds of the engine. "Way more, my boy, but that gets me out of here. I'll sell this car down at the station unless you want to buy it?"

Red shakes his head.

"I'll sell it at the station then. I'll really get something for it now that you have it running so sharp. Clem and I are off then to California. I'll be in touch. Join us for the groundbreaking? Give me a few months. Hockey is the future."

Pyle puts the car in gear and drives it in a circle in the parking lot to point himself back out in the direction he came before pausing one last moment.

"You know what time it is, don't you?" Pyle says, putting on his goggles.

"I'm afraid I do," Red replies.

"Showtime," Pyle utters with that winning grin while speeding away, which causes the green feather from his hat to sail off into the air.

Red could have easily caught it, but he doesn't even make an effort.

CHAPTER 61

Norman, taller now than when Red first met him, runs out for a pass. He's wide open, ready to catch it, when something distracts him, and the football bounces right off his chest.

The other boys start to get mad until they realize what made him miss the ball. A Stutz Bearcat is roaring down the street. It skids to a halt. Norman limps over to the car with the other boys following.

"Figure out that spiral, yet?" Norman asks.

"It's a work in progress," Red replies. "But I have a little friend helping me."

Red scoops his dog out of a box in the passenger seat.

"He's a killer. I'd run if I were you, boys," Red says, placing Pal on the ground.

The moment he does, the boys take off running. Given his limp, Norman is the easiest for Pal to catch, tugging at Norman's pants, knocking him down, and then licking his face. One by one, Pal tackles all the boys and licks their faces until they bounce back up, and the game starts over.

Red grabs a few bags of groceries he'd tied down to the passenger seat and limps toward Lillian's house.

Helen's gang of angry brothers has assembled on the porch. Red scans the scene. Despite holding the groceries, he's agile enough to fend them off, but he had already decided to take the licks instead. Just as he's about to be punched in the face, Lillian steps out on the porch and shoos her sons away.

315

"Get. Go! All of yous," Lillian says before looking sternly at Red. "You're a fool. They could have beat you silly."

"I'm here to do whatever it takes to see Helen."

"And the baby?"

"And the baby," he clarifies. "And I brought you a peace offering."

"Me? What could that possibly be?"

"This…," he says, reaching into a bag and pulling out a large wheel of cheese.

It takes her a moment to register the significance of their conversation all those years ago.

"What kind?" she says.

"Good question," he says. "I'm not exactly sure what the moon is made of. Swiss? Regardless, I bought like seven different types."

She considers the gesture for a moment.

"It's a start. Better would be if you quit playing children's games for a living and got a real job," she says, taking the groceries from him. "I'll tell her you're here, but that's it."

She carries the groceries inside, leaving him on the porch. While waiting, he turns around, noticing the boys return to playing football. He loves watching Pal tackle whomever has the ball and observes that Norman is no longer the only one with a limp.

He had recently read a story by Warren regarding a phenomenon that has been happening since he returned to the Bears. Little kids all over Chicago have begun limping on the playground, pretending to be Red Grange.

"A stage dog and an assortment of cheese?" Helen says, having stepped out on the porch behind him.

Red turns to find her holding an almost two-year-old adorable Princess whose hair is as red as ever.

"Please don't tell me you also brought a Red Grange Doll," Helen says, motioning to the bag Red is still holding.

Unfortunately, Red can't hide that his replica doll is precisely what's in the bag as he instinctively closes it and holds it at his side. Fixating on the baby, however, gets him over his embarrassment.

He's mesmerized by watching Princess cling to her mother, clearly wondering who he is. It dawns on him that everyone in Chicago knows him except his own daughter.

"What's your big plan showing up today?" Helen asks. "You always have a plan. One more year of this. Two more years of that. It always revolves around Red, Red, Red. Go on, let's hear it?"

"I don't have a plan."

"I'm to believe Red Grange doesn't have a plan?"

"I didn't even know if I'd make it past your brothers…or your mother."

Helen nods, indicating that's a fair point.

"I just…," Red stutters. "I just…I just want to do what's right."

"For who? For you?"

"For the baby, for starters. And, for you, if you'll let me."

She thinks for a moment.

"That's it? That's your big speech? After a year of my resolve not to write back to you but wait to see if you ever show up on your own accord. That's your big speech?"

"Well, in case you didn't know, I'm a football player. We're not exactly known for words. Or brains."

"A football player? I thought you were a celebrity. A film and stage actor. After all this time, you didn't plan what you would say if you got this far? You could certainly afford for someone to write you a soliloquy."

"Come on, I don't even know what that is. I'm trying to live in the present, you know. I've done a lot of soul-searching. I'm an athlete, not an entertainer."

He can tell by her face that isn't good enough.

"Okay," he says, "I guess I have a few thoughts rattling around, but it's not rehearsed."

"Let's hear it."

Red takes a deep breath to muster the courage. Too shy to look at her, he simply says what is on his mind.

"I think of Princess every night before I go to bed. I wonder how big she's getting. If she says words yet. If she's athletic. If she's tough. If she's sassy like you. Smart like you. Determined like you. Hoping she's all of you and maybe just a little bit of me. If I have any good parts."

He glances up to find Helen is still listening.

"And I wonder if you appreciate that I turned down New York offers and took a job in Chicago so I can be part of her life."

He thinks he sees a hint of a nod. It's enough, at least, to give him the courage to keep going.

"And I'll admit my thoughts often also go to you. Would you allow me even to visit the baby? Would you be a part of the visits? Would Norman? Would your parents? Your brothers? Could your family be mine, too?"

She's still with him.

"And then, after all that, I ask myself the toughest of all questions. Could you ever trust me again? And, I continue to have the craziest thought of all."

He really has to muster up the courage for this one.

"Could I ever win you back? I'm good at football, but I'm the best when I'm with you."

That one garners a smile.

"But mostly," he says, "I lay in bed at night wondering if I were ever to take another acting gig…if you think I might be ready to branch out from lipstick?"

That registers a laugh.

"Mascara, maybe?" he suggests. "In my heart of hearts, I really think I'm ready to take it to another level. And you'd be the one to get me there. What do you say?"

"I say no," she promptly replies. "I mean yes to most of what you said. I tried to be tough this whole time, but I loved every word of it. I loved it all. Especially the you're great with me part. But, no."

"No?"

"No, you are not ready for mascara."

One thing is for sure: she'll always make him laugh. Simply being near Helen and the baby makes Red feel alive. Smiling feels even better.

"Seriously," she continues, "the key to makeup starts with a good foundation. Let's get that right and see where it takes us."

He nods. Makes perfect sense. Everything is finally making sense. *This is living.*

"You want to really take your game to the next level?" Helen asks. "Learn to change a diaper."

OVERTIME

George Halas, nicknamed Papa Bear, coached the Chicago Bears for 40 years, winning 341 games. He described Red as "a fine, honest, and modest man," and said, "no player has had a greater impact on the game of football, college or professional, than Red Grange." Halas often referred to Red as the greatest running back he ever saw.

Halas' eldest daughter, Virginia Halas McCaskey, runs the Bears today. She was born the same year as Red's sophomore year of college and turned 101 on January 5, 2024. George Halas passed away in 1983 at the age of 88.

The 1926 American Football League wasn't Tim Mara's only battle with the AFL in New York City. A second upstart league named the AFL operated in 1936, and a third called itself that as well in 1940. The Giants were also challenged by the All-America Football Conference from 1946 to 1949. Mara won all these wars, maintaining supremacy in New York City, before passing away in 1959 at the age of 71. His grandson, John Mara, serves as the president of the Giants today.

George "Wildcat" Wilson played in the NFL from 1926 to 1929. His only requirements for playing in exhibition games against Red were to be paid upfront and given a decent offensive line. After his football days, he worked on the docks in San Francisco. Wilson passed away in 1963 at the age of 62.

George Trafton played in the NFL from 1920 to 1934. Red called Trafton the "meanest, toughest player alive." It was said of Trafton that he was strongly disliked in every NFL city except Green Bay, "where he was hated." He was also credited with being the first center to hike the ball with one hand. After football, he was a boxer and a wrestler. Trafton was elected to the NFL Hall of Fame in 1964 and passed away in 1971 at the age of 74.

Earl Britton played for six professional teams from 1925-1929. Red and Earl's exceptional freshman squad at Illinois also included players who transferred out of Red's shadow to become All-Americans at other schools. Earl could have been a superstar elsewhere, but elected to stay at Illinois and unselfishly block for Red. After football, he worked in sales and passed away in 1973 at the age of 70.

Garland Grange, nicknamed Pinky, played for the Bears from 1929-1931. In a 1978 interview, Red said, "We used to have some of the greatest arguments, Gardie and I, when working on the ice truck. We're out in the country, and I remember this so well, we stopped the truck and turned it off and got out into a field. We had the doggonedest fight you ever saw. We both are bloody. We clean up, and get back in the truck and go to work. We worked all day together, the both of us."

Red also said, "My brother was an entirely different type of personality on the football field than I. While I was a quiet sort of player who could feel it inside, he could stimulate the entire team with his enthusiasm. He breathed fire and brimstone, and before a game, we almost wanted to tie him up for fear he might go out on the field and kill somebody."

After his playing days, Garland moved to Miami and worked as an executive for a department store. Garland passed away in 1981 at the age of 74.

Bob Zuppke, nicknamed Mr. Razzle Dazzle and The Little Dutchman, was born in Berlin and coached for twenty-eight years at Illinois, retiring in 1941. During his tenure, the average attendance at Illinois games rose from four thousand to sixty thousand fans. The playing field at Memorial Stadium was dedicated to him in 1966.

Zuppke is credited with inventing football mainstays such as the huddle, the screen pass, the spiral snap, and, perhaps the greatest trick play in sports, the flea flicker. He won national championships in 1914, 1919, 1923, and 1927.

In 1929, a Carnegie Foundation report accused many colleges with prominent athletic programs of recruiting athletes, giving them cushy jobs, paying them, and other violations. In only 21 out of the 105 American colleges and universities which the Carnegie Foundation visited was no evidence found that athletes were subsidized by any group or individual. Illinois was determined to be free from transgressions.

However, Zuppke's staunch refusal to recruit out-of-state players, as other colleges routinely began to do, hurt his winning percentage in the 1930s. At the same time, other high-profile programs continued to bend the rules. He was fired in 1941.

Zuppke is quoted as saying, "I will never have another Grange, but neither will anyone else. Generations to come will produce their great runners, but only Grange's name will be immortal." In later years, he even named his dog Red.

Zuppke passed away in 1957 at the age of 78. His wife, Fannie, passed away in 1936 while he was still coaching. For Zuppke's funeral, Red sent a statement saying, "I have lost my closest friend, and football has lost its greatest genius." His artwork can be found throughout the University of Illinois, including the painting of a dejected player on the bench.

Helen Flozek successfully divorced Leo Flozek and officially changed her last name back to Morrissey. Unfortunately, her relationship with Red didn't last. The reasons why are lost to history. Helen married Jeremiah Francis O'Dea in 1941 and had a third child, Marjorie.

Rose Maria, Princess' daughter, said Princess maintained a relationship with Red until she turned twelve, and they spoke again briefly when she turned eighteen. She also said her mother's birth certificate reads Princess Rosemary Morrissey. It never read Haroldine Grange, despite what was said in court.

The family has memories of Red bringing food, clothes, and presents to Lillian's home and staying with them. They often said they wouldn't have been able to get through the Great Depression without him. They also remember Red playing with children in their neighborhood and the kids faking limps to emulate him.

Rose inherited the aquamarine pendant and bracelet Red gave to Helen, also worn by Helen in newspaper photos of the court proceedings. Norman passed away in 1976 at the age of 52. Helen passed away in 1982 at the age of 73. Princess passed away in 2014 at the age of 85.

C.C. Pyle is widely considered to be the first sports agent. Professional team owners of all sports so strongly hated the concept that they banned agents until the 1960s. After Red and Pyle were no longer partners, Pyle ended up managing a "Ripley's Believe it or Not" exhibit at the Chicago World's Fair. His fourth wife, Elvia Allman Tourtellotte, was also an actress and comedian, best known as the no-nonsense boss in the famous *I Love Lucy* candy factory episode. Pyle became president of the Radio Transcription Company, a position he held until his death of a heart attack in Los Angeles in 1939 at the age of 56.

In 1970, Red said of Pyle, "If he was around today, wouldn't he have a field day with all the big money rolling around? You hear all this talk about the Houston Astrodome these days, but I'm talking about in 1926, he had a set of blueprints made up. It had a roof you could open and close. The aisles were escalators, helicopter pads, and many more ideas. Pyle made a million three or four times over and lost it. He was a great guy to have on your side."

Red rarely said anything negative about Pyle publicly and stayed in semi-regular touch with him until he died.

Harold "Red" Grange played for the Bears from 1925 to 1934. He threw that famous touchdown pass to Garland on October 27, 1929. Two days later, on October 29, the stock market crashed, kicking off The Great Depression. Like many Americans, Red is said to have lost, in that single day, the bulk of the money he had saved. He credits George Halas for giving him a "job" to play for the Bears that sustained him through the depression years.

After his playing days were over, he started an insurance agency, later becoming a television broadcaster. Red has said in interviews that owning his own insurance agency was the portion of his career for which he was most proud.

In 1931, Red starred in a twelve-part series that played in movie theaters on Saturday mornings called *The Galloping Ghost,* which can be seen on YouTube today. It was one of the early films to utilize sound. Though he never finished his degree, he did serve on the University of Illinois Board of Trustees from 1951 to 1955.

In 1941, Red married Margaret, nicknamed Muggs. She was a flight attendant he'd met on a plane. They were together for almost 50 years until his death, and they had no children together.

Later in life, after saving enough money, Red vanished from public life to a retirement community in Florida to play golf, enjoy long boat rides, and feed birds. He only resurfaced publicly on the rarest of occasions.

It is said that Red and Margaret displayed no football memorabilia in their Florida home, with the exception of a painting by Zuppke of Red in uniform. Red died in 1991 at the age of 87. Margaret passed away shortly after him.

In 1963, the first NFL Hall of Fame class of seventeen was considered the most influential in founding the NFL. Among the seventeen inducted were Tim Mara, George Halas, Ernie

"Big Dog" Nevers, Jim Thorpe, Commissioner Joe Carr, and Harold "Red" Grange.

In 1991, S*ports Illustrated* declared Red's four touchdowns in twelve minutes against Michigan to be "The Most Unforgettable Moment in Sports." The one-hundred-year anniversary of that game will be October 19, 2024, at the University of Illinois Memorial Stadium Rededication against Michigan.

The NFL's 1926 Red Grange Rule lives on today, making Red the last player to play college and pro football in the same year. Athletic scholarships were not given to college athletes until the 1950s. In 1972, freshmen were allowed to play on varsity. In 2021, a Supreme Court decision allowed college athletes to earn compensation for their name, image, and likeness. In 2024, the NCAA settled a multi-billion-dollar landmark case, threatening the end of amateurism by paving the way for universities to pay athletes directly.

Walter Camp's rule book changes every year. In 1927, the goalposts were moved to the back of the endzone. In 1933, they were returned to the goal line. In 1974, they were sent back again. In 1934, the size of the football was reduced to make passing easier. In 1941, free substitution was allowed, creating the specialization of offensive and defensive players; although, it took coaches five years to widely discover the benefits. In 1949, coaches were allowed to stand up from the bench during games. Starting in the 1960s, they were allowed to coach from the sidelines, and, around that same time, plastic firmly replaced leather helmets.

Black college football players became more prominent over time and began being honored with end-of-year recognitions more frequently beginning in the 1950s. Black players sporadically played in the NFL from 1920 to 1932. There were none, however, from 1933 to 1945. During that time, George Halas publicly talked about Black players returning to the league.

Shortly after the Bears' 1925-1926 "barnstorming tour," the NFL changed their scheduling procedures to try to limit a team's schedule to no more than two games a week. Even today, the timing of Thursday Night Football makes limiting to just one game a week tricky. It's hard to fathom, but during Red's tour, there was a stretch of four games in five days. Four times on the tour, games were played on back-to-back days in different cities.

In the 1970 book *The Game That Was*, Red is quoted as saying, "When I watch football, I can't watch the ball carrier. I pick out a lineman and watch the blocking because that's what makes a football team. You see, the guy who makes the touchdowns is very unimportant. It's a heck of a lot easier carrying that ball than blocking, believe me. Blocking is the toughest job in the world."

In 2009, a one-ton statue, eight times bigger than he was in real life, was erected in honor of Red Grange outside Memorial Stadium at the University of Illinois. During his lifetime, Red is reported to have objected to any proposed statue of himself, saying, "Nobody's great in football. You're only as great as the other ten guys make you."

ABOUT THE AUTHOR

Doug Villhard is a professor, entrepreneur, investor, and philanthropist. After decades of starting and selling companies, he is supposed to be retired but instead is having too much fun heading the #1-ranked entrepreneurship department at the Olin Business School at Washington University in St. Louis.

Doug, Diane, and their four children live just outside of St. Louis in Glen Carbon, Illinois, where they co-founded Father McGivney Catholic High School.

When Doug isn't writing, teaching, investing in startups, or serving on boards, he's perpetually working toward achieving a respectable golf score.

Visit DougVillhard.com to:
- Watch a video of the author discussing what was fact and what was fiction in the telling of this story and his other novels, *Company of Women* and *City of Women*;
- View photos of Red, C.C. Pyle, Helen, Garland, Zuppke, Clem, and other real-life characters from this book;
- Download a book club discussion guide;
- And, schedule Doug to attend your next event.